BIRTHDAY
GIRL

BIRTHDAY GIRL

An Elliott Nash Thriller

MATTHEW IDEN

THOMAS & MERCER

Text copyright © 2018 by Life Sentence Publishing LLC
All rights reserved.

Published by Thomas & Mercer, Seattle

www.apub.com

Amazon, the Amazon logo, and Thomas & Mercer are trademarks of Amazon.com, Inc., or its affiliates.

ISBN-13: 9781542045889
ISBN-10: 1542045886

Cover design by Shasti O'Leary-Soudant

Printed in the United States of America

For Renee, who continues to make the whole thing possible.
For my family.
For my friends.

PROLOGUE

The Children

Sister came home as the last slanted rays of sunlight squeezed their way into the house through small gaps and holes. The deep, greasy odor of fried chicken wafted upward from the foyer to every corner of the old four-square.

"Charlie, Charlotte, Tina!" she singsonged as she made her way down the dark, musty hall on her way to the kitchen. "Buddy, Maggie! Come to dinner! I've brought a treat."

Five pairs of feet stampeded to the kitchen from bedrooms and the cellar, books and toys dropping in the rush. The children—blond and brunette, pale and dark, brown- and blue- and green-eyed, but all dressed in poorly fitted hand-me-downs—came to a skidding halt just inside the doorway, bunching up comically, then shuffling forward in half-steps, eyes and mouths wide in anticipation of the rare extravagance.

Sister, still in her work clothes, leaned against the Formica counter, a gentle smile on her face. She'd already placed the white bucket, mounded high with crispy brown wings and thighs, on the scarred farmhouse table like a trophy. Stacks of lily-white napkins rose on either side of it, begging to be made dirty by oily little fingers.

"Take your seats," she said with a clap of her hands. "And no sneaking a bite!"

Their bare feet made slapping noises on the green linoleum floor as they moved to their places. Following the clatter and screech of chair legs, the five climbed into their seats around the table, then turned their heads in her direction, eyes downcast, unblinking.

Sister watched in approval, then addressed the children. "What do we say before we eat?"

"Grace," Charlotte mumbled. Like the others, she snuck glances at the bucket.

"That's right, we say grace." Her eyes flicked over their faces, looking for black eyes and bruises that were the signs of rough play. She'd forbidden it, but it still happened from time to time, a consequence of young, energetic bodies being cooped up while she was at work. Finding nothing out of the ordinary, she still frowned. "Charlotte, did you wash your hands?"

"Yes, Sister." The girl's golden hair, hanging long past her shoulders, bobbed with her head.

"But I didn't hear the water running."

"I was quick." The answer was straightforward, but the slightest undercurrent of sarcasm colored every word.

"I guess you were," Sister said, smiling, but with a gleam in her eye that meant she didn't believe the answer for a second . . . or appreciate the tone in which it was delivered.

She took her seat at the head of the table, taking stock. Charlie, as the eldest, sat to her right, then Charlotte, Tina, and Buddy, until they wrapped around the table, with Maggie to Sister's left. Overhead, a clear jelly-jar lamp, dead bugs littering the glass bottom, hung from the ceiling. Its single bulb cast a harsh light that threw their shadows onto the table's surface in sharp lines and gleamed on the chrome handles of cabinets and drawers that were rarely, if ever, opened.

As they sat, enduring her inspection, Tina darted her hand out and pinched one of Buddy's large ears. The boy yelped but, instead of turning and hitting her like any brother would do, kept his eyes locked on the table in front of him.

"Tina," she said reprovingly, but nothing else. The girl flushed, dropping her head with the ghost of a grin. Everyone knew she wouldn't get in trouble. Tina was Sister's favorite. Buddy, his face burning, scowled. The rest sat still and silent.

When she was sure order had been restored, Sister leaned over. "It's your birthday soon, Charlie."

"Yes, Sister," he mumbled, looking down at his hands. They'd had a disagreement that morning, and he'd actually yelled at Sister over breakfast. About what was unimportant; in this household, talking back was unheard of.

When Charlie said no more, Sister looked around at the others. The children had their hands folded as she'd taught them and looked sufficiently penitential, even while she knew the smell coming from the bucket of chicken, sitting within arm's reach, was driving them to distraction.

She watched them for a moment longer, then said, "Let us bow our heads."

Obediently, the crowns of five heads tipped forward and five pairs of eyes shut. Sister began the prayer but kept her eyes open, watching as Maggie, the youngest at six, darted her dirty little hand forward and tore off a strip of chicken skin, jamming it in her mouth.

"Amen." Sister ended the prayer, and as one, five heads came up and stared at the bucket. "Charlie, would you serve your brother and sisters?"

"Yes, Sister."

She pushed her chair back and stood. "Maggie? Help me get something out of the oven."

"Sister?" the little girl said, confused, glancing from the fried chicken to the other children. Next to her, Buddy's eyes widened with excitement; last month, Sister had brought enough store-bought cupcakes for each of them to have one. Buddy had made his last a whole week. But Sister never used the stove.

"Help me with the oven, Maggie," Sister said again, patiently. "I hid something special in there before you came into the kitchen."

Maggie slid off her chair as Sister came around the table and then opened the door to the ancient white porcelain stove. A ripple seemed to pass through her as she touched it. Inside, the racks had been removed, leaving just a dark, black, empty box. Maggie peered inside.

Charlie started to say something, but Charlotte reached out, grabbed one of his clenched fists, and silenced him with a look.

Sister, a hand on Maggie's bottom, lifted her off the floor and into the oven. Her shriek startled the other children; they froze, hunks of chicken in their hands and mouths. Sister slammed the door shut and backed her weight against it as the little girl began to scream and kick from the inside.

Sister smiled beatifically, then raised her voice to be heard over Maggie's wails. "Eat up, everyone! There's plenty of food for those who follow the rules."

1

Elliott

This is the way it happened.

They're at the playground. Cee Cee's legs are dangling off the edge of the bench, and she's kicking them in short, angry flicks of her feet. He's had to put her in time-out because she punched the Gilmer boy for pushing her into the dirt. Appearances have to be maintained—he should act upset, both for Cee Cee and the other parents—but he is secretly pleased because Patrick Gilmer is a little shit who will grow up to be a much bigger shit if someone like his daughter doesn't put him in his place.

Cee Cee knows he's faking. Even as she kicks, her face breaks into the smile she likes to use on him, catching her lower lip with her teeth as she grins. Locks of curly red hair—mysteries that he and Marilyn, both of them brunettes, have pondered the origin of—drop in her face, getting in her eyes, and she brushes them away with a knuckle, a gesture he already knows she'll keep and use as a teenager, a young woman, a mother. He smiles at her, unable to keep up the sham, and she winks back at him.

"Come push me, Daddy!"

"In a second, honey," he calls. He's got a particularly thorny problem at work to solve, so he's put his head in his hands to think when there's a tremendous crash behind him. He literally jumps in the air.

A panel truck has slammed into an oncoming car by the edge of the playground. Glass shatters and metal squeals as it is torn away from fenders and bumpers. Children, scared by the noise, are screaming before their parents scoop them up in their arms, afraid, perhaps, there will be an explosion or just out of instinct. Elliott is looking directly at the wreck, but it seems indistinct, lacking detail.

He sprints to the edge of the lot anyway, jumps the twisted border fencing. Bystanders are milling around, tending to the drivers. He has no medical training, so he turns instead to the scene by the jungle gym. Kids are screaming. He moves from parent to child to parent in a blur, reassuring and offering a hand. "I'm a psychologist," he says. "Maybe I can help."

Sirens wail. Ambulances arrive. Children are distraught. There are tears and murmurs and embarrassed prayers of thanks that it wasn't them, it wasn't their children. The parents shoot him reproachful looks that he doesn't understand. He'd tried to help, hadn't he? Rebuffed, he turns away, then freezes.

Cee Cee isn't on the bench or on the swings.

She isn't in the playground.

She's gone.

He lurched upright, gasping, his heart lodged high in his throat like he'd swallowed a baseball. Wide-eyed, he glanced around in the dark, trying to place himself. Awareness returned reluctantly in a slow trickle and it was a long minute before he remembered where he was, when he was, who he was.

My name is Elliott Nash. I am—was—sleeping. A car has crashed nearby.

He eased himself back to the dry earth, feeling his heart settle into a weird arrhythmia, a syncopated triplet that made him simultaneously edgy and hopeful. Flat on his back, with the ball of his thumb pressed to his sternum, he stared upward at the struts and cables of the cathedral-like underside of the bridge. Dust rained down as he listened to the aftermath of the traffic accident above, trying to push away the shreds of his nightmare and separate fact from fiction.

Yes, he and Cee Cee had been at the playground, all those years ago, but there'd been no car crash, no heroic parents staunching the flow of blood. His brain, wonderfully resilient and creative, had simply used what it could find lying around—his bottomless well of guilt, his sensitivity to the world around him, the crash that had just occurred above his head—to cobble together a new and improved nightmare for him. A dream featuring *sensory incorporation of external stimuli*, as he and his old psychology textbooks had once called it.

In truth, he'd probably brought it on himself, priming the pump of his guilt with his little nightly ritual of saying good night to Cee Cee before drifting off. Thing was, each night for the last eight years, she'd said it right back, as clearly as she'd ever said it in life. Until recently. Her voice had begun to fade, and for several weeks now, his nightly farewell went unanswered. In turn, his nightmares had become more frequent, more punishing.

His former self smiled patronizingly and reached for the textbook again. Flipped to the glossary in the back, stopped at *T* for *transient auditory hallucination*.

Voices in your head, is that it, Dr. Nash?

"No!" he said aloud. *That "hallucination" has kept me alive for eight years. And it will kill me if I never hear it again.*

A high-pitched wail split the air and his heart started to bang away again, a three-legged horse trying to burst out of his chest. He put his hands over his face. *Please, no screams.* It was a selfish thought, one he should've been ashamed of. Someone might be dying or hurt up there. But over the years he'd learned to be greedy, at least with his emotions. Not just because the screams were bad—of course they were—but, when muffled or heard from far away, they sounded like the cries of children.

The wail changed pitch and his shoulders slumped in relief. Not screams, just an ambulance, maybe two, rushing to the scene. The sirens piled on top of each other, different threads of sound in a tapestry of disaster. He lay for a moment, listening, but the intimation of injury and death nearby quickly became too much to take.

Kneeling in the dirt, joints creaking, he rolled the quilted freight blanket into a spiral, brushing it clean before cinching it tight with an old belt. He ran a hand over the dirty knapsack he used as a pillow, having been robbed before with his head still on it. It didn't matter what was in there; people would steal anything because value was irrelevant. When you had nothing, anything was a prize.

He slung the bedroll and pack over one shoulder, sparing a quick glance around the abutment that had been his home for a few hours. Before he'd bunked down, he'd cleared the area of the bottles and flasks lined up against the abutment wall, pitching them into the river rather than be tempted by the few drops left in the bottom. With the trash gone, it was a good spot—he'd been lucky to have it to himself—and would be claimed by someone else before too long. Nights were getting colder, and when the wind picked up along the Potomac and the autumn rain came thrashing down, it could literally kill you to not have a roof over your head. But it wasn't worth fighting someone for it. He didn't have the energy and, anyway, there was nothing sadder than a fight between bums. Plenty of other places to hole up out there.

He climbed the embankment next to the bridge, emerging close to the road like a mole popping out of the ground. He glanced across the water at the bright lights of Washington, DC. Traffic already choked the parkway in a bright line as far as he could see, four lanes of cattle nosing their way out of the city after a hard day's work at a desk. Music and muffled talk show nonsense *wah-wahed* through closed windows. He kept his back to the wreck, but splashes of blue and red reflected off bumpers and fenders. To his right, a panel van changed lanes at a crawl, easing through the spaces in a futile attempt to make headway. His stomach clutched at the sight and he had to turn away.

The driver closest to him caught his eye. A young woman, late twenties. Talking on a phone, a look of irritation on her face. Hair, a perfect bob. Clothes, a white blouse underneath a no-nonsense blazer. The hint of a necklace at the throat. Armed and armored from doing battle in the District for some law firm or lobbying group.

Their eyes suddenly met. In the instant before she looked away, he saw the array of emotions he'd come to expect. Pity. Revulsion. A flicker of apprehension, though not much.

What she lacked, he could see, was curiosity. Did she wonder who he was or had been? How he'd gotten here or where he was going? Whether he would live through the night, the week, the year? Did someone care for him or had he cared for someone else in turn, with a love so desperate that it would drive her to tears if he had just a minute to tell her about it?

But why should she care? Maybe he'd asked those questions himself, once, sitting in his car, watching a bum trundle by or hustle to clean his windshield. Maybe he hadn't. He couldn't remember.

He dropped his gaze and put one foot in front of the other, grinding out the steps along the parkway that would take him to the path that led to the town where he would look for a meal or a handout, for a bed or a box. Or, like last night, just a quiet patch of dirt.

But his feet took a detour that his conscious brain hadn't intended. Forty minutes later, from a bench in the far corner of the Alexandria Presbyterian cemetery, Elliott looked out over the shoulders of granite headstones, immovable sentries marching away from him in columns and rows. Unlike the chaos on the bridge, the night here was cold, quiet, and still.

Ornately fashioned streetlamps, meant to evoke Victorian gaslights, perhaps, were placed sporadically along the road leading to the cemetery, but there were none in the graveyard itself, leaving the middle spaces dark and surrounded by silent, skeletal trees.

He avoided the cemetery during the day. Dog walkers and joggers had reported him before, finding his violation greater than their own. Once upon a time, he'd tried to avoid them by going to the far corner of the massive grounds, a muddy niche out of sight of the gravel path, but he'd realized his mistake staring down at the rain-drenched Barbie dolls and decaying stuffed animals, soggy handwritten notes and chipped plastic tiaras—it was the children's cemetery. Gulls wheeled and screamed in the sky. He'd fled, certain he was going to lose his mind.

Later, however, he found that the center of the cemetery was a place of peace after sunset, where he could sit undisturbed and watch the night unfold.

Tonight was exceptionally clear for November, and the oncoming winter sky with all its stars was open to him, obscured only intermittently by his clouding breath. Leaves of birch trees, curling and brown but stubbornly holding on, rattled nearby.

Eight years ago, the wounds had been raw and wide. His little girl gone, his marriage dissolved, his career a fast-fading memory. The one thing that would stay constant, he knew even then, was the pain. He'd thought about his life, before and after, looking for meaning. Nothing had come to him and, for no particular reason, he'd decided to carry on until, in time, persevering itself became the purpose. Had it been courage or cowardice? He still didn't know.

Learning to survive on the streets came incrementally. A lesson here, a beat down there. He'd accepted it all until he found a kind of equilibrium—don't expect too much, take what you can, move on. He managed to stay alive and, for a time, he even fooled himself into thinking that he'd found a sliver of purpose. Reaching out to the homeless around him, he'd started using old skills again, talking to them or, more often, listening. Trying to help. Throughout it all, Cee Cee's voice kept him going.

As time passed, however, he began to see the same people begin to slip away—to drugs, to booze, to crippling mental health problems.

There were no long-term solutions for street people, only temporary stays. He watched an endless procession of damaged souls walk the streets, get help, only to wind up back on those streets again.

His drive to help them withered away and with it went Cee Cee's voice until, a week ago, it had culminated in him sitting here, in this very spot in the cemetery—as dead inside as any body in the ground around him—thinking about what the last eight years had yielded. The pain had devolved into the dull ache promised on daytime talk shows, but that only described its intensity, not its persistence. His work on the streets, if you could call it that, had amounted to nothing. He had never done less with his life. He'd never been worth less in his life.

As if in a trance, he'd stood and shuffled out of the cemetery toward the downtown area. Drinkers and diners had been out in force. A couple, holding hands and with eyes only for each other, had crossed in front of him and opened the door to a restaurant. Laughter and voices, the clatter of dishes and glasses, had splashed onto the street, then were cut off as the door swung shut.

The vitality of so many people had overwhelmed him. He'd ducked into an alley to escape. Threading his way past dumpsters and loading docks, he'd crossed one last street before finding himself near the train station.

He'd jumped the fence and skulked toward the tracks, timing his movements so the station attendant wouldn't see him. A pile of railroad ties had given him a place to hide. He'd squatted there until the rumble of an oncoming engine vibrated up through his feet; then he'd crawled forward, his heart thrashing in his chest. Down the line, a train ground its way along the track at a glacial four or five miles an hour. Slow, but enough to do the job.

Swallowing convulsively, he'd lowered himself to the track and placed his head on the rail, his cheek resting on the cold steel, facing the train as it came into the station.

The single headlight, a blinding eye, stared back at him.

Vibrations ran down the rail, so strong they rattled his teeth and bruised his cheek.

The noise of the engine was the sound of a thousand horses, a rock slide, the crash of a tidal wave.

The instinct to run had been overpowering, and he'd fought to keep his head pressed to the rail. He forced himself to watch as it came closer, the bones in his body turning to jelly. Despite the fear coursing through his body, he'd smiled. Eight years of pain, seemingly so unnecessary now, about to disappear in an instant.

He closed his eyes, then said goodbye to Cee Cee instead of his normal *Good night, baby.* It was the closest thing to prayer or a wish he'd made in all that time. Hoping to hear her voice one last time.

But there was no answer.

Why? He almost screamed it. *Why won't you talk to me?*

The roar of the engine filled his mind, invaded every part of his body. The train was almost on top of him.

Suddenly he was off the track, rolling in the cinders, thrusting himself out of the way of the train, yelling, screaming at the top of his lungs. The heat of the engine had scorched him as he'd kicked and bucked away from the rail.

Lying on the berm an arm's length from the track, he'd cried, bawled like a baby, because he wanted to live, he just didn't know why.

He sat in the cemetery now, remembering that night. Somewhere above his head, a mockingbird trilled a nighttime song.

Elliott reached up and touched his face. His beard was still singed from the heat of the train. That's how close he'd been.

Why not end it all, Dr. Nash? What are you holding on for?

He had no answer. But one thing he did know: if he was going to go on living, he needed to hear his little girl's voice again.

2

Amy

With one foot mashing the clutch and the other braced against the dashboard, Amy gritted her teeth, grabbed the shifter in both hands, and leaned back. It was her third and probably final try to move it back to "R." Behind her, the cars that had piled up waiting for her to park began honking, unaware that it was a minor miracle that the little car had managed to cross the river from DC to Virginia in one piece.

The stick wiggled in her hand, then chunked into gear. Humming a prayer of thanks, she hauled on the wheel with a practiced move, punched the gas, and slid her little rust bucket into the space. The Celica didn't mind drive as much as reverse, and she straightened the car out and shut the engine off in a snap.

As the convoy of cars slid past, she turned in her seat and flashed each of them her sweetest smile of apology. The last driver, a pale, fat guy crammed into a yellow minivan like the cream filling in a Twinkie, yelled something obscene as he passed her. She offered him the same smile she'd given the others. What had she read in the paper the other day? *Share a piece of your heart instead of your mind.* Then again, she'd also read, *Whatever gets you through the day*, so she flipped off his rapidly disappearing bumper.

The driver's door hadn't worked for months, so she grabbed her pack of Marlboros off the dash and began the contorted dance across the seat to the passenger's side, arching her back to avoid getting jabbed in the kidney by the emergency brake.

As she wriggled across the seat, her pocket rattled like dice in a cup. Inside was a little, ugly, orange plastic bottle with its awkward, child-proof, adult-accessible cap, and inside that were seven white, oblong pills. They'd been in there, untouched, for almost a year. The sound sent a ripple of disgust through her, and she put a hand over her pocket to quiet it, but made no move to leave the bottle in the car. It belonged in her pocket as much as the crystal around her neck or the ankh tattooed on her wrist.

She hopped out, slammed the screeching door, and headed east toward the water. No need to lock it; there was nothing to steal, and she couldn't afford to fix the window if someone broke it trying to get in. They were welcome to the handful of candy wrappers and the dream catcher hanging from the rearview mirror.

Then again, Old Town Alexandria didn't look like a neighborhood with those kind of problems. It was a hamlet of fired bricks and cobble-stone streets, with businesses that could afford to close for lunch and boutiques she could only dream of visiting. They had garden tours and parades and bakeries for dogs marked by signs designed to look like pink bows wrapped around a bone.

It was nothing like her own tiny studio in a corner of DC, where sometimes the electricity worked and sometimes it didn't, and some-times the trash was picked up and sometimes it sat on the curb for weeks on end. Where you went when you had just enough to get by, but definitely not enough to get ahead.

No, people here turned up their collars on their trench coats when a gust of wind kicked up dirt and leaves with a sound like running water. They stepped carefully over puddles to keep their shoes dry. More importantly, they looked like they had somewhere to go and were on a mission to get there. Where Amy lived, almost no one moved with purpose; entertainment was to sit on the front stoop and watch the world leave them behind.

But in Alexandria, it was a sunny, crystal-blue morning, gorgeous as November days went, though unpredictable—fast-moving clouds shrouded the street in shade every few minutes. Amy pulled the long sleeves of her sweatshirt over her hands, then shoved them into her armpits, twisting her arms tight into her center, trying to trap the warmth there.

She took her time on King Street, peering into the windows, considering purchasing things she had no money for, keeping her head down as she passed. She was stalling, she knew, an attempt to warm up to the job she'd given herself.

It wasn't the mechanics of the task—she knew what to do. Detective Cargill had given her directions, told her what to say, even let her know where to park. She had questions that desperately needed answers, and this was her best shot to get them, now that the police had officially given up.

Francis House wasn't what she'd imagined. From Cargill's description, she'd pictured a medieval monastery, all dark stone and fake arrow slits, like the churches she remembered from her childhood in Ohio. Instead, what she found was a sand-colored, institutional-looking building from an era when funding was as scarce as imagination, squeezed between two other more modern office towers. Anonymous and unremarkable, it could've been a school or the sewer authority or the county unemployment office.

A knot of men and women of all ages and races huddled outside the building's double doors. Each wore layers of accumulated clothing: shiny jogging shorts over dirty jeans, or a sweater with a vest and a turtleneck. Some stood, some leaned, and some slouched, but the way they did all these things made it evident they were tired, both in the short haul and the long run. They were secondhand parts in a broken machine.

One or two swayed in place, a hand pressed to the wall for support. They had the look of old pros. It was late morning, the lowest point of the day—they were caught halfway between the damage of one drink or one pill and the bliss of the next. As she walked toward them, her mouth puckered and her heart slammed a quick dozen beats in her rib cage.

Sliding a hand into her pocket, she grabbed the pill bottle and gave it a little shake. The rattle gave her the tiniest peace of mind she needed, and her heart slipped back to its regular rhythm.

"Ain't open until eleven, miss," a man in a green poncho said as she walked up. A large wen on his forehead stood out above soulful eyes.

Amy's heart sank. "It's not open?"

"*Kitchen* ain't open," an older white woman sitting on the steps corrected. Frizzy gray hair stood out in tangles from her scalp. The collars and cuffs of three different coats peeked out from under one another. The pile of clothing made her already broad shape indistinct along the edges. "You can go in, you got business, but Sister Madeline will shoo you out if you're here for the food. They don't like no one trying to get ahead of no one else."

She thanked them and passed through the glass doors as the conversation veered toward other topics. Inside, the building was as functional and institutional as the outside, with a long central hall branching off in three different directions. Clouds of bleach and old coffee sat on the air. Unsure where to go, Amy stood in the foyer. She flinched at the distant clash of dishes, then jumped at the even louder sound of metal pans hitting the floor immediately after.

A door in the hall opened and a woman's head, adorned in a nun's habit, popped out. She had turned automatically to the right, toward the source of the noise, then came fully out into the hall. As a reflex, she glanced toward the front door and started when she saw Amy standing there. Her face, doughy and wrinkled, held the businesslike expression of those who dole out kindness on an industrial scale.

"The kitchen's not open—"

"Until eleven. I know," Amy said. "I'm not here for the food, Sister. Detective Dave Cargill sent me."

The sister, already moving toward the source of the noise, stopped and pivoted at the unexpected answer. "How can I help you, then?"

"I'm looking for a man named Elliott. Elliott Nash. Detective Cargill said he might be able to help me."

"Help you how?"

"He . . . he might be able to find someone I'm looking for."

"Yes?" the nun prompted. "Find who?"

She swallowed and the lump in her throat, almost a year later, was instantly there. Answering a thousand times hadn't made it any easier. The nun looked at her, her eyes wet and unblinking, a fish-eyed stare that was neither unsympathetic nor impatient; she'd simply heard and seen too much.

Amy breathed in slowly, then exhaled her answer, giving life and sound to her last hope. "Almost a year ago, someone very special was taken from me and hasn't been seen since. The police have closed the case. And the last person who might be able to help me is Elliott Nash. That's why I need to find him."

The nun's stare softened. "Then I guess we'd better find him for you."

3

Sister

Sister stared up at the coffered ceiling. High, thin windows let in a milky light that illuminated crown molding, the flags in their brass stands, the hard, marble floor. The floor she was sitting on right now.

Why was she sitting on the floor?

Flat, clapping footsteps came close, rousing her. "Hon, are you all right?"

Sister looked up, but the face didn't register right away. It never did.

The face loomed closer, but it was still as featureless as an egg. A tentative hand reached out to touch her shoulder. "Hey, it's me. Denise."

Where am I?

By force of will, she bore down on the fear, clamping down on it long enough to get her bearings. Where was she? She was sitting on the corner bench by the elevators. No. No, she wasn't sitting on the bench, she was squatting next to it like an ape, one hand grasping the hard oak arm for balance.

Her thighs were burning, so she must've been down here for a while. Her legs were splayed open by the position. A compromising situation that should've embarrassed her—it would've mortified her mother's social and religious sensibilities—but in a lifetime of setbacks and horrors, it was not something that even registered.

Besides Denise's questions, the only other noise was a reedy whistle that, she realized, was the sound of her own breathing, passing in and out of her open mouth. Tears had slipped down to her nose to join the snot, and the combination had cascaded down to merge with a thin line of saliva that had escaped her lips.

The voice came back. "Do I need to get security? Did someone . . . were you assaulted?"

Assaulted? What a meaningless, inadequate word. How did you explain that a Friday afternoon office prank, meant in good fun, was enough to send her right up to the edge of sanity, close enough to look over the lip, in fact, where she could see firsthand what would happen if she let go?

A couple of young idiots, excited by the prospect of the weekend, had gotten carried away, laughing, pulling her by the arms into the elevator. *Come to happy hour with us! Forget the stairs. Get in here!* But all she could see was a miniature steel cube, stuffed with people, and growing smaller by the second, ready to trap her, to suffocate her.

It was a special thing, this fear of hers. Like a time machine, but one that only went back to a single place, a special little Hell specially made for her, a three-by-three-by-three metal box where the door slowly closed on her life . . .

A tiny, far-off voice reminded her she'd done the same to little Maggie in the name of discipline. *Wasn't it a horrible thing,* the voice seemed to say, *that you were so very willing to visit this same terror upon her?*

She pushed the thought out of her mind. A single episode was nothing compared to the horror her mother had exposed her to, time and again. Maggie would recover and, in time, appreciate the . . . correction.

Sucking in a deep, clean, mind-clearing inhalation, she smiled and forced herself to pull the face in front of her into focus. It was Denise, just like she'd said, the young girl from Document Control.

"Thank you, Denise." She wiped the back of her hand across her face, ignoring the smear it left on her blouse, then pushed herself to her feet and sat on the bench. "Oh, I must look like a mess."

"You could say that. What happened? Are you hurt?"

"You know," she said, wiping the tears away with a finger, careful not to smear her mascara, "about ten years ago I hurt my back lifting a box of those damn legal books, and it hasn't been the same since. The doctor said it was a slipped disc and tried to get me into the OR, but who wants to have back surgery?" Her voice was high pitched, she knew, but she couldn't control it. Close to babbling, snatching at any idea that would sound halfway sane, she forced herself to slow down. "Anyway, sometimes I have a spasm at the worst time. I was standing here at the elevators and it just went *snap!* like that. The pain is incredible, but if I wait long enough it gets better on its own."

Denise looked at her skeptically. "Slipped disc?"

"Yes. Terrible thing to have. I hope you never suffer from it."

The woman bit her lip, struggling with something. "You know, my husband was an infantryman in Iraq for three tours. And about once a week, he wakes up in a panic, with the same look on his face you had just a minute ago. Like he's being hunted."

"Is that so?" *Please go away.*

"And then he dives under the bed for cover until I coax him back out."

"What a terrible thing to go through."

"What I'm saying is, you look like you've got something terrible going on. Not just something physical; something inside of you. My husband was diagnosed with PTSD, but combat isn't the only way you get it."

"I'm fine, really," she said. Tottering in place, she patted her hair and smoothed her skirt with her hands. She smiled at Denise, who had an expression of worry bordering on action. *She knows you're lying. Say something!*

She sighed, then looked the woman in the eye. "You're right, Denise, I don't have a slipped disc. I'm terribly claustrophobic. It's not something I like to tell people, but I've been afraid of small spaces since I was a child. Before you came down the hall, Noah and all the other interns wanted me to get a drink with them—me! Going to a bar, can you imagine?"

"What happened?"

"They tried to pull me into the elevator. It was all I could do to keep from screaming. The doors shut, and that's all I remembered until you came to my rescue."

A light bulb went on for Denise, and her mouth made an "O" of discovery. "Is that why you take the stairs?"

She nodded. "It's all I can do to stay in the office, it seems so small to me sometimes. And an *elevator*?" She shuddered. "I'd rather die."

"I think I'll be having a talk with Mr. Noah," Denise said grimly. "He and those other monkeys probably didn't give it a second thought."

"That really is so kind of you, but I'm afraid if you said something to them, they'd either torture me with it or think I'm crazy. They're so much younger than I am, I feel like they barely listen to me as it is. Please, let's just keep it our secret."

"You're sure?"

"Absolutely."

"And you don't need to see a doctor or anything?"

"I'm fine now. Truly."

"You better not be kidding. You know this place would shut down without you." Denise reached out and patted her hand. "It's Friday. Why don't you knock off early, try to forget about it? Make it an early weekend. Go home and spend some time with your family."

The bland words had been meant as a kind of generic sympathy, but she could feel her heart grow lighter at the thought. She gave Denise a wide, genuine smile. "Yes, I think I'll do that. I'll go home and see my family. You know, I have so much to do when I get home, but that's just what the doctor ordered."

4

Amy

The wind-whipped day that had started cheerful and bright had given way to a bruise-blue veil as the sun dipped over the horizon. Streetlamps flickered to life, and anyone left on the street now had their heads down and shoulders hunched, with a firm destination in mind and people to go home to. Amy cruised Old Town slowly in the failing light, looking for the landmarks Sister Madeline had given her.

"From the end of Union Street," the nun had said, "with the river on your left, look for a ragged dirt path. Follow it far enough and it should lead you to a homeless camp. There's a good chance Elliott will be there. He tries to help some of the other homeless folks. Talking to them, listening to their problems. During the winter, he does it at the shelters, but in the fall months, the best place to find the most homeless souls is that little shanty village."

"He talks to them?"

"Yes. He was a psychiatrist or psychologist before . . ." She cleared her throat. "Well, before whatever happened, happened."

"That's kind of him."

"It is, although I think it helps him, as well. To be needed, I mean." She sighed. "At least, it *did*."

"What do you mean?"

The nun wrung her hands. "For the past couple of months . . . well, I don't wish to violate his privacy. We try to look out for him, but . . . we can't always be there."

"We?"

A rosy blush touched the edges of her face. "Detective Cargill calls from time to time, asking about Elliott. I think he asks the local police officers to keep an eye out, as well. Elliott has people who care for him; if only he'd do the same for himself."

Now Amy stood at the head of that path, a patch of woods dead in front of her. To the left was a new townhome community. **HOUNDSTOOTH PIER**, gilt letters, begonias surrounding a faux gatehouse, a colonial motif. Wedges of warm lamplight spilled out of windows. Beyond, visible through a gap in the rows, the river slopped against an elaborately bricked quay. It seemed strange to think there was a homeless community five minutes' walk from these million-dollar homes, or that the people in them were oblivious to the fact.

Amy pulled her sweatshirt tighter around her body, then crossed the street. The path was muddy and narrow, but well used. In the twilight, the contrast of gray and green—trees and shrubs—was the only guide she had. She hadn't thought to bring a flashlight, naturally, and her little flip phone was so ancient it didn't have a light. Soon, however, she saw the sharp, industrial glint of the Wilson Bridge towering above and ahead.

She stood for a minute, listening. The constant hum of traffic was a lonely sound. A horde of people, rushing home, unaware that she looked up at them from a hundred feet below.

On the far side of the bridge it was more of the same, but she was much closer to the edge of the Potomac and could see the sluggish movement of the water through the trees, illuminated by the distant lights of the malls and parks across the river.

A low murmur reached her ears and she tracked the noise to her right, pushing forward until she saw a subdued glow, like polished brass. The glow turned into one, then three, then five small fires, each with a handful of forms huddled around it, alternately holding their hands or feet toward the flames. Behind or beside each person were mounds, some rectangular and towering chest-high—shopping carts, she realized—others a single backpack or piece of luggage kept close.

The closest gathering looked her way as she came close. A form, rotund in layers of swaddled clothes, struggled to its feet and waddled close. The smell of moldy sneakers and body odor was overwhelming. "Gemmy? Is that you?"

"No," Amy said, taking a step back. "I'm sorry, I'm not Gemmy."

"Then who the hell are you?"

"I'm looking for someone named Elliott," she said. "Elliott Nash."

"The shrink?"

"I . . . yes, guess so."

"Didn't see him come in, but you can try over there." The figure raised an arm.

Amy shuffled toward the row of fires. Heads turned in her direction as she passed, and she suddenly lost confidence as she looked back at the faceless black forms. Her voice caught in her throat as she spoke, and she coughed twice before she could speak again. "I'm looking for Elliott Nash."

Murmurs rose as they discussed among themselves. A knot of figures shouted at her to speak up.

She raised her voice and tried again. "I said, I'm looking for Elliott Nash. He's a . . . he was a doctor. A psychologist."

A deep pause followed and she realized her mistake. Many homeless people had been diagnosed with mental illnesses, might've been *made* homeless by that diagnosis. Psychologists might've been who institutionalized or medicated them, separated them from family or friends, from parents or children. Declared them mentally unfit to act as husbands or wives or children. She could sympathize.

A lanky form stood up at the farthest edge of the makeshift village, where several people circled a fire. The voice, low but powerful, carried across the huddled homeless. "I'm Elliott Nash."

Amy moved forward awkwardly, unsure whether to shake his hand or what, so she went with the simplest approach. "Dr. Nash—"

"Elliott." Nash's face, long and gaunt, was pulled even longer by a beard that hung almost to his chest. Dark eyes and a slightly hooked nose gave him the look of a hermit or a medieval crusader.

"Elliott." She paused, pulling her thoughts together. "My name is Amy Scowcroft, and I've come to ask you to help me find my daughter."

He opened his mouth to answer, but a crash of thunder obliterated whatever he was going to say. A second later, rain swept through the trees with a sound like a breaking wave. Amy hunched her shoulders instinctively as the drops fell like pebbles.

"What did you say?" she yelled.

"I said, I can't help you."

"Why not?"

"I don't help people anymore."

"But you haven't even heard what I have to say!"

"I don't need to."

She fought to keep her voice even, logical, but the panic rose in her chest. *If he won't even listen to me* . . . "Dr. Nash, Elliott, whatever. Please. My daughter's been missing for almost a year. The police have given up. I am out of options. I was told you were the only person in the world who might still care enough to help me." Her eyes flicked back and forth, trying to read his mind. "Please. I don't have anyone else."

He stared at her. Rain collected on his brow, dripped off his nose. "Who sent you?"

"Detective Dave Cargill."

His face flickered for a moment. Or it might've been the distant flash of lightning. He looked to the side, as if considering, then grabbed a grubby knapsack off the ground. "Follow me."

They slipped away unnoticed, leaving the other homeless men and women huddled in miserable bunches under the leafless sweetgums and sycamores. Elliott led them along a barely discernible path through the woods, away from the river and the camp.

In time, they came to a line of ragged fencing marking a rectangular plot of land cleared on the edge of the woods. In the corner of the plot was a shed made of weather-beaten boards and a corrugated roof tilted at a rakish slant. Mopping the rain from his face, he grubbed around in his knapsack, then pulled out a flathead screwdriver with half the handle missing. Ignoring the lock on the door, he popped the hasp instead.

The door swung open like the cover of a book, and Amy had to turn her head sharply at the fecund scent of fertilizer. Elliott ventured inside with his hands outstretched, disappearing into the shed's gloomy interior. She heard a bump, the sound of falling rakes and shovels; then the tiny space was filled with a low-wattage glow from a utility lamp. It swung in a small arc, sending shadows around the walls. He gestured impatiently for her to come in and she did, closing the door just as the rain doubled in strength, drumming a loud tattoo on the roof.

She looked around at the tools leaning in a corner, the neatly stacked plastic bags of mulch and soil. A rough potter's bench had been knocked together with a few pieces of scrap wood. On it was a shoe box with paper seed packets, their corners peeking out.

She slicked her hair back with one hand. "Community garden?"

He nodded. "The last squash came up two weeks ago, and no one's thought about coming around since. It's not the Taj Mahal, but it's dry and out of the wind."

"Sleeping on mulch can't be too comfortable," she said with a small smile, looking for something to say.

"If you think so, you've never slept on a sidewalk." Her face must've looked pained, and he grimaced. "I meant that it's not so bad. Mulch isn't a feather bed, but it's actually better than the cots at the shelter . . ."

His voice trailed off awkwardly. Looking nonplussed, he turned and punched a comfortable depression in one of the bags and sat. After a moment, she matched him, sitting between two stacks of potting soil like it was a throne. They looked at each other for a moment. The shadows on his face curved down from his cheeks like bird's wings, becoming indistinct when they reached the jungle of his beard.

She was poor, he would think, and undernourished. Maybe the ragged sweatshirt and ripped jeans were masquerading as shabby chic and the thin face with the sharp cheekbones just the results of the latest fad diet, but surely he'd seen enough poor people to know the difference between fashion and circumstance. Her long blonde hair was chopped unevenly—anybody could see it had been a quick job with a rubber band and a pair of scissors—and she knew she lacked a certain polish, which told others she either didn't have a job or couldn't hold one. Hollowed-out eyes and a perpetual frown told him more, she was sure. So many people had stopped her in checkout lines and in the stores to ask her what was wrong that she'd taken to lying, telling them she was sick, letting them think she had cancer, just to get them to stop asking.

He gave a cough, as though to knock the rust from his voice. "Your name is Amy Scowcroft. Your daughter is missing. Dave Cargill sent you to me. You think I can help you. Do I have it right so far?"

"Yes."

"Give me the rest." His voice was gruff. "Keep it short."

She composed herself. "We live in DC, in Southeast, in a tiny studio, just the two of us. Lacey looks like a miniature me, even down to the gray sweatshirt." She raised a sodden sleeve. "But from there the comparison stops. She's cute. Smart. Headstrong. A little too headstrong, sometimes, maybe. Focused. She never made friends easily, but once she did, it stuck."

"How old?"

"Ten."

He nodded, then gestured for her to keep going.

"Just under a year ago, Lacey was walking home from a friend's house when she didn't come home, that night or . . . after. She simply disappeared, right off the street. She hasn't been seen since."

"No witnesses?"

Amy shook her head. "She vanished. I canvassed the streets passing out fliers, going door to door, calling radio and TV stations with her description. No one ever came forward to say they'd seen her abducted."

"So, no AMBER Alert?"

"No."

"And a . . . body was never found?"

"No."

"What about the police? You said they'd given up."

She folded her hands and looked into a dark corner of the shed. "They tried for a while, but one of them finally told me they'd been ordered to move on, that the case had been officially closed for months, but a few of them were logging extra hours anyway, hoping for a break."

Elliott said nothing.

"I begged them to stay on the case. I didn't understand how they could let my child, any child, just disappear. Then they told me that Lacey was one of hundreds of children who go missing, and she was, at the end of the day, just a number."

"And you wouldn't take no for an answer?"

"In a manner of speaking." She gave him a weak smile. "I broke down, then, I guess. Really lost my squash, as my dad used to say. I cried, I beat my chest, I think I even threatened to go to the media and expose them as lazy good-for-nothings. I was . . . escorted from police headquarters more than once."

"But not before they told you to come find me?"

"One of them, the kindest one of the bunch, the one who tried longer than the rest, told me about you. Someone who might be able to help me, who would understand what I was going through."

"Dave Cargill."

"Yes."

"Did he tell you why?"

"He said you were a psychologist. That you had worked for the police as a consultant profiling criminals, testifying, helping the cops see past the crime to the criminal, I think is the way he put it. Really talented." She hesitated. "He wanted to say more, but something stopped him."

She watched as he closed his eyes, let the air leak out through his nose. He stayed that way for a minute, then opened them and looked at her across the shadowy distance. "It's been eleven months, nearly a year since your daughter went missing?"

"Yes."

"And you think she's alive?"

"Yes."

"The statistics alone should tell you that your daughter is beyond help."

She leaned forward. "I know the statistics. Believe me, I know. Every cop and social worker I met made sure I knew. But I'll tell you what I told them: an infinite space still exists between Lacey being just another number and still breathing."

"Not infinite," he said, a cruel thing to say. To test her? she wondered. To test himself? "What if they're right? What if she's gone?"

"I choose to believe they're wrong."

"Choosing to believe a reality and living it are two different things," he pressed. "You might not have the luxury of simply ignoring the truth."

She took a moment before answering. "When I was very young, we had a pet toad. I named it Hoppy and doted on it. After a year or so, it died a natural death. Absolutely normal, but its short life span came as a total surprise to me. I had made goofy, elaborate plans for our life together."

Elliott said nothing.

"So, there I was," Amy continued, "looking down at his little, deflated green body, and I asked my mother, 'Where'd Hoppy go?' I should say that my mother was an adjunct professor of philosophy at a local community college and liked using her education to instruct outside the classroom. She called it 'applied philosophy.'"

"As though belief and thought are distinct from life."

"Exactly. So when I asked her about Hoppy, she pursed her lips and asked, 'What is the nature of your question, dear?'"

He snorted. "How old were you?"

"Five. A bit too young for existential questions like 'What is death?' or 'What is the meaning of our existence?'" She was silent for a moment. "Ten years later, my dad was killed in a car accident, and I wanted to ask some of those questions again. *Where is Dad? When will I see him again? If he's gone, why can I still sense his presence?* I felt my mother's eyes on me, wanting me to ask her."

"But you didn't."

"No. Because by then I knew her philosophies couldn't encompass the response I needed or wanted. I required a better answer than she could provide." Amy thought about it. "So, now, when people seem to be saying *your daughter is gone, give up*, I want to say, if Lacey is dead, why can I still feel her? Still sense her? Feel the impression of her head on my breast and her breath on my face?"

Elliott smiled thinly. "What is the nature of your question?"

"The nature of my question is, *What else am I supposed to do?* Until I see her body or until I get her back, Lacey is alive to me. She has to be. Statistics, philosophies, history—they're all useless." She pounded a fist to her chest. "The connection between me and my daughter is what matters. The only thing that matters."

Elliott put his head back until it rested against one of the giant bags of dirt. Seemingly unaware of what he was doing, he raised a hand to his face and touched his own cheek, then let it drop. Overhead, the rain drummed steadily on the corrugated roof.

"Elliott? Dr. Nash?"

He cleared his throat, still looking at the ceiling. "Can I ask you something?"

"Sure."

"Do you . . ." His voice faded. "Do you ever hear your daughter?"

"Hear her?" she asked, her voice catching in her throat.

Elliott looked away, embarrassed. "Forget I asked."

"If I say yes, you won't think I'm crazy?"

"I was a psychologist. Crazy is a relative term for me," he said.

"I can still hear Lacey sing to herself, very late at night. Almost to keep herself brave. But when I told the police I could hear her, I could feel her emotions, they started to shut me out."

He stared back at her. "Does Lacey . . . speak to you?"

"Directly? No," she answered sadly. "It's like I have a connection, but it's only one way. I hope she can feel me, hear me, too."

He sagged back into the bags and sighed, a long rattle that started in his chest and worked its way up his throat. "Why me, Amy Scowcroft? You have no family, no friends?"

Her expression was bleak. "No, I . . . don't have anyone else. All the resources that were brought to bear—the police, the press, the community—they've moved on. I can't afford to pay anyone to look for my daughter, and I can't talk anyone else into helping me. All I've got is myself—and you, if you'll help me."

"What makes you think I can do anything for you?" He gestured at himself. "I'm a wreck. I sleep in boxes. I beg for food. I'm worse than nothing."

"Detective Cargill is a good man. He wouldn't tell me to reach out unless he thought you could help me. Your skills as a psychologist, your experience understanding criminals, your empathy . . . I don't know, he saw something, remembered something, that told him you'd be able to help me find out who took my daughter."

Before he looked away, the stoic mask he'd been wearing slipped and she flinched at the pain and sadness she saw there, a physical match for the grief she felt herself.

"That's a good reason for Amy Scowcroft," he said. "But why should I help you?"

She leaned in and pinned him with her eyes. "Something terrible happened to you, Elliott. I don't know what it was, but I know you're searching for a way to make sense of it, of how this . . . *thing*, this horrific event, fits into your life. Or how your life fits into it."

He snorted, but she pressed on, moving closer.

"Listen to me. Maybe you've given up and you think there's nothing left for you, or maybe you're just . . . tired of asking *why.* I get it, believe me. But if you think there's a chance, any chance in the world, that your life could use a guide or a goal or a purpose right now, there's this. There's Lacey. There's me, sitting here, asking you. Help me find my child, Elliott. She's alive, I know she is. But for how long?"

5

The Children

It was Charlie's birthday and they were having a party.

Sister had sent them to their rooms and instructed them to stay there until she called, her eyes gleaming with a feral green light. It was a look adults got from time to time. They'd all seen it before, not that that made it any less scary. That glint said they weren't being seen as children anymore, but as objects, as things.

Huddling in their rooms, they waited for the small brass bell to ring—though, when it came, none of them moved until it rang a second time, insistent and angry. Since the night she'd brought fried chicken home, Sister had been increasingly taciturn with them, even mean, and they'd found it better to stay out of her way, but there was no ignoring this summons. They met in the hall, then shuffled to the landing at the top of the stairs. As they began to descend, Charlotte looked back. Maggie hadn't moved.

"Come on, Maggie," she said, holding out her hand. "We have to go."

"I'm scared," the little girl whispered.

"We won't let her hurt you again," Charlie said, but his voice broke on the word "again." He gave Maggie a weak smile, then held out his hand, too. "We'll go together. It's my birthday, after all."

Charlotte gasped as a thought occurred to her. "Is this . . . ?"

"I don't know," he said, and it was then she could see how scared he was. "What choice do we have?"

Feeling sick, Charlotte grabbed Maggie's hand, coaxing her down a step, then reached back and grabbed Buddy's sweating hand. He held it tight, even though he was a boy. Tina trailed behind, but wouldn't have held hands anyway. Linked, they descended one step at a time.

"Come to the kitchen," Sister called, and they trooped barefoot—none of the old shoes fit them, and they never went outside—down the hall to obey. She stood next to the old soapstone sink, watching them as they filed in. Her hand rested on a large plastic grocery-store clamshell on the counter. Noses lifted. They could smell the sugar in the icing, but they kept their eyes averted.

She told them to sit at their assigned seats, everyone except for Charlie, who was given Sister's chair at the head of the table. Sister was thin and, to them, very tall, with shoulder-length hair parted in the middle and streaked with gray. Sister smiled at them, causing Charlotte to shudder: the gleam in the woman's eyes was gone, replaced by the hollow stare of a predatory bird.

At each place setting was a fork, a small glass of milk, and a battered plastic party hat, oft-handled and missing the original foil fringe. Stained crepe streamers hung from the ceiling, and a cardboard banner pronouncing **Hap y Birthda !** had been strung from the tops of the cabinets so that it hung over the table. Sister put Charlie's hat on for him, fussing with the elastic string under his chin, then stood behind him, one hand on his shoulder. He looked as though he had a stomachache. A large glass of milk, a special treat, sat next to his paper plate.

"It's Charlie's birthday today." The waxy skin of Sister's face was drawn tight over cheeks that shone like market apples. "Put your hats on."

Sister pulled the cake out of the clamshell with a loud pop and set it on the table. She squared it just so, then crossed the floor with jerky movements like she was being pulled by invisible strings.

The lights flicked off and, in the darkness, Sister had to shuffle carefully back to the table, where she fumbled with something that rattled like small bones in a box. The match struck with an orange light that flared harshly in the darkness and filled the room with a sulfuric stink. One by one, she lit the candles.

"Sing to Charlie," Sister commanded. They began to sing then, their high, thin voices never rising beyond a whisper. Sister pushed the cake closer until thirteen candles bathed Charlie's face in their glow, revealing the start of peach fuzz on a face so pale that the veins were visible in his cheeks. He kept his eyes locked on the table in front of the cake.

The song ended and their voices died off. Sister prodded Charlie, who leaned forward and—needing three weak tries—blew the candles out, plunging the room into darkness again. The sharp, sweet smell of smoke filled the room, and the embers at the tips of the candles were tiny orange points of light that died out, one by one.

"Eat your cake and drink your milk, everyone," Sister said in the swiftly fading light. "Today is a very special day for Charlie."

6

Elliott

Elliott stretched long legs out to the sidewalk, warming himself in the sun, trying to leave his inner turmoil behind for once and lose himself in what would probably be one of the last pleasant days of the year.

After a night spent in the shed, he'd set out for Alexandria's shopping district to ease his mind. There was a café where the baristas, some of them just a bit of scratch away from hitting the streets themselves, would pour him a cup if the boss wasn't there and even look the other way when he shambled to the back to perform a quick washup in their only restroom. If the owner walked in, he'd have to dodge out the back and into the parking lot, but even if he got caught, the guy would just growl at him to keep a low profile next time. In fact, Elliott was sure it was the boss who approved the free coffee. People were generally kind. They just weren't always sure how much they should express it.

Today, the young barista had handed him a day-old pastry with the coffee, but asked in a whisper that he please not eat it in the shop. He'd nodded, thanked her, and slipped it into a pocket. As he left, she gave him the sweetest smile he'd seen in a month, and he turned away before she could see what it did to him.

From there, he'd shuffled to one of his favorite spots in town, a set of park benches close to the main street, but with enough distance to keep from scaring people. Elliott sipped his coffee, munched his pastry, and stretched out to enjoy the day until the lack of sleep and sun-filled warmth made him drowsy. Shadows played on the street and sidewalk. With the cup growing cold in his hand, he let his eyes droop.

Of the simple comforts in life, he thought sleepily, there were things he'd forgotten and had learned to like again. A cold glass of water on a hot day. Staying dry under an overhang while the rain fell a foot from your face. Pure sunlight hitting you slantwise on a breezy November day.

Objects meant little to him now that he'd discovered that he could lose nearly all of them without the sky falling, like cars and phones, though it helped when you had nowhere to go and no one to call. Money, it had turned out, was surprisingly unnecessary, though it had taken him years to find ways to manage without it.

Then there were the things you never thought you needed but longed for anyway. Naturally, that particular list could go on and on, but what he really missed, Elliott thought, were keys.

He missed their sound, the jangle that was a particular music different than anyone else's. He missed how he could twirl the ring of them on a finger like a cowboy's six-shooter, holstering them in his pocket as he walked into work. He'd had a dog—Marilyn had taken him when she'd left—that had known the sound of those keys through the door or from the curb. The dog, a collie, would come to the window as soon as he pulled the keys from his pocket and stare at him as he walked up the driveway, prancing in place like she was standing on a hot plate.

After years of living on the street, Elliott had come across his share of discarded keys and toyed with the idea of putting together a fake set, just to hear the jangle once again. But he'd tossed the idea as quickly as it had come to him. Coping mechanisms were nice, but complete fictions were dangerous. It was a short trip from fake keys to an imaginary dog; he'd seen it happen. The healthiest alternative was to take the good things—genuine and unaffected, even if they were humble—as they came to you.

That's what had bothered him about Amy Scowcroft. Her belief she could find her daughter was nothing but a wish. Heartfelt? Of course. Genuine? Certainly. But, in the end, still just a wish. Constructing a set of beliefs around cosmic connections and a mother's intuition didn't change that. It was a delusion.

Like hearing your dead daughter's voice in your head? Nothing like that, is it?

"No, it's not," he snarled. An old man walking by glanced up, alarmed, and took a wide step toward the street. Elliott sagged back against the bench.

The sound of Cee Cee's voice was enough to get him through the day, that's it, that's all it was. A small patch of fabricated reality to help him get by was not the same thing as a life-altering self-delusion.

Life altering? Like the kind that makes you lay your head on a train rail? Choo-choo, Dr. Nash!

He groaned and rolled onto his side on the bench.

He wished Amy Scowcroft well, he really did. But nothing he did for her would matter, and he couldn't face the idea of her fantasy coming unraveled while he watched, sit there while her life burned when the truth was revealed. She could do it on her own, if she wanted. But he simply didn't have the courage to bear witness while it happened.

God damn Dave Cargill for sending her to him. Dave, a good Samaritan even when he *wasn't* being a cop, would've been simultaneously embarrassed and thoughtful, wanting to give her a reason for hope while not quite revealing why it would make sense to seek out a penniless bum for help.

What Dave had remembered was that Elliott had testified in dozens of cases, studied hundreds more, and could read the criminally insane like a road map. He knew the psychological contours of the Ted Bundys and Luis Garavitos and Karl Denkes of the world better than he knew his own family. He'd written for journals, spoken at conferences, and taught at universities. But when the theoretical had become real—very real—for him, none of his training or education or experience ended up mattering one tiny bit. That's the part Dave had forgotten.

He took a moment, willing his irritation to dissipate. To his surprise, it did, and he drifted back into a pleasant dreamy state.

In fact, he felt like he'd been welded to the steel seat, stationary and immovable. *Hypnogogic paralysis*, a distant portion of his mind reminded him, an intellectual remnant of his former life that would take a lobotomy to remove. The same puddle of knowledge also contained the always-entertaining party trivia that some claims of alien abduction could be blamed on a variant of what he was experiencing right now, *hypnopompic hallucination.* He'd actually interviewed an avowed abductee who swore he'd been taken to Neptune and taught to breathe underwater.

But did you remember, a dark memory whispered in his ear, *that a less amusing cause of sleep paralysis is childhood sexual abuse?* The recollection rose like a tide, threatening to drown him, but he gently shoved the thought away, willing it to drift downstream as he'd done with his anger at Dave. Once again, it worked, and he watched his anxiety, whispers fading, float into the distance.

A truck wheeled past, its big engine roaring as it took a right onto Route 1 south, out of town. Someone had the volume on their rap music turned up, but then the light turned green and the sharp, angry lyrics dopplered away. Pedestrians chatted away on their cell phones, a monologue that was not too different from some of the more disturbed homeless he knew.

Elliott's stomach growled as the smell of burned sugar suddenly pushed the stray thoughts aside. A small coffee and a stale pastry didn't amount to much halfway through the day. He sat up groggily.

"What wrong with him, Daddy?" The voice was close enough to be in his ear. Elliott surfaced like a fish on a line.

Standing at the corner, waiting to cross, was a young father holding hands with a little boy on his left and a little girl on his right. Each of them held an ice cream cone only slightly smaller than their heads. The boy looked over his shoulder at Elliott as he took impossibly large licks off the cone. Half of the ice cream made it onto his tongue, the other half onto his face. Elliott tried looking away, but his gaze was pulled back magnetically to the little girl.

As he watched, the top scoop of ice cream slipped off her cone and hit the pavement with an audible splat. She stared at it unbelieving for a moment, then started howling.

"Oh, Taylor," the father said when he saw the catastrophe. "Why couldn't you be more careful?"

The accusation brought on a fresh wave of tears. The father realized his mistake and let go of the boy's hand to kneel and see what kind of triage he could perform on the rapidly melting scoop.

The brother, oblivious to his sister's anguish, tottered over, holding the cone out. "Want some?"

Elliott opened his mouth—*no thanks*—when the father looked up from where he was trying to console his daughter. The man's eyes flickered from his son to Elliott and back again. Emotions played across his face—alarm, guilt, fear—then the father lunged for his son's arm. "Sam, *no!*"

The man yanked the boy away hard enough to make him cry. The father began a whispered lecture, his face down and turned away from Elliott. Behind the unfolding drama, however, something more interesting had caught Taylor's eye: the little girl, ice cream forgotten, turned to watch a dog and his owner sprint across the street on a yellow light, barely missing the red. Smelling the ice cream, the dog strained toward the little girl.

At the sight of the dog, a grin split her face.

Head down, the father lectured his son.

The girl ran.

Crossing traffic surged, a pickup truck roared, the engine impossibly loud. A hoarse shout—*mine?*—ripped the air. Elliott was on his feet and off the curb. The sole of his left shoe came loose, the end flopping open like a drunk's mouth, the tip of his sock lolling like a tongue, hampering him. He was running, reaching, diving.

Muscles he hadn't used in years stretched to the breaking point, screamed as his hands cupped the air. The little girl's face, fear present in every line, was suddenly very close. Green eyes, a snotty nose, sugar-sweet breath.

The squeal of tires.

His reflection in the chrome of a bumper so close.

Elliott folded the little girl to his chest, turning his body, grunting as he took the sharp, wedged impact in the flesh of his upper arm and shoulder.

Both of them were screaming and squirming as he tumbled to the asphalt with the little girl cradled to his chest. He was still flat on his back when the father ripped her from his arms. Elliott's hands remained in position like he was holding a prize—*she was this big*. Traffic was in chaos, pedestrians on the corner were shouting. The driver of the truck was half-out, one foot on the ground, his face pale and sick-looking. Horns honked farther up the line as irate drivers demanded action.

From the ground, Elliott turned his head to see the man hugging both of his children, squeezing them hard, all three of them crying. He rolled over and pushed himself painfully to his feet. His arm and back throbbed like he'd been hit with a bat, but it was the touch of the little girl that had left him dazed. A distant siren brought him to his senses. He hurried to the bench, slung his knapsack across his back, and started to shuffle off.

"Wait!"

Elliott turned. The father, his face tearstained, walked toward him. Elliott began to move faster, expecting an angry accusation or reprimand.

"Please . . . sir," the man said, holding a hand up. "Thank you. That's all I wanted to say. Thank you so much. I can't believe what almost happened. If you hadn't been there, I would've watched—I mean, I shouldn't have taken my eyes off her for a second. If you hadn't been there . . . I would've never forgiven myself. It's all my fault. She could've . . ." He stopped, choking at the thought.

The man's face was grief-stricken, and it was clear he thought he knew what he'd avoided. For a split second, Elliott considered telling him the truth, that the man had no idea how narrowly he had missed a lifetime of self-recrimination and pain. But it would be self-indulgent and cruel and wouldn't make any difference in the long run, anyway.

He sighed. "It wasn't your fault. Nothing happened, which is the way it should be."

The man stared as though he couldn't believe Elliott could speak English. He flushed, then fumbled in a pocket, and for a sickening second Elliott knew the man was going to try and give him money. He held up his palm to turn him down, but a crumpled twenty had been shoved into his hands before he could form the words.

"Please, just take it," the man said, choking. "If you hadn't been here, my life would be . . . I'd be . . ."

Like me? Elliott looked at him, tired. "Look, just . . . learn from this. Cherish your children. Keep them close. But forgive them, forgive yourself. Help someone else. Live your life."

The man started to stammer something else, but Elliott was already moving. He felt the eyes of the street on him. It was time to go. He walked away, leaving the buzz of conversation behind, but unable to ignore the tingling in his arms where he'd cradled the little girl for a few precious seconds. His mind was a riot of emotions.

The girl's body was real. Her life was real. As they'd lain on the road, her chest had expanded and contracted as she'd breathed, her heart had beat fast against his breast. The feeling of the train track, cold on his face, passed through his mind, warring with the human warmth of the little girl's cheek where it had pressed to his, present and alive.

Alive. Because of him.

It isn't enough to be. *You have to* do. *Find purpose by making purpose, by accepting what is offered.*

Something brittle deep inside him snapped and he changed course in midstride, heading for a place where they'd let him use the phone. He had a call to make.

7

Charlotte

It wasn't the bed that bothered Charlotte (although the mattress had lumps the size of her fist and smelled like damp towels), or even the fact that she had to share it. Like the rest of them, her bedmate, Maggie, was skinny from lack of food and exercise and was small, even for six, so she barely took up any space at all. She cried in her sleep sometimes, but everyone cried here.

And she wasn't bothered because the house was dark all the time. Sheets of plywood covered every window, nailed to the outside of the frame, while on the inside, the curtains were pulled tight and tacked to the rotting trim. On the rare occasion sunlight entered the house, it came in slivers formed by warped boards and crooked sills. As long as Sister wasn't looking, they would let the thin, warm wedges of sun play over their faces. But the darkness didn't bother her, not anymore.

What she hated was how quiet the house was, especially at night. There was never an outside noise—not a bird or a car, not the honk of a car horn—and the furnace almost never ran; Sister turned the heat down so low at night that sometimes there was frost on the inside windowsill. But even that would've been all right if there'd been something to hear.

Sometimes she lay so still the blood began to pound in her ears as she tried to catch a sound from the outside. A car. A distant plane. A dog barking down the street. But there was nothing. The silence in the house was so thick that it took on a sound of its own, a low whine that seemed to grow, fade, then begin again.

For all that the house was quiet, it was the silence of a held breath, a tension that held an expectation of release that never came. Lying in bed, stiff as a board, she would wait for something to happen, knowing that just because it hadn't yet didn't mean it wouldn't, or that it wasn't torture waiting for it.

Punishment awaited the first one to make a noise, she was sure. So, if the moldy old sheets brought on a sneeze, she'd pinch her nose and hold it in so tightly that stars would light up in her eyes, careening and crashing in the dark. When she wanted to roll over, she did so in tiny increments so that the springs wouldn't squeak. On most nights, she would lie on her back, staring at the ceiling and listening to the house breathe and sigh, creak and crack. And, naturally, once everyone had turned in for the night, she wouldn't have left the bed for anything less than the house burning down.

Only once—recently—had she been tempted to break her own rule. A wave of cramps had hit her, a feeling like her guts were being pulled out from the bottom up. She'd been seconds away from running for the bathroom, no matter what the punishment, when the pain finally passed, though not without a . . . problem. She'd slid out of bed and did the best she could to clean herself up with some tissues she'd had in her pockets. Instinctively, she'd hidden everything from Sister and the others, although she'd seen Maggie's little eyes glinting in the dark. That had been a month ago, and she was terrified the feeling would return.

And tonight was especially a night to be quiet.

The birthday party had ended in chaos and fear. They'd watched in horror as Charlie had strangely slumped to the kitchen floor. There'd been a frozen moment of shock, then Sister had screeched at them to go to their rooms, screaming and dragging them out of their chairs when they hadn't moved quickly enough, actually swatting Charlotte when she wouldn't stop staring from the kitchen doorway. Charlie was just sick. Very sick. Everything was going to be fine.

She shivered now, thinking about it. Charlie was the oldest and the bravest of them all, always willing to talk back to Sister when she lost her temper and threatened to hurt one of the other kids. Charlotte, wanting to emulate him, had stuck up for Maggie and Buddy when she could, but Sister seemed to have taken a particular dislike to her, and things that Charlie managed to get away with had resulted in slaps and skipped meals and threats of the cellar for her.

The mutual suffering had only served to bring Charlie and Charlotte together. Without actually talking about it, they'd come to consider themselves the protectors of the others. But there was no way she could do it on her own and, after seeing Charlie lying on the floor, her first thought was, *He's gone.* She'd spent hours in bed fearing for him, wondering if Sister would come for her next.

So, when she heard the first bump, her heart skipped a beat. The bump was a heavy, meaningful sound, one that none of the others in the house would normally dare make. On the other hand, she reasoned, Tina had fallen out of bed once, and Charlie had farted once so loudly that they'd heard it from all the way down the hall. The giggles had been unstoppable, breaking into laughter so long and hard that they'd been in tears, until Sister had run from room to room screaming at them that it was a disgusting thing to do and that if they didn't go back to sleep she'd punish them, she'd punish them all.

She hung on for long minutes for another sound, but all was quiet. Despite herself, her eyes began to droop and Maggie's soft, even breathing beside her began to lull her to sleep.

Then the hair on her neck rose at the sound of a different noise, a sliding, hissing noise like a bag of laundry being dragged across the hardwood floors of the old farmhouse.

She raised her head off the pillow, straining to hear.

A grunt was followed by a soft murmuring. She eased out of bed, slipping like a snake from under the covers so that she wouldn't wake Maggie. Squatting in the total darkness, she ran her hand over the floorboards, so buckled by age and humidity that the seams and splits were easy to tell by touch. Once she knew where she was, she stood and, placing her feet carefully on certain boards she'd long-since memorized, moved toward the door. Going side to side and even backward as needed, she crossed the six steps in a noiseless, slow-motion game of hopscotch.

The sliding and murmuring had continued, growing louder as whatever or whoever it was began to pass by her door. She froze, however, as the sound stopped. Risking the noise, she took two long steps back to the bed and vaulted under the covers just as a soft, persistent, mechanical clicking told her the doorknob to their bedroom door was being turned. She squeezed her eyes shut and buried her face in the crook of her elbow, pretending sleep. Her cheek was pressed against the sheets, and the smell of mold and dust was strong, tickling her nose.

The door stopped, open a mere sliver. It stayed that way for a long, bloated moment; then, through cracked lids, she watched as a dull light played over her face and body, flicked to Maggie's, then away. The knob turned again in a slow-motion cycle. She smothered a gasp as a sharp clack told her the latch hadn't caught. After a long pause, the hissing sound continued.

Heart pounding, she was slithering out of bed once more when Maggie rolled over and mumbled her name. The name Sister had given her.

"Charlotte?"

"Shh. I just have to go to the bathroom," she whispered. "Go back to sleep."

Maggie mumbled, then went quiet, leaving her to pad back to the door and run her fingers along the frame to explore the opening. Unlatched, the door had swung open about an inch.

The sliding sound had stopped again, but was replaced by soft, rhythmic thuds. She put her eye to the slim gap and looked out. It was still pitch-black, but the same soft, muddy light that had examined her was bobbing up and down on the steps in time to the thumps. With her heart in her throat, she pushed the door wider yet again, just enough to squeeze through. Thinking catlike thoughts, she slipped to the edge of the staircase, pushed her face into the gap between the spindles of the banister, and looked down.

Sister was descending the stairs backward so she could drag a large bundle, something long, wrapped in a blanket, and heavy enough that she was having trouble even lifting it. She held a tiny flashlight between her teeth, and the light, though dim, put the lines and wrinkles of her face in sharp relief: the puckered skin of her brow, the deep lines carved to either side of her mouth.

Sister paused, leaning against the wall, then set to again, hauling her burden backward down the steps. It was difficult, obviously, and not helped by the fact that she was trying to keep the blanket wound tight around the bundle. She was nearly to the first floor when she stumbled slightly and sat down heavily on the last step with a curse.

Sister lost her grip on the bundle and snatched at it desperately.

Charlotte covered her mouth and scrambled back to her room, slipping into bed, unable to stop shaking and crying.

He really is gone, she thought. *And I'm next.*

8

Dave

Out of habit, Detective Dave Cargill of DC's Metropolitan Police Department Youth and Family Services division ran a hand over his balding head, then stopped ruefully. It had been a full head of hair when he'd started this job twenty years before and had thinned incrementally, pulled out over many nights just like this one.

It was 8:32, hours past quitting time for normal people, and reports were due by 9:00. He had two down and five to go, a record of procrastination even for him. The bull pen was empty except for Fracasso and Carter talking hockey, trading jabs over the cubicle wall.

"Hey, Dave, how 'bout those Caps?" Fracasso said, trying to suck him into the conversation. His partner, born and bred in south Philly, bled black and orange. "You going to win the Cup again this year?"

Hearing the air quotes around the word "win," Dave grunted and held up a middle finger without looking away from his screen, eliciting a laugh from Fracasso. To his relief, they went back to harassing each other about NHL standings and Corsi ratings. At forty-three, Dave had a single life uncomplicated by a wife or children—he was still undecided on the merits of family—and he wanted to reap the rewards of being alone: if he got the reports done, he could get home, park himself in his easy chair, and watch bad television.

So, when the phone rang, he didn't bother to look at the face of his department-issued cell phone; he simply fished it out of his pocket as he read the last sentence on his computer screen.

"Youth and Family Services. Cargill," he said absently into the mouthpiece.

"Dave?" His name was a bug's squeak from the distance.

"Yeah?" He put it up to his ear. "Who is this?"

"Elliott."

"Elliott who?"

"Nash. Elliott Nash."

"Elliott? My god." He almost dropped his phone. "How are you? Are you . . ."

"Sober? Yes." There was a pause. "I spoke with Amy Scowcroft."

"Yeah?"

"She said you sent her to me."

Dave paused. "I did."

"You want to tell me why?"

"Because you can read insane and perverted and criminal behavior like you're psychic. If there's anyone who could take the pieces of her case and put them together, it's you."

"That doesn't really answer my question. I don't work with you anymore. I don't work, period. So why now?"

"We're off the case. It's closed and cold."

"You're off a lot of cases. Why her? Why me?"

Dave tapped the pencil on his desk, watched it bounce. He sighed. "I don't know, Elliott. She's in pain. There's no one to help. The dad is a deadbeat and out of the picture. No family to speak of. She's lived off her savings the whole time, is *this* close to being on the street . . ." He trailed off, embarrassed. "She needs help."

"Help with what, Dave? Every statistic out there says her daughter is dead or being pimped out somewhere a million miles away. Either way, she's gone. And you knew that when you gave her my name."

Dave considered how much to reveal, then said, "When we first started working together, I told you I was a foster kid. I didn't tell you more because I don't like talking about it. It was not a good life. No, it was hell. I bounced from home to home. They were rough years, shit years. And what I came from was . . . worse." He paused. "Look, I know what it's like to be little and lonely and scared. It's why I work where I do, why I do what I do. If there's a chance, no matter how small, for Amy Scowcroft to find her daughter, I want her to have it."

"Even if that chance is a washed-up psychologist living on the streets?"

"You were the best at decoding criminals that I ever worked with, Elliott," Dave said. "You're smart, compassionate, skilled. If anyone can help her find Lacey, now that we're out of it, it's you."

"What if I don't *want* to help her, Dave? What if I'm tired of helping? Tired of being needed? What if I'm just . . . tired?"

A long silence filled the line. The guys on the other side of the room yelled Dave's name, pantomimed lifting a beer. He shook his head and sketched a wave as they left.

Finally, he said, "I spoke to Sister Madeline."

"Sister Madeline, my monitor."

Dave threw the pencil across the room. "Goddamn it, she checks on you because she cares. Like I care. And she told me about . . . how you . . ."

"You're doing what we used to call 'avoidance coping,'" Elliott said. "You can say it. I tried to kill myself."

"You want to talk about it?"

"Getting into psychotherapy now, Dave?" Elliott gave a dry, humorless laugh. "I don't recommend it. It'll ruin your day."

"Elliott, what's going on?"

"I can't hear her anymore, Dave. I can't hear Cee Cee. And she's the whole reason I've been sticking around."

"It's been eight years, man. There's got to be more to life than just hanging on. If you could find—"

"Dave," Elliott interrupted. "I'm going to do it. I'm going to help Amy Scowcroft find her daughter."

"You are?"

"Yes."

"Does *she* know that?"

"Not yet. I wanted to get straight with you, talk it out, understand your motives. Hell, understand mine." Elliott coughed. "You're right. I've got to find something else, find another reason for being alive. At least for now."

Dave exhaled. *Thank you.*

"But," Elliott continued, "you have to come clean."

He swallowed. "About what?"

"About the other reason you picked me to help her."

"What other reason?"

"Come on, Dave. If we don't find Amy's daughter, who better than a bereaved parent—who happens to be a psychologist—to help another bereaved parent. Am I right?"

It was what he admired and loathed about Elliott, Dave thought. He *was* almost always right. "If anyone can find Amy's daughter, it's you. But, I've seen a lot of Laceys, and there's a big gap between 'can' and 'will.' So . . . yes. If things turn out badly, it would be good if Amy didn't have to face that reality cold."

"I can help her cope," Elliott said. "But I'm not exactly the poster boy for successful grief management."

"Just give it a shot. Help her, help yourself." *Hell, help me. Let me feel better about myself.* Old feelings of guilt washed over him. "I guess

I should warn you, though. She's got some . . . odd ideas about how to go about finding her daughter."

"Odd how?"

"She's a hippie chick. Divination, crystals, numerology. All that crap. Claims she has a psychic connection to people and things. You'll have to cut through all that to get anywhere."

"That's . . . interesting. I'll have to deal with it as it comes." Elliott paused. "How much official information have you shared with her?"

"What, like files? Reports?"

"Yes."

"Some, but not much. When Lacey's case was active, we told her what we were doing, of course. She asked for more—files on other missing kids and such. Trying to make some kind of connection, I guess. When she started talking about divining the kid's whereabouts, though, we turned off the tap, if you know what I mean."

"I get it, but I need to work from something if I'm really going to help her," Elliott said. "I need names, dates, locations if I'm going to build a profile of the kidnapper."

"That stuff only comes from case files."

"Correct." There was dead air for a minute. "I know it's not policy—"

"Policy? It's illegal!"

"—and that it could be your job. If you got caught. I get that. But without some hard data to work from, I can't do anything for her. So either I'm actually helping her find her daughter, or I'm pulling a con to help her cope with the assumed death of her daughter. And I'm not going to do that."

The pause was longer this time. "You're really going to help her?"

"Yes."

Dave glanced at the clock and groaned. 8:57. Elliott was asking for years of files, notes, case summaries. It was a good bet that neither he nor Amy could access email or a computer, so everything would have to be printed. As for finding the information, Dave would have to avoid getting sucked into old failures and successes and just focus on the cases relevant to Lacey's disappearance, then organize everything so that two smart and driven, but untrained, would-be detectives could use the information in some meaningful way.

"You better let me go, then," Dave said. "It's going to be a long night."

9

Sister

She'd only used this section of the city once before.

Her life had been spent in and around Washington, DC, and she knew most of it like the back of her hand, but the east side of the city was a mystery to her. Over the years, portions of it had fallen into decline, risen in a temporary renaissance, only to fall back into poverty again. It was in one of those declines now, and many parts were still poor and, to her mind, quite dangerous, so she'd avoided traveling there, even if having a new portion of the city to . . . use would've been helpful.

She'd briefly toyed with going as far as Baltimore, even breaking out a map and scouring the various streets and neighborhoods for a suitable spot. Barclay. Allendale. Pratt Monroe. Her favorite had been a neighborhood called simply Pigtown. *An alley in Pigtown,* she said to herself. It had a Dickensian ring to it, which suited the nature of her mission. Dickens, who wrote about the lost and the orphaned, the living and the almost dead. It seemed . . . appropriate.

But there was always so little time and, anyway, Baltimore was a strange and dangerous place to her, a city that had grown organically rather than by intent. The buildings there were towering, intimidating, not hampered by the artificial restrictions of the capital that kept the city manageable. No, she would put this to rest nearby. At home, as it were, even if this section of the city was as strange to her as the dark side of the moon.

From the Beltway, she squinted in the dark, trying to find the exit she needed. This was always the saddest and most frightening part of her task—a hum she'd maintained since leaving the house grew into a soft wail as she drove. But she pushed forward, making headway at exactly the speed limit. It was three in the morning, and she had a task to accomplish before getting into work by seven. She'd have no rest before putting in a full day at the office, but that was the nature of her work. A soft rain speckled the windshield, causing the pinpricks of white and amber light atop the distant buildings to grow and twinkle before the rhythmic thump of the wipers took it away.

She had just spotted her exit when her heart suddenly leaped in her throat. A police car—brown and blue, lights flashing, no siren—flew by in the inside lane, its tires slicing through the rain with a sound like cloth ripping. A ripple passed through her as she watched its taillights dwindle in the distance. One minute she was alone on a four-lane highway; the next, her car was rocking side to side, almost sideswiped by a police car. It was too much.

She faltered then, and nearly turned around. Had he started to follow her or even just slowed down, it would've been the end. She would've pulled over and confessed everything. Her anxiety was so strong, it was crippling.

Compensating the only way she knew how, she took the long, sharp nail of her right index finger and dug it into the scrawny flesh of her left forearm. Scar tissue there kept her from feeling anything at first, and she pushed harder until, with her gasp, the pressure blossomed into very real, very sharp pain. The nail never broke the surface of her skin, but dozens of small crescents tattooed her arm from the wrist to the inside of her elbow. She sighed as the anxiety faded, letting her continue on.

The street she was looking for was clearly marked, though she was disappointed to see her chosen target wasn't the urban slum she'd expected, just a neighborhood in transition. It had its share of broken-down blocks of low-income housing, but also parks and murals and even an elegant old pile that might've been a theater or community playhouse. She'd been hoping for a desperate ghetto like the kind she'd seen in the newspaper.

Still, there were a number of shady characters walking the streets and hugging the corners of row houses, dark figures with nothing to stop bad weather and life except rounded shoulders and an attitude. With the cold rain coming down in needles now, you had to be desperate or dumb or both to be on the streets four hours before dawn.

Just what she was looking for.

The alley was behind a short block of restaurants and tenements, a squat little drive attached to a parking lot, which made her nervous—lots meant cars, cars meant people—but pavement instead of mud also meant no tire tracks, or, alternatively, so many that hers would be lost. A dumpster took up half the width of the alley. Much of it was blanketed in shadow. Lights had only been spared for the lot, not for the passageway to the street.

She pulled into a stall, then turned off her lights and settled in to wait. She'd flipped her collar up and hugged her arms to her chest when something caught her eye in the rearview mirror. Her exhaust, steaming in the cold. She turned the car off and burrowed even deeper into her light jacket, wishing she'd thought to bring something heavier.

Lights in one tenement window winked off, on, then off again, but no one appeared silhouetted and suspicious, peering out to see who was crazy enough to sit in the cold in the middle of the night. When her fingers began to go numb, she leaned forward to start the car again, then froze. Another police cruiser, this one a red, white, and blue MPD sedan, slid through the parking lot like a shark. It slowed as it passed each row of cars, paused, then moved on.

She slithered down into the footwell, her heart slamming in her chest, crouching beneath the steering wheel and resting her head against the cold vinyl of the door. Tears streamed down her face, and her breath came in short gasps.

She heard the purr of the cruiser as it pulled close, and her imagination filled in the rest: a lone officer, bored, hoping for something to liven up a graveyard shift, happy to shine a spotlight on anything, hoping to find a crime in progress. Her heart popped into her throat: her car had out-of-state license plates. Was that enough to catch a policeman's eye, make him get out and investigate?

And there, *there*, looking just like she thought it would, a sharp, bright light passed through her window, turning the driver side of her car into a sheet of white. She pressed her face and her head into the gap between the seat and the door like a frightened dog, jamming her feet up against the floorboards near the pedals to make herself as small as possible.

The light stayed on her car for a long minute, pinning it, scouring it, until—in a blink—the light went off, plunging the car's interior into darkness. The low burble of the cop car faded away, punctuated by the slow crunch of cinders and gravel.

She didn't move for many long minutes. Finally, with her legs going numb, she uncurled from under the steering wheel and crawled up the seat like an animal coming out of hibernation.

With her eyes just above the horizon of the dashboard, she looked out. The lot was empty. The night was silent, cold, and dark. The few lights that had been on when she'd arrived were out.

She pulled herself fully upright behind the wheel, started the car, and maneuvered it until she could back up into the alley, very near the dumpster. She left the car running, then got out, trotted to the back, and opened the trunk.

Inside was the long, blanket-wrapped form. Grunting and straining, she pulled it out and dumped it onto the ground. Letting her fear fuel her, she dragged it to the dumpster, then tugged the blanket away.

Working quickly, she rolled Charlie off the blanket, folded it, then threw it in the trunk. She arranged the body into a seated position against the rough brick wall behind him. She tried to fold the hands in the lap, but the·slack fingers refused to stay intertwined, and the arms fell to his side.

Biting her lip, she cupped one cheek in her hand, then leaned forward and kissed the young man's forehead. He smelled faintly of buttercream icing. She looked at the wispy beginnings of a mustache barely visible in the little light that reached the alley. The face was both familiar and strange to her, a melding of all the boys and brothers and men she had known over the years.

She frowned.

His lower lip seemed to tremble. She blinked, passing a hand over his mouth, wondering if she imagined a feathery breath on her wrist. But there was a slight breeze in the alley that stirred plastic bags and fast-food wrappers. She leaned forward, staring at the pale blue vein in his temple, looking for the suggestion of movement. Did it pulse slightly?

"No," she whispered. *Impossible. I measured carefully, accurately. I've always done it right.*

She went to feel for a pulse in his neck when a siren split the air on the street at the end of the alley. With a cry, her last nerve frayed, she fled to her car and slammed it into gear, leaving the lot and the body behind.

10

Elliott

This is the way it happened.

Marilyn is on his case again—he's working too much, he's never around, his daughter never sees him. So now he's at a playground instead of the office, sitting on a bench while Cee Cee is on the swing. But his cases are piling up and his phone is ringing, ringing, ringing as people in the office try to reach him.

They're in the corner of the tot lot. He woke this morning with a head-ache and doesn't really feel like making small talk with the other parents, who look at him with judging, sidelong glances, anyway. For what, being antisocial? For keeping his kid away from the others? Who knows.

His head is in his hands, trying to think through a particularly thorny problem at work, when a knocking sound distracts him. He looks up, irritated. A jumble of kids are sitting at the top of the sliding board, jostling and pushing. One of them, grinning like an ape, is pounding on the board with his fist.

The sound fills his head, impossible to ignore. Elliott gets up to ask the kid to stop when the slide begins to crumple and tip. Screaming, the kids tumble to the ground. There is crying and yelling from parents and children alike. Elliott stumbles across the lot, intent on helping, but stops short. The situation is in hand, and the nearby parents who see him approaching shoot him dirty looks. Rebuffed, his head pounding, he shrugs and turns to go back.

Cee Cee isn't on the bench or on the swings.

She isn't in the playground.

She's gone.

◆　◆　◆

The night had been hard, one of the hardest he could remember. Amy Scowcroft's corner of southeast DC was unfamiliar territory, and all his comfortable go-to spots were miles away across the river.

Years ago, he'd mistakenly tried to make DC his home, hoping to lose both himself and his memories in the city's urban mass. But he'd been beaten and robbed too many times to stay, and he'd found out that he hadn't actually wanted to forget. Scratching out an existence in sedate Old Town had kept him alive, which, in turn, let him remember.

He'd gotten lucky this time—searching the streets got him a dry, secluded spot under the exhaust vent of a rundown neighborhood bakery. It had been an inspired choice, since work started at two in the morning, blowing warm air out through the vents and directly over where he lay huddled, teeth chattering.

On the downside, the air was sweet with the smell of rising dough and baking bread. When he woke, his stomach had nearly turned itself inside out. He found a half-eaten bear claw in the trash that he paired with a small coffee he begged from a convenience store clerk. Exhausted, he sat on a park bench across the street from the bakery, sipping his coffee and letting the day begin around him.

A church or town hall clock bonged the hour, startling him. Eight o'clock, he guessed. Time for him to start the first morning of his redemption. He got to his feet and shuffled the six or seven blocks to the address Dave had given him, a tiny apartment hanging on to the end of a rundown row of tenements. Even in the poor part of the city, the duct-taped repairs on his old jacket caught a few glances; he kept his head down as he walked. Police cars passed frequently, but they were looking for bigger fish.

He stood at the bottom of the steps and looked at the cheap vinyl screen door, hesitating. His beard was stringy and halfway down to his chest. His hair was lank and greasy and hung past his shoulders. If he were being honest, he couldn't remember the last shower he'd had—the rainstorm he and Amy Scowcroft had run through had been the closest thing he'd had to a bath in weeks. If he smelled like a barnyard, he was lucky.

A small smile split his face. *Butterflies, Dr. Nash? You're here to help this woman, not to take her out on a date.* He shook his head and mounted the steps, knocked, then retreated to the street. He'd found that people appreciated distance when dealing with the homeless.

A minute passed before Amy opened the door, keeping it in front of her like a shield. A rat, flushed by the noise, scurried along the front of her porch and turned the corner. She frowned, confused. "Mr. Nash?"

"Elliott," he corrected her, then struggled to find more words. "Can we talk?"

He watched as hope flickered across her face, then disappeared as reality and experience stepped in. He knew what she was thinking. *The nights are getting colder . . . a homeless man . . . this is awfully convenient.* "About what, exactly?"

"I wanted to talk about your . . . about Lacey."

"Didn't we already have that conversation?"

He turned and looked down the street again, then back. "You're not happy with me. I made it clear that I didn't want to help."

"Yes, you did."

"I'd like to change my mind."

"You would?"

"Yes."

"Why?"

"I . . . ," he started, then shook his head.

She waited, but he seemed to be unable to say what he came to say. "If you came up here for a handout—"

"No! No. That's not it at all." He swallowed and seemed to be struggling. "I know my change of heart seems strange. Suspicious. I wouldn't trust me either. But I have my reasons. All I can tell you is I don't want anything from you. Except to help. I've lived on the streets for eight years." He put a hand to his head. "I didn't say that for your sympathy, I mean I don't need anything, from you or anyone. Just the opposite, in fact. I . . . I haven't needed to help someone *else* for a long time. Please. I'd like to help you."

His mouth went dry, surprised to find that he was terrified that she would turn him away. She seemed to search his face for something.

Finally, she gave him a cautious smile and opened the door wider. "If you're willing to help me find Lacey, I wouldn't say no."

He nodded. "I don't know what I can do for you. But, whatever I can offer, it's yours."

Inside, a futon with a purple covering kept company with a home-made coffee table made from milk crates and a piece of plywood. It was stacked high with papers, binders, and manila folders. The smell of incense hung heavy in the air, tickling his nose. The only decorations were a tie-dyed sheet hung with thumbtacks on the wall and a dead spider plant sharing space in the kitchenette sink with several dirty coffee cups. He could've made it to the sink and back in four steps.

He sat gingerly on the edge of the futon. Amy shut the door and there was a thick moment of silence.

"Nice place," he said at the same time as Amy blurted, "Can I get you anything?"

They each gave an awkward laugh. "I'm sorry," she said. "I'm not used to this. I haven't had anyone here since . . . for, well, forever."

"I haven't sat on a cushion in forever, so we're even." He started to say something, stopped, then rested his forehead on the heel of his hand. "Look. If it wasn't obvious, I haven't worked, if that's what you want to call this, in eight years. Most of my conversations have been about shelters and free meals and where I can spend the night. I'm not even sure I can speak to you like a normal person. I might be very . . . honest with you."

"I need honest right now."

"I'm saying it might hurt," he said. "And I don't have the skills to soften the blow. Not anymore."

She looked him in the eye. "Elliott, I can take it. I'll do anything to get Lacey back. And, believe me, I've found 'normal' conversation overrated. I want you to speak your mind."

"You're okay with taking advice from the crazy homeless guy?"

"I wouldn't have looked for you if I didn't," she said, then gave him a small smile. "And, for the record, you don't seem that crazy to me. But I've been told I'm not a good judge of character."

He snorted. "Then I guess we should get started." He glanced at the stack of binders, notes, and newspaper clippings. "Your research?"

"All of it."

Elliott raked a finger down the stack. "Files are good to have, but if I'm going to help you, I need to know more. Tell me about Lacey, about yourself. About the day Lacey was taken. Give me the details, as much as you can stand."

Amy paled, but collected herself and started talking. Details began spilling out. The dry, technical points at first—her age (ten), her hair color (blonde, like her mother), her eyes (blue)—in the litany she'd had to repeat countless time for the police. Memories slipped in. The two of them walking to school, watching TV at night, falling asleep on the couch together.

The good times merged with the bad ones. How Darren, a deadbeat not ready for fatherhood, had left the picture. How she'd worked a succession of low-paying jobs, having to move into smaller and smaller apartments, eventually winding up in the closet they were sitting in now.

When Lacey turned ten, Amy began letting her ride to friends' houses alone, even though they were in one of the worst neighborhoods in the city. But you couldn't lock a ten-year-old girl up forever. On a clear Saturday in June, she went out on her bike and never came back. Calls to the friend's mother revealed that, yes, she'd been there . . . she'd just never come home. Frantic, Amy called the police.

"Right after Lacey was taken," she said, "the police were like a swarm in here. I was terrified, of course, but the sheer activity was reassuring. They asked questions, they put out bulletins, they contacted the press."

"When did the investigation wind down?"

"After a few weeks, when we didn't get any results, the energy started to drop. They went from calling several times a day to once, then to once a week. From the start, I'd kept my own notes and cribbed information where I could, but when they stopped taking my calls I knew I had to do it all myself. For months, I was out beating the streets every night, working with child-abduction watch groups, building my own files. I even crawled through some pretty horrible websites and chat rooms just, you know, in case . . ."

Elliott nodded, then gestured toward her tower of notes. "This was the result?"

"I call it my database," she said, resting a hand on top of the two-foot stack. "It's anything and everything I could scrap, salvage, print, or steal on child abductions in the DC area for the last five years. Every night before the trash is picked up, I rifle through my neighbor's recycling for the paper and pull out any articles I think might even remotely fit Lacey's case."

"How have you organized it?"

She lifted one binder as tall as her fist to her lap. Papers, tattered and stained, stuck out from the pile. "This file is my MISSING: FOUND. It contains all the runaways, throwaways, and others who eventually made it back." She riffled through the papers and Elliott got the impression of blurry grade-school portraits and line upon line of text.

She put the binder aside and picked up another, much smaller, binder. "This is my MISSING: NOT FOUND file. It contains dozens of children between eight and fourteen who simply disappeared."

"Is Lacey's case in there?" She looked away. "I'll take that as a no."

"I keep it separate. I study the others constantly, hoping some little piece of information might've been overlooked or misfiled, but I haven't found anything yet. I've been stumped for weeks."

"Which is where I come in."

"Yes."

"I don't want to waste time going over what the police did. Dave Cargill is a good cop, works with good people. They know what they're doing, and I'm not going to second-guess their methods. They obviously thought they took Lacey's case as far as they could and came up empty. That doesn't mean they didn't miss something, but let's assume they did their job."

"Okay."

"You don't agree?"

"I like Detective Cargill."

"But?"

"He didn't seem to look for anything beyond the obvious, and I think the other detectives followed his lead. They questioned me, they talked to my ex, they scoured the neighborhood. Those are all good things, I guess, but they never talked about whether there were other connections."

"Connections?"

"The tissue that keeps all in touch. There are cosmic strings, webs between us all."

Elliott pressed a finger into his temple, made small circles there. "I . . . like what? Could you be more specific?"

"I don't think Lacey's kidnapping was a single event," she said simply. "I have a feeling that she was part of a larger scheme and that other kids may have been kidnapped, as well."

"A larger scheme? Like trafficking? A gang?"

"Or a cult. Or a single crazy person who's done this before. As far as I know, the police spent a day or two on the idea, then dropped it and focused all of their energy on hounding my ex and my neighbors. It's been up to me to look for that connection."

"Have you found it?"

"Not yet. But I'm hoping with your help, we can." The look on her face was fragile. "Do you think we have a chance?"

He was quiet for a moment. Like he'd told Dave, he wasn't here to con her, to pretend to help while waiting for her to get over it. If he was in, he was all in. Finally, he said, "If I'm here to help you, we have to work under the assumption that Lacey is alive and that there's a way to find her."

"Thank you, Elliott." Amy's eyes were shining and he dropped his gaze, embarrassed. After a moment, she said, "How do we start? Should I take you through my notes?"

He cleared his throat. "I think we should look through everything you've got, but not before we have a chance to review—"

A heavy knock on the door interrupted him. Amy, confused, stood and answered the door. Standing on her porch, his arms full with banker's boxes, was Dave Cargill. He peered at them from around the stack.

"Someone order delivery?"

11

Charlotte

"But *why* does *i* come before *e*?"

She and Maggie were sitting on the couch in the living room, reading *Melton Goes to Montana*—Sister's favorite book as a child, she'd said, and the one she'd told her to teach to the younger girl. "What do you mean, why?"

"Why can't it be the other way around?"

She looked down at the page in front of her. Melton was a platypus who traveled the world discovering objects and learning new words, but the book was so old it was hard to recognize some of things that the author took for granted. It also smelled bad, like a box that had been left in the basement for too long, and the cover was peeling at the corner, exposing a thousand leaves of paper.

"I don't know. It just is."

"Why?"

She made a face. Maggie could be a whiner, and if she started the "why" game, it wouldn't end until she got tired of it or you told her to shut up—at which point she'd burst into tears. "It's just a rule, Maggie. Like when Sister tells us we can't go outside."

Maggie pouted, sensing that her game was going to be cut short. "But *why?*"

She raised an eyebrow. "Do you ask Sister *why* when she tells you to do something?"

"No." She dropped her eyes to the ground.

"This is the same thing. Just treat it like a rule."

"But we don't tell Sister everything," Maggie said, suddenly struck by an idea. "Like you haven't told her about—"

"Let's just read the next page," she said, talking over her.

"Told Sister about what?" a voice from behind them asked, making them jump.

Tina looked down at them from behind the old floral couch. The girl was tall and as thin as a stick. Her long limbs made her gawky and a little clumsy, but she could be surprisingly quiet when she wanted, which was often, since she liked to sneak around the house. Catching one of the others breaking a rule and tattling on them was one her favorite things to do. The only time you knew Tina was coming was when she sang to herself in a high-pitched whisper.

I'm older than her, Charlotte told herself. "None of your business. Anyway, Sister told me I'm supposed to teach Maggie reading every day. Do you want to tell her that you didn't let me do that?"

Tina paled, but then her face got mean and, quick as a snake, she reached out and pinched Maggie's upper arm, hard. The little girl's eyes widened for one quiet second, then she screamed bloody murder.

Tina slipped away, cackling as she fled to the kitchen and down the basement steps. She spent most every day down there, had explored every nook and corner setting up booby traps and playing her own dark games. No one went after Tina once the cellar door had banged shut.

Charlotte tried to comfort Maggie, but her concern turned to disgust when she saw the pinch hadn't even left a mark. "Oh, grow up," she said when Maggie wouldn't stop crying, but that just brought on a new burst of tears, followed by a round of screamed accusations that faded as Maggie fled upstairs to her room.

Charlotte curled up in a corner of the couch, drawing her knees to her chest and rubbing a cheek against the rough, worn fabric of the cushion. Exhausted and depressed, she let her eyes droop, but Charlie's pale face appeared in her mind's eye and they flew open again.

Charlie had been her first real friend in a long time, even counting the days before . . . before Sister. It had taken weeks for the shock of her abduction to finally fade and for her to settle into her new existence, but throughout it Charlie had looked after her, showing her small kindnesses that meant so much living under Sister's iron rule. She'd tried to return the favor, and eventually they'd forged a kind of alliance that had been sealed with a whispered conversation in his bedroom.

"Maggie and Tina and Buddy . . . ," she started, hesitating, wondering if it was even a mistake to ask. Sister had special punishments for those who mentioned the past. "Those aren't their names, right? Their real names?"

He looked at her, his gaze wide and very still. "Why do you think so?"

"They don't sound right," she said. "And, well . . ."

"What?"

"*My* name isn't Charlotte," she blurted.

Charlie slid off the bed and checked the door. He came back and, leaning close, put his lips next to her ear. "I know. My name isn't Charlie."

They stared at each other; then, silently daring the other, both blurted their names at the same time. It made her want to laugh and cry at the same time—saying her name out loud was the first real thing she'd felt in weeks. She shouted it over and over, unable to help herself.

He clapped a hand over her mouth and they sat there, terrified. It didn't matter that Sister wasn't home—her presence seemed always around them, the threat of her anger hanging just over their heads.

Long minutes passed and nothing happened; then the words began to tumble out of Charlie, though in a whisper so light, she had to lean in until their faces almost touched. He told her about his life before and how much he missed his parents, even though they were divorced and fought all the time. Charlotte started to tell him about herself, but her throat got tight and scratchy.

He was reluctant to touch on some things, like how long he'd been there, but she wheedled and pleaded. *Four years,* he finally told her, *so long that I've forgotten what outside looks like.* He got excited, realizing she could tell him about all the things he'd missed, like what the cars looked like and what music was popular and what his favorite baseball team was doing. She exhausted herself, telling him as much as she could remember, though it made her sad when she realized she'd eventually lose those things, too.

His stream of questions were endless, and she finally stopped him with one of her own.

"I'm not the first Charlotte, am I?"

He looked at her strangely. "Why?"

"We have to wear these weird clothes," she said, plucking at the ancient blue blouse Sister had insisted she wear, then pointing to his green button-down. The sleeves stopped three inches short of his wrists. "These were someone else's, right?"

"I guess." His eyes slid away from hers.

"So what happened to them? Where are they?"

He was quiet for a long time. "There was . . . another girl. She waited all day for Sister to come home, hiding in the hall; then she tried to just run past her. I guess she thought maybe Sister would be so surprised she wouldn't know what to do. But Sister caught her by the neck before she'd made it out the door."

The blood drained from her face. "What happened to her?"

"Sister tied her to a post in the basement," Charlie said grimly. "And left her there for a week."

Charlotte covered her mouth with her hands.

"She cried all day the first day and some of the second. Then . . . nothing."

"Is she still down there?"

Charlie snorted. "Do you think even *Tina* would go to the cellar if she was? Sister snuck her out while we slept."

"She killed her?"

Charlie shrugged. "She never came back."

"She couldn't just . . . murder all of us. There wouldn't be anyone left."

He looked at her sadly. "There's always someone new, Charlotte."

"What do you mean?"

"You showed up the next week," he said and touched her arm as if to make sure she was there.

She let his words sink in. "She *replaces* us?"

"I think so. I've been here so long, I've known different Buddys and Tinas and Maggies and Charlottes. Two Buddys, actually."

"Hasn't anyone tried to escape? I mean, *really* escape . . . something smarter than just running out the door?"

His voice dropped even lower, and he told her of all the things that kept them prisoner. About the triple locks on the front door and the plywood-covered windows, about the bars on the basement windows and the coal chute that had been welded shut long ago. That there were **No Trespassing** signs posted everywhere, and Sister had threatened to shoot the last stranger who had come to the house.

"You made that last part up," Charlotte accused. "How do you know there are signs if you haven't been outside?"

"I told you, I've been here four years. How else could it be that no one's come to the front door in all that time?"

Her heart sank. "So there's no way out?"

"It's all been tried before," he said, then added mysteriously, "but I've got some ideas."

But what they were, he wouldn't tell her, and as far as she knew, he hadn't attempted to escape since their conversation. And now Charlie was gone. His fight with Sister, followed by his birthday party, had happened suddenly, surprising them all. Just like the Charlotte before her, apparently.

She sat up. Which meant whatever Charlie's *ideas* had been, he hadn't had a chance to put them into action. And, between whatever she'd been up to late last night and having to go to work this morning, there'd been no time for Sister to clean his room or search his things.

Charlotte slowly uncurled and slipped off the couch. Padding quietly into the kitchen, she pulled a chair over to the basement door and jammed it under the knob, locking Tina in the cellar. Next, she crept up the stairs and peeked into her own room, where she found Maggie—exhausted by her tantrum—sprawled facedown on the bed, breathing deep. She backed away and padded down the hall. Through a crack in the door, she saw Buddy on his bed, reading a book by the light of the tiny overhead lamp Sister had allowed him.

She was lucky everyone was so lazy; exploring was a favorite pastime when boredom took over. Each of them had crawled all over the house, deciding that someone, or many someones, had lived there once upon a time. The furniture was chunky and ancient, of course, and the house smelled like old people. But if you searched long enough, you could find keepsakes—pennies, the stub of a pencil, a tiny spoon—tucked into secret places. Intrepid and inquisitive, they'd found notes stuck in cracks in the paneling behind the couch or rolled into tubes and slipped into hidey-holes. "My name is drew I miss my cat" on a piece of scrap paper taped to the back of a dresser. A simple, red-crayon "Help me" scrawled on the wooden underside of a dining room chair.

Charlotte crept to the end of the hall where Charlie's and Sister's rooms—the latter a thick oak door that was always locked—faced each other. Interior doors, even bedrooms and bathrooms, remained unlocked except when Sister distributed punishment by isolating one of them in a room for a day, a week, or a month. The rest of the time, the thick skeleton keyholes watched them unwinkingly, a reminder that even the little bit of freedom they had, to roam about the house, could be taken away. Feeling like a thief, she slipped into Charlie's room.

She'd been there before, of course, and the first thing she always noticed was the smell. With all the windows in the house shut and boarded, there was never any fresh air, and the smell here was a strange musk of body odor and dirty socks and . . . *boy*, a different kind of odor than she was used to. It mixed poorly with the recycled air that came through the registers, the crude oil and rust smell of the old furnace in the cellar.

She turned to search the room. The bed was unmade. The pillow was on the floor, the sheets were tangled, and the blanket missing. She crept closer to look at the bed, then wrinkled her nose. Maggie had wet their shared bed a few times, so she knew what the puddle-shaped discoloration was. She left it alone.

There were no closets, only a wardrobe in the corner with a flimsy wooden door that squealed as she pulled on the knob. Inside were the clothes she'd grown used to seeing Charlie wear: a pair of patched and stitched jeans, more gray than blue. Brown corduroys that she knew he'd hated because of the swishing noise they made when he walked, despite most of the ridges having been worn away. Two white undershirts, stains at the pits. One plaid shirt that he'd been unable to button because it had been bought for someone even thinner than he was, and you could almost see through him. His favorite clothes, a pair of green work pants and a faded cowboy shirt, were missing.

Charlotte was about to close the door when she noticed a tiny piece of fabric hanging down from the top of the opening of the wardrobe. Curious, she reached up and felt along the inner frame. Her hand encountered a square lump the size of a few slices of bread. She tugged at it—it was hung from a small nail or thumbtack—and pulled out a hand towel, torn in several places, that had been folded and tied to form a hobo's bundle.

Inside was a thin cotton handkerchief, balled into a knot. Charlotte unwound it, revealing seven dull quarters in the center of the knot. She gasped. No one was allowed to keep money, and she hadn't seen anything more valuable than a penny since she'd been in the house, which meant Charlie had either stumbled across a small stash or stolen it. A cold tingle ran up her spine as she imagined rifling through Sister's purse while the woman herself was just around the corner.

She put the quarters aside. Also in the bundle was a small paring knife that had gone missing months ago—Sister had been furious when they couldn't find it—three cookies that were now just a pile of crumbs, a set of three matches, and, finally, a brass skeleton key, polished to a dull shine and rounded in places. There were no markings on it and nothing to identify what it unlocked.

Her pulse pounded in her head as she stared at the odd collection. Since the moment she'd been brought here, she'd been allowed no personal items besides her clothes—which she didn't want anyway—so finding Charlie's tiny stash was like discovering buried treasure. But it was a treasure that could mean big trouble, maybe the worst.

She jumped as, downstairs, Tina started kicking the basement door. Moving quickly, she pocketed the key, folded the towel, and placed the bundle back in the corner of the wardrobe the way she'd found it. A key she could hide, but if Maggie saw the bundle in their room, the secret wouldn't last for a minute. A wave of nausea raced through her at the thought of Tina or, god forbid, Sister finding the key.

Charlotte took her time making sure the package was just like she found it, then shut the door to the wardrobe. She took one last glance at the disheveled, soiled bed, then crept out of the room before one of the others caught her, her mind swirling with possibilities.

12

Elliott

"This is the best I could do on short notice," Dave said, dipping his hands into the first box and picking up a thick sheaf of papers. "It's a mishmash of cases going back five years. If you want to go back further, I'll need more time to pull it all. I figured you'd want to get started right away."

"Five years is a good sample size," Elliott said. "Hopefully it's representative of case types and enough, maybe, to start looking for patterns. What's the origin of the files?"

"Some of them are from my own collected notes; the rest are summary case files I printed out late last night or early this morning. And, sorry, but a lot of it has been sanitized for public consumption, so there were redactions even in the photocopies. That info is gone unless I really dig."

"Still, this is . . . incredible," Amy said, her eyes wide.

"Yeah, well, don't get too excited. Bear in mind these are all summaries and truncated files. If I'd printed out all of the information for each case, it would fill this room. You're going to have to piece together a lot of it to get a complete picture."

He went on to explain the organization scheme. Red-tagged folders, two hundred and sixteen sheets in all, represented five years' worth of missing children cases that had been successfully closed. They were summaries of summaries, with as many as ten blurbs per page, representing over two thousand individual kids. Most, Dave explained, were either runaways who had returned to the families or abductions by a family member, usually an estranged parent, where the child was found and returned.

The two remaining sections were categorized as "abductions by strangers" that had been solved and the small group of cases where the child hadn't been found alive. The latter had dates of discovery as well as basic biographical information.

Blue-tagged folders were open cases where the child hadn't been found. The summary consisted of a paragraph, a last known address, and a cryptic string of sentences that seemed to include the name and district of the officer who had taken the initial report and a reference number for more detailed history. Each ended with the statement, "No additional information."

"So we have names. Addresses. Dates of discovery," Elliott said, flipping pages. "Cause of death and location for the ones who didn't make it. And summaries if we need more information."

"Pretty much," Dave said. "Any idea how you're going to tackle it?"

Before Elliott could open his mouth, Amy said, "We have to convert all the numbers into Abjad values, naturally; then we can work out patterns from there."

The two men turned to her, blank.

"Sorry?" Elliott asked.

"The Abjad value," she said. When their faces remained confused, she turned to her tower of papers and pulled out a laminated reference sheet that she handed to Elliott. He turned it over in his hands. Signs of the zodiac lined the bottom, and each corner sported an astrological symbol. In the center was a large table with columns for both Western and Arabic letters, as well as numbers.

He raised his head and glanced at Dave, then back at Amy. "Is this supposed to explain something?"

"Abjad is a divination system that comes from the number you get from a word. Ancient Sufis used them to discover the deeper values hidden in common meanings. Like this." She picked up a tablet of paper from the floor. Simple but lengthy addition problems were scribbled in every open space. She flipped to a fresh sheet and began jotting down letters, then consulted the reference table she'd handed to Elliott. "See, E-l-l-i-o-t-t gives a score of 19. N-a-s-h is 188. Add them together and your name has a final value of 207."

Dave snorted, but Elliott kept a straight face. "What do you with the number once you have it?"

"Look for more connections, try to find intersections with other names or places."

"The values aren't consecutive?" Dave asked, bemused. "Like A is worth one, B is worth two?"

"Oh no. The values were determined long ago and are nonlinear. And they're case sensitive. It's all very complicated." She held up the laminated sheet. "That's why I need this."

Elliott gave her a look. "It's a . . . magic number?"

"Not magic. Numerology. A tool for finding those connections I told you about, underneath the surface of things. But permutations can make the calculations a little hairy."

"Such as?"

"Well, the value for R-o-b-e-r-t is 209, but it could also be Bob, which has a value of two, see? Or maybe you shouldn't be using Abjad at all. If the person was Jewish, you would use the gematric value. Or you could go all the way back to isopsephism. There are as many schools of arithmancy as there were cultures—it could take a year to translate all of the cases into every school. But Abjad is the most powerful."

Elliott blinked. "Of course. How do you handle dates?"

"You calculate the Abjad value of the month and add the numeric values of the day and year. Let's take January 24, 1985." She consulted the table again. "The Abjad value of January is 143. Add that to 24, add that to 1985, and you get 2,152."

"What's so special about January 24, 1985?" Dave asked.

"It was the first sighting of Halley's comet on its last return to Earth."

"Sorry I asked."

Elliott pointed at the numbers on her tablet. "Why not the numeric value of the month, so that January was just worth one?"

She pursed her lips, considering. "We could do that, but I think the name of the month has more spiritual heft than the number. Like, June is named for the goddess Juno, which has actual meaning and history, right? But the number six, not so much."

"Spiritual heft?" He stroked his beard. "Numerology?"

She nodded.

"Arithmancy?"

She nodded again.

"And you think this works?"

"Sometimes."

Dave coughed into his hand, giving Elliott a knowing look, then turned to the door. "I'm going to have to take off. Good luck. Both of you."

"Thank you, Detective!" Amy called as he let himself out. He threw a wave over his shoulder and shut the door. Amy turned back to Elliott. "You seem to be having second thoughts."

"No, no, that's not it. I'm just having trouble believing this is an . . . effective way to go about finding your daughter."

"It's not that different than what the police do. They ask a question and grab a piece of information, then see if it leads to another, right? Or psychology. You ask a question, put that answer in a category, then look to see if it links to something else. Ask questions, compare information.

Find clues that pull you in the direction of something else that you didn't know existed."

Elliott opened his mouth, then shut it. "All right. Dave's files give us a lot of material to work with. How do you want to move forward?"

She smiled, enthusiastic and energized. "Calculating the Abjad numbers can be a drag, but with two of us on the job, I think we could get through it in a few hours. How about I read off the files, compare it to the table, then you add the numbers?"

He glanced around. "You're doing this without a computer?"

"I had to pawn it to pay the rent. We'll have to do it by hand."

"So I'm a . . . calculator?"

"Yes. But only at first."

"I'm not sure that's putting my psychology degree to best use."

"You might be surprised," she said. "Help me with this; then we'll do the psychological mumbo jumbo after."

"Mumbo *jumbo*?"

"Just teasing." She flipped over a fresh sheet on the tablet, handed it to him with the pencil, then picked up the case files and looked at him expectantly. "Ready?"

13

Sister

Sister stared at the stove, not sure why it had caught her attention. She'd slept poorly the night before, dreaming of Charlie, and now she was late for work. The children had been fed and sent off to their chores or play—Charlotte to teach Maggie more *Melton*, Buddy to read, Tina to the cellar—and she had no time for distractions.

But still . . . the stove had caught her attention. Maybe a whiff of gas or a stray thought had made her look over, suddenly making conspicuous what had been invisible to her for the better part of forty years.

Her eyes ran over the ancient Wedgewood with its fat, round dials, the white porcelain top, the thick steel burners. She had never used it to cook. Touching it to push Maggie into it had taken every ounce of willpower she'd had. Most days, touching it made her physically ill. To even walk near it caused a shudder to go through her.

For all that, she couldn't abide it getting dirty, just like Mother, who would get on her hands and knees to wipe the undersides of things, places where no one would ever see. She made the others take turns cleaning it.

The thing squatted in the corner, taunting her. A memory, held at bay in the corner of her mind, suddenly wriggled to the front, displaying itself obscenely. She began to shake.

Why, Mother?

Because you didn't listen to me, dear.

I promise I won't do it again. Please.

Of course you would say that now, dear. The guilty always repent once they see the punishment that awaits. But the virtuous do what is right without prompting, with no expectation of reward or fear of punishment.

Please, Mother. I didn't know it was wrong!

You will now. The craven will burn in Hell.

Please, Mother. Please!

"Please." She whispered it and blinked. She was standing in front of the stove now, her fingers caressing the wide chrome handle. She snatched her hand away. When had she moved? Against her will, her hand floated downward, resting on the handle again. Her breath came in erratic gasps, as though someone were choking her, then letting go.

Pulling with a slow and steady pressure, she hoped to avoid the squeal of springs, but the sound was in her head anyway. She shivered like she had a fever. A strange sound filled the air, and she realized her teeth were chattering. Unable to stop herself, she yanked the oven door open all the way.

Staring back at her, eyes wide and bright as new quarters, her hair hanging down like a curtain, was a little girl.

The girl opened her mouth.

Please.

She screamed and squeezed her eyes shut hard, slamming the oven door and stumbling backward until she crashed against the heavy farmhouse table. She slid to the ground, screaming into her hands and retching.

Light footsteps pattered in the hall behind her.

"Sister?" Tina.

She had to make herself pull her hands away from her mouth. "Not now."

"But I heard—"

From the floor, half turning, the words were ripped out of her. *"I said not now!"*

The footsteps retreated.

She put both hands across her mouth again because, if she screamed or cried, Mother would turn the dial. Never too high and never for too long, but she could still feel the heat on the skin of her palms and knees, blooming and growing all around her until an animal fear filled her, thrashing and hysterical, pushing and kicking on the door while her mother held it shut, the woman leaning her whole weight against it until she'd decided her willful, sinful eldest daughter had learned her lesson.

She crawled across the floor. Hand quaking, she reached out from where she lay sprawled and gently pried the door open again. She flinched once more at the squeaking spring, paused, then yanked it open until the oven gaped like a whale's mouth.

The stove was a simple black box, the racks taken out long ago and lost, smelling faintly of char and gas and fear. Scratches marred the speckled black surface of the interior.

It was empty.

But the little girl with the eyes like quarters had never gone away. She was just inside her, all the time.

Forever.

14

Elliott

It took the rest of the afternoon.

As soon as the door shut, they dove into the boxes, pulling out folders, wrapping their heads around the mountain of information. Pure determination got them through the first few hours, but as the rays began tilting through the window into the little room, Elliott nodded off, eventually falling asleep with the pencil still in his hand. He woke when Amy gently pulled it away, his eyes popping open and his hands balled into fists.

"It's okay," Amy said, backing away. "Elliott. It's me. Amy. It's okay."

His head snapped back and forth in a panic; then he took a deep breath and his hands relaxed as he got his bearings. He groaned and sat up.

Amy looked at him with concern. "Can I get you something to drink?"

"Yeah," he said in a tight voice. "That'd be great."

She busied herself a few steps away in the kitchen. In a moment, the steam rolled out of the pan, announcing the water was ready. Amy poured for two, stirred, then brought the coffee over to him. "It's instant, sorry. I don't have anything stronger."

He took a sip, then glanced at the mug. It had a unicorn jumping over a rainbow on the side. "This is fine. Thank you."

Out of the corner of his eye, he watched as she blew into her coffee, letting the heat wash across her face as she peered at him over the rim. Without raising his head, he said, "Go ahead and ask."

"What?"

"You want to ask me something," he said. "So ask."

She looked away. "It isn't fair of me. You're extending yourself to a stranger, with no promise of payment—"

"I'm not looking for payment."

"I know. Not of the monetary kind. But I feel like I need to know more about you."

"Why Dave Cargill told you to find me? And no one else?"

She shrugged, embarrassed. "Yes."

He tightened his hands around the cup, choosing his words. "When I worked with Dave, I was a forensic psychologist, helping the cops and the courts with the criminally insane. Questioning, diagnosing, recommending. Sometimes I helped put them away for good, sometimes I got them treatment that turned their lives around. The word 'forensic' sounds quite clinical, as though I plucked minds out of heads and unlocked their mysteries by holding them up to the light. A real scientist. In reality, I was in court half the time, maybe more. I gave my testimony, answered the DA's questions, and promptly forgot about the rest."

"What happened?"

"What happened was not everyone forgot me." He rubbed a hand over his face. "John Jeffery Kerrigan was a thirty-seven-year-old serial pedophile whose childhood history read like a horror movie. As did his rap sheet. When I took the case, I tried to be impartial, scientific, but what I learned made me hope he'd get put away for life."

He shrugged. "Colleagues told me it was my best performance on the stand. There are well-known precedents for passing abuse from parent to child. It's called 'intergenerational transmission of violence,' and I made sure the jury knew exactly what it was, that Kerrigan was both a victim and a perpetrator of it, and he wasn't going to find treatment—and no child would be safe—if he was put back on the streets.

"There was a moment of high drama when Kerrigan threatened me from across the courtroom, but I didn't take it to heart. Plenty of defendants did that when I testified. But Kerrigan was a special case. I'd done my homework on his abusive father and difficult childhood and laid it out for the jury. He never forgave me for describing it so thoroughly. On top of that, my testimony was the most damning part of the prosecution, and Kerrigan knew it.

"But, in the end, my 'performance' didn't matter. Skimpy evidence and prosecutorial screwups meant Kerrigan went to a halfway house and then was out. When I heard the verdict, I was bitter, I was disappointed, but I let it go—the system had failed like it sometimes does, but we'd get the next one, right?"

Outside, a car horn honked. There were shouts, laughter, then silence.

"A year later," Elliott continued, "my daughter Cecilia—Cee Cee—and I went to a nearby playground. She was abducted, in plain sight of everyone there, including me. We never found her."

He swallowed loudly, coughed.

"There was no trace of her until her clothes turned up in a park in Virginia months later, covered with her blood and . . . evidence from Kerrigan. The courtroom threats became relevant. After they arrested him, he admitted kidnapping her, doing things to her, killing her, though they never found her body. Witnesses later remembered seeing a blue panel van—like the one Kerrigan owned—hanging around the park. I still can't see one without getting tied into knots. So, between the evidence and the confession, they threw the book at him this time, but of course it didn't matter. Like so many other things we do, it was too late."

Amy put a hand over her mouth.

"We tried to have another child. It was a disaster. We separated and Marilyn left DC. By December, I'd stopped working—I couldn't take the stand without seeing Kerrigan across from me. By March, I'd been evicted and started sleeping on couches. By June, I was on the streets. Lucky me, I had a few months to learn to live off the grid before it got cold. That was eight years ago."

A silence fell between them.

"So, now you know. That's why Dave sent me to you. I'm a kindred spirit. With a psychology degree. I know what you've been through. I know the kind of mind that would conceive of taking your daughter." *And, if the worst should happen, I can warn you just how deep you can sink.*

"Elliott, I'm so sorry," Amy whispered.

He nodded, not trusting himself to speak for a moment, then sighed and shook himself. He drained his coffee and put it down with a bang. "Let's get back to work."

They took their places on the futon, and Amy resumed the process of taking dozens of dates from Dave's files, turning them into numbers from her Abjad chart, then reciting the values to Elliott. He, in turn, jotted them down, added the results, then recorded the final figure in her homemade spreadsheet, a yellow legal tablet with hand-drawn lines. The work moved along in a steady drone, punctuated by Elliott's sighs as they added what seemed to be an endless succession of nonsense numbers without context. He reminded himself that this was part of Amy's coping strategy, a way to take control of her situation. There would be time later to add some intelligence and deduction to the search.

He dutifully scratched the figures onto the paper. *509 plus 9 plus 2015 equals 2,533.*

Next.

110 plus 16 plus 2014 equals 2,140.

Next.

618 plus 31 plus 2013 equals 2,662.

Elliott scowled, his pencil hovering over the paper. *618 plus 31 . . .* Something about the combination plucked at his memory. "What category are we on?"

Amy looked back at her work. "The dates they . . . discovered the bodies."

"We're into the kids who didn't make it?"

"Yes. Why?"

Elliott looked at the tablet. There was hardly a space on the paper that wasn't filled with scribbles, but he looked at the total for the last addition problem and circled it, then scanned the cramped sheet until he found another, circling it, as well. He frowned. *That's not it.* Something else had caught his attention.

"What was the calculation before that?"

Amy consulted her book. "The birthdays of the victims. Why, did you find something?"

"Hold on."

His eyes skimmed left along the row to the first column. *Cameron King.* He swallowed so hard his throat made a clicking noise. Putting a name to the numbers was painful. But he willed his eyes to trace the row to the right, reading the numbers that summed a child's life. Born in March—a Pisces, Amy had already noted in the margin, of course she had—and only eight years old when he'd been reported missing seven years previously.

His birthday calculation was 618 plus 28 plus 2001 equals 2,647.

He glanced over at his "date of discovery" calculation: 2,662.

He tapped the number with his pencil. In a vast spreadsheet where nearly all of the entries differed in value by the hundreds, this one was off by fifteen.

Holding his place with a finger, he nodded at the red-tagged stack of folders. "Can you find Cameron King's case file in that mess?"

Sensing his growing excitement, Amy slipped the sheet out and handed it to him. He read the summary, piecing together a narrative in his head from the handful of facts.

Cameron King's body had been found behind a dumpster near an exhaust grate on Georgia Avenue. New track marks on his arms had suggested a recent, sickening addiction to heroin—Elliott swallowed; that clicking noise again—at just twelve years old, a legacy of a child's life on the streets. At the time of the discovery, the mother had been in jail for solicitation and possession. The father, unknown. The mother was released in custody long enough to identify the body. Cameron was written off as a throwaway-turned-junkie and the case was closed. Or, more accurately, never opened. A young boy, nearly a teen, dead sadly close to his birthday.

Elliott froze. How *close* to his birthday?

He squinted at the abbreviated police report. The body had been found by a beat cop in the predawn hours of March 31, already in the early stages of decomposition. The coroner had put the date of death seventy-two hours earlier.

Subtract three from the date of discovery and Cameron King had died *on* his birthday.

Somewhere between Elliott's heart and his stomach a vacuum took hold, a falling feeling that wouldn't go away. He took the spreadsheet he'd recorded his final numbers on and folded the paper like an accordion so that the column marked "birthday" was now butted against "date of discovery." He felt Amy's eyes watching him. With a finger, he traced down the paper, comparing the Abjad numbers in each column, then glancing at the victim's "age" column for confirmation. Each time his finger stopped, the two Abjad numbers were nearly identical.

Why not identical? Well, different years, first of all. And assume that not all bodies are found immediately. The date of discovery would naturally be a few days after the actual death, which was not explicitly listed in Dave's files but implied in the coroner's reports.

If you took that slight margin of error into account, then the exact difference between the victim's birth date and the day they died was their age.

He raised his head and looked at Amy. His heart was hammering in his rib cage. A large part of his calculus for getting involved in Lacey Scowcroft's case melted away. While his offer to help find Lacey had been an honest one, at least a part of him thought that his real challenge would be to lead Amy gently back from the edge when they learned that the worst had happened, that Lacey was dead. To convince her to fold her past away and accept a different future before she ended up like him, or worse. All that evaporated in the face of what he was reading on the pages in front of him.

She looked at him, anxious. "Elliott? What is it?"

"There's a connection."

Her face paled. "Show me."

He pointed to the columns, having a hard time containing his excitement. "Your crazy Abjad numbers, for the vast majority of these kids, bear no resemblance to each other. Which makes sense, of course. The dates these kids were born have no connection to any other date, so the Abjad values are wildly different from each other."

"Right."

He pointed to Cameron's row. "But these values are close. *Really* close. Meaning the dates they were derived from are very similar. I didn't notice because I wasn't seeing the actual days, the months and so on. I was just adding numbers."

"Those are the birth date and date of discovery Abjad values," Amy said, then frowned. "They're close, but they're not exact."

"No, they're not, but that's the date the body was *discovered*. If you assume the victim actually died a day or two or three before they were found, then the values are only off by Cameron's age, which means . . ."

"He died on his birthday," she finished for him, then paled. "How many did you find?"

"Six. About five too many to be a coincidence."

Amy's eyes widened. "Oh my god. Someone's killing them on their birthdays?"

"It seems that way," he cautioned. "It's only a pattern at this point."

"But how did no one see that before?"

He gestured to the files. "Six kids across dozens, maybe hundreds, of cases? Over a five-year spread? Not to mention . . ."

"What?"

Elliott hesitated, then made a face. "Cameron was the throwaway kid of a junkie mom and an absent father. My guess? When he disappeared, his case got bounced back and forth between CPS and the MPD. The cops glanced at it and threw some manpower at the case, but not a lot—check the shelters, watch the street corners, keep an eye out."

"And when his body turned up and the examiner called it an overdose . . ."

"The cops filed it 'closed' and moved on to the next one. Why would an already overtaxed police force have any reason to look for random correlations between birthdays and death dates?"

Suddenly, Amy gasped and grabbed a fistful of his jacket.

"What's wrong?" he asked.

"Elliott," she choked. "Lacey's birthday is in ten days."

15

Dave

"I'll take a large coffee and a marble frosted—aw, hell . . ."

Dave glanced over as the radio on Fracasso's hip barked. His partner's face, lit up for once in anticipation of a donut and a coffee, fell back to its pouchy, hound dog look as they listened to the call come in.

"Baker 37 and Baker 36, respond for a possible overdose on the fourteen hundred block of Levis Street in the Trinidad. A white male approximately twelve to fourteen years old was seen lying on the ground unresponsive. Medics are staging."

Fracasso turned the volume down as other customers glanced up. A minute later, the response came back.

"Baker 37, 10-4. I'm en route."

Ten seconds later: "Baker 36. I'm busy with an assault in Edgeworth. Anyone else in the vicinity?"

They were on a lunch break and weren't a patrol unit, so they wouldn't be expected to respond to a radio call . . . but they were six blocks away. Fracasso looked at the donut case longingly. "Do we gotta?"

"Tony, we're Youth and Family Services, remember? Forget the donut."

Fracasso sighed, but grabbed the mic. "Cruiser 553. I'm in the area of that last call. Go ahead and hold me out."

They jogged out to the car and hit the street, making it to the Trinidad neighborhood in three minutes, even with traffic, but were stymied by the collection of small, urban streets. Bent over the steering wheel to better see street signs, Fracasso hummed and muttered to himself. "Levis, Levis, where are you, Levis?"

Dave poked at the GPS. "Two blocks up, take a left."

When they got to Levis, Fracasso gunned it, spotting a group of people knotted up by the curb of what they assumed was the fourteen hundred block. Fracasso swung to the curb. They jumped out and were ready to run when Dave stopped short.

"They said overdose, right?"

"Drug kit, good call." Fracasso swerved back to the cruiser and popped the trunk. He snatched out a small black duffel bag. "Got it."

The people shouted and pointed toward the back of a low row of tenements. The last house appeared abandoned, with broken windows and a boarded up door. They sprinted down a narrow walk squeezed between the house and a rotting fence to the backyard where, propped up against a brick wall, was a young man—stick thin, pale, head lolling. They knelt to either side of him.

Dave swore as he snapped on plastic gloves, then lifted one of the boy's eyelids. The eyes were wide and blank, with pinpoint pupils. Sirens in the distance. Fracasso had two fingers on the kid's throat. "Dave, no pulse."

"Do the NARCAN anyway."

Fracasso broke open a small plastic box from the duffel bag, then pulled out a slim paper sleeve. Ripping it open, he slid out a thick-bodied syringe with a wedged white plastic head.

"Hold his head," Fracasso said through gritted teeth. Sweat beaded along his hairline in the chilly air. "Where's the freaking medic?"

Grabbing the chin and top of the skull, Dave positioned the boy's head so that his partner could place the syringe just inside the right nostril. With steady pressure, Fracasso depressed the plunger halfway down, then switched nostrils and emptied the rest of the syringe. There was no apparent effect, and they began rubbing the boy's wrists and ankles.

Which is when Dave noticed that the boy's clothes were odd even for a young teen junkie or tweaker. He was wearing faded green work pants, like the kind old men preferred, worn smooth at the knees and the inner thighs. His top was a blue, long-sleeved plaid shirt with a wide cowboy collar and sleeves that fell several inches short of the boy's wrists. Across the shoulders was a stylized yoke with decorative white stitching. The material was so thin the boy's ribs were visible through the fabric.

Dave frowned. "I think I—"

Heavy footsteps thudded as two EMTs rounded the corner wheeling a stretcher. They brought it as close as they could, then ditched it when the ground got too rough. They jogged over to the cops, dropping kits and bags next to the boy.

"James," Dave said, recognizing the bigger of the two EMTs.

"Hey, Dave. What's happening?" James said as he knelt, his eyes never leaving the body. The two cops backed away to give them room. "We got ourselves a case of the ol' meanie greenies?"

"Maybe. Didn't have time to check the pockets. Reported as an OD. Dilated pupils, clammy skin, unresponsive. We did the NARCAN thing."

James frowned. "How old is this kid?"

"Peach fuzz says teen, but he's skinny as shit," Fracasso said. "I bet I weighed more than him when I was born."

"He still high?"

Fracasso snorted. "Don't know if he's still *alive*."

James glanced at the other EMT, who had a stethoscope out and on the kid's chest. The EMT nodded. "He's alive. Well, a little bit of him, anyway. We'll grab the Reeves and haul him out of here. The

NARCAN'll keep him breathing till we can get him to Mercy General." He grinned humorlessly at the two detectives. "Fourth one we caught today!"

"That a record?"

James gave a derisive snort. "Not even top ten. But you gimme till suppertime, I'll let you know."

Baker 37 pulled up and started interviewing the small crowd on the street while Dave and Fracasso watched the medics slide the boy's body onto a Reeves device, a flexible orange sling with straps, and from there onto the wheeled stretcher. James lifted the boy tenderly from the Reeves sling onto the stretcher.

"See this shit all the goddamned time and I still can't stand it," Fracasso said.

The words barely registered for Dave. He couldn't stop staring at the boy's ridiculous, ill-fitting shirt, a raggedy old thing too short at the wrists and stretched tight across the bony shoulders. It stirred a childhood memory so long forgotten he was wondering if he was just imagining it, filling in blanks of his mind that he didn't know were there. He'd seen it, he was sure, as a child. Maybe on a TV show or in a comic? A cowboy shirt with a wide collar . . . it had the taste of something familiar, an object that had been in his vision all the time once. Then, nothing. An absolute blank.

Fracasso nudged him. "Everything still working in there?"

Dave shook himself. "Sorry, Tony. Guess I'm not used to it myself."

"Hey, at least he made it this far," his partner said as they watched them roll the teen around the building and to the ambulance waiting in the street. "Fingers crossed he'll pull out of it in the hospital."

"Yeah."

"So," Fracasso said. "We going back for those donuts or what?"

16

Evan

Julie leaned over and shouted at Evan above the applause. "It's going to be a total madhouse out there!"

He nodded wearily and kept clapping until his hands stung. The kids—dressed in their turkey, Pilgrim, and Native American costumes—looked dazed at all the attention. No surprise—they were on their third curtain call, but no parent of a Saint Andrew's student wanted to be seen as anything less than insanely enthusiastic. Especially if your ex was somewhere in the audience. With her new husband. He fought the temptation to look over his shoulder to see how hard *she* was clapping.

Julie nudged him. The Pilgrims had come back out onstage for their bow, and his son was looking right at him. Evan waved like he'd never seen him before. Jeremy, wan and willowy but tall for ten, would've been mistaken for one of the middle-school chaperones if he hadn't been dressed like a sixteenth-century Dutch Master, complete with buckled shoes on his feet and black sugarloaf hat sitting atop his burst of red hair. Shifting from foot to foot, the boy held on to a papier-mâché blunderbuss with both hands like it was a life preserver.

To the relief of every adult in the massive theater, the overhead lights came on after the last bow and the children trooped offstage. The sounds of general bustle followed as everyone reached for their coats and began filing out of the rows and into the aisles.

The Thanksgiving extravaganza was a two-part affair, with half the children at the school having given their performance the previous night, so what could have been an orderly process disintegrated into complete chaos as the kids in the audience—made to sit still and quiet for nearly an hour—exploded out of their seats and began tearing around the space, hooting and whooping at each other. Behind him, a kid let out a scream like he was being disemboweled, then vaulted over the row of seats so he could run pell-mell along the row with three other friends who had done the same.

Julie shot Evan an over-the-shoulder look as they shuffled down the row. "I know," he said. "Madhouse."

He smiled at her back, wondering how he'd gotten lucky enough to find a woman willing to enter a relationship with a ten-year-old already in the picture, to put up with Lydia and *Graham* when they came over for their custody visit, or to put up with *him* when he fell into a funk about how things had worked out.

The memories still stung, the accusations Lydia had leveled at him, the hell she'd put him through, but all that mattered was that he'd been cleared. The last year had been rough going—the hearings especially so—but the problems finally seemed to have worked themselves out, and life was moving forward. He'd never be happy with *Graham* in his life in any capacity, but the guy wasn't the worst thing that could've happened, and, he had to admit grudgingly, that as bad as Lydia had been as a wife, she was a doting mother.

Julie took his hand and squeezed as they finally made it into the aisle. They headed up the ramp to the lobby with everyone else. "No moping, right?"

He squeezed back. "No moping."

◆ ◆ ◆

Jeremy

Jeremy ducked under Ms. Parson's outstretched arm, but he forgot about his hat and his social studies teacher clotheslined it clean off his head.

"Mr. Weir, there is no running," she called, giving him a hard look that normally made his stomach turn to water, but he was half-crazy with adrenaline and he just laughed as he sprinted down the narrow corridor created by the layers of stage curtain. She clapped her hands and called after him, "Your parents are waiting for you in the lobby!"

He and Will and Trey horsed around for a while, but eventually enough teachers showed up to herd them into the music room to get changed out of their Thanksgiving costumes. There was still plenty of screaming and shouting, but he was definitely ready to lose the Pilgrim outfit. The material was something cheap and scratchy, and he already had a rash around his neck from where the high white collar had chafed.

Despite how much he hated the costume and how much he'd hated being in the stupid play, he folded each piece of the outfit carefully, matching seams and smoothing out each wrinkle, then placed it in the bag so that nothing would crease. If he didn't, his mom would freak, and that meant a lecture and maybe worse. It look so long, in fact, by the time he was changed, Will and Trey were done and he was the last one in the music room. He snatched up the garment bag and ran out.

The hall rang with the distant noise of conversation filtering down from the lobby. He hurried toward the noise, past glass cases full of trophies and bulletin boards with blue-and-gold construction paper cutout letters cheering **GO SAINTS!** He glanced at the case as he hurried past—he was fascinated by the old pictures of football players with their slack faces and leather helmets—and dropped the bag. He cursed and knelt to grab it, scared that he'd undone all the good work to keep the costume wrinkle-free.

"Jeremy?"

Startled, he looked up. An older woman stood in front of him, smiling, with her hands on her hips. She was dressed like a teacher—long plaid dress and sweater top with a frilly collar, just like Ms. Parson—but he'd never seen her before.

She arched an eyebrow. "It *is* Jeremy, isn't it? Jeremy Weir?"

"Yes, ma'am," he said automatically. Mom didn't like when children didn't answer correctly.

"Well, I'm glad I found you in all of this mess. Your father said you'd be back here," she said. Her smile was genuine, but tight, as if it were hard for her to keep on her face. Wrinkles around her eyes reminded him of his mother, but where his mom's eyes were gray, these were dark and intense, like buttons on a coat. "Apparently there wasn't any parking out front, so he wants you to meet him in the bus lot."

"He does?"

She ignored his question and pointed at the garment bag. "Did you fold your costume correctly?"

"Yes, ma'am."

"Give it to me," she ordered, holding out a hand. He surrendered it to her and she pulled the flaps up to take a look, then tsked and straightened out several of the folds. "It'll do, I suppose. I'll carry it for you."

"But . . ."

The smile disappeared as she gave him a sharp look. "Do you always talk back to adults, Jeremy?"

A flush crept up his neck and he shook his head.

"Then we'd better get you to your father. Are you ready?"

He looked over his shoulder, but there was no one else around. He turned to meet the stare of the woman, expectant and waiting.

"Yes, ma'am."

Evan

Evan rocked in place, dazed. He'd thought the inside of the theater was chaos, but nothing could prepare him for the scene in the lobby. Sounds piled on top of each other in so many layers that he wasn't going deaf—he was going crazy. Children from three to thirteen were running across the lobby at track-meet speed. Buckles and bonnets littered the ground to join dropped gloves and winter hats and programs. Parents, many of whom had never been anywhere but the guidance office, hovered and chatted around the edges of the maelstrom.

Out of the mess, Lydia appeared next to him, suddenly and without warning, and he had to smother the bitterness and anger that welled up every time he saw her. Trailing her, storklike and severe, was Graham in all his crew cut and Burberry glory.

"Evan," his former wife said. She'd cut her hair, he noticed, her beautiful black hair, something he'd asked her not to do while they'd been married. It was an angular pageboy cut that put her looks on par with Graham's.

"Lydia." He pivoted a quarter turn. "You know Julie. Julie, this is Graham."

Julie was gracious as always, with a genuine smile that made Lydia's grimace dull in comparison. He noted grudgingly that Graham, despite his Marine Corps demeanor, was pleasant and his smile sincere as he shook hands with Julie. *Well*, he thought, *it's not like they have a history.*

"Jeremy did well," Julie said. Evan winced, waiting for Lydia to pounce. If it wasn't a superlative nor a criticism . . .

"I suppose." Lydia pursed her lips. "He forgot one of his lines and threw off the poor thing after him."

"It's an elementary school play," Evan said. "I thought he did fine."

Lydia shrugged with a look that said, *Of course you would*, and turned to glance at the lobby. Threads of people were slowly making their way to the exits, although the lobby was still packed with kids, parents, and teachers.

"You did a nice job on the blunderbuss, Evan," Graham said with a smile.

"Thanks," he said cautiously, trying to decide if he should read anything into the comment. "I was just happy it didn't break in half when Jeremy shot the turkey. It's been a while since I messed with papier-mâché."

"Like thirty years, I guess?"

Evan relaxed and offered a small smile. "Something like that."

"The only thing I learned in art class was how to eat paste," Julie offered, and the three of them laughed.

Lydia turned in a circle, a sour look on her face. She checked her watch. *Her new diamond watch,* Evan noticed.

The conversation continued along safe lines—sports, traffic, work— with only the occasional barbed comment from Lydia and the riposte from Evan. He found himself laughing at one or two of Graham's jokes and wondered how he ever thought the man was a humorless government hack. *Divorce proceedings following hyperbolic charges of child abuse will do that,* he thought. He might even have Graham to thank for Lydia finally admitting she'd exaggerated a few details here and there. As in, made them up.

"Where *is* that boy?"

Evan looked over at Lydia, startled, then around the lobby. Most of the crowd was gone, he saw with surprise. He'd had the impression it would never actually empty. "He'll be along, Lydia. Relax."

"Don't tell me to relax," she snapped and just like that, the tension was there. Not just emotionally, but physically: his neck seemed to fuse with his skull into a single plate. Julie's hand appeared at the small of his back, tracing tiny circles.

"He's probably screwing around with Will or Trey."

"I'm sure that's it," Graham said, squeezing Lydia's upper arm. "How often do kids get to mess around in school after dark?"

"Why don't we split up and look for him?" Julie suggested. "There are only these two main corridors leading from the lobby into the school. We'll find him in ten minutes, I bet."

Graham led Lydia away to one of the halls before she could comment, while Evan and Julie took the other. Somewhat self-consciously, then more boldly, they pulled on doors and peeked down halls, calling Jeremy's name. The burr of noise that had seemed so aggravating not long ago had faded, and the only sounds were the sharp clap of their footsteps on the tile floor and the echo off the institutional walls.

"The music room?" Julie said in front of a set of double doors. "Jeremy said they'd be changing here, I thought." But there was no one inside, just the smell of disinfectant.

Evan felt the first prickle of uncertainty. *Someone has to be last*, he tried to tell himself, but the halls felt inert, abandoned. Their footsteps were hurried now, just under a jog.

"Maybe Lydia and Graham found him first," Julie said, trying to sound hopeful. "You know she'd take her time chastising the poor kid."

Evan didn't answer. He'd heard a rattle like a chain hitting metal somewhere up ahead. They turned the corner to see a stooped man in gray-green overalls drawing a portable security fence, like a metal accordion, across the mouth of a set of glass double doors.

"Excuse me!" Evan jogged up to the man, hating the high pitch of alarm in his voice. "Excuse me. I'm looking for my son. He was in the play tonight. About yea tall? Pale? Red hair and freckles?"

The man looked at him from the other side of the gate like a prison guard. "Well, a woman came through with her son a little bit ago. Seemed a bit old for him, but that's not for me to say. I tried to tell her she wasn't supposed to come through here, you know, 'cause this entrance is for the principal and the teachers—hey!"

Evan yanked the gate wide enough to squeeze through. The man yelled for him to stop, but Evan was already at the glass doors, throwing them open and sprinting out into the night. Cold lights shined onto an empty lot, and his breath steamed in white clouds. He turned to his right, just catching sight of a big boat of a car leaving the parking lot.

"Jeremy? Jeremy!" He sprinted after the car, screaming his son's name as the bright red brake lights turned the far corner of the school and disappeared.

◆ ◆ ◆

Jeremy

"Where are we going?" His words came out slow, like he had a mouthful of peanut butter.

"I told you," the woman said patiently. "I'm taking you to your family."

Jeremy looked out of the window of the car, trying to concentrate, but the bright orange and white lights of the school seemed to dim and enlarge, shrink and grow, going from pinpoint stars to diffuse planets. His head lolled on top of his shoulders like a broken action figure.

The lady was next to him, driving the car. They'd waited for a minute or two for Dad to show up, but nobody used the back lot except when they had gym class outside and the weather was nice. He was screwing up the courage to tell her he thought he should go inside when she'd reached into her handbag and offered him some hot chocolate from a thermos. It felt impolite to say no, he was cold, and besides she had his costume, which he couldn't leave behind.

He wasn't even done with the cup before he started feeling strange, like his feet were floating skyward past his shoulders, while the rest of this body stayed still. He felt nauseous and giddy at the same time. The lady had led him by the elbow to an ugly old car like his grandmother drove, then buckled him into the front seat before climbing in herself. Fear tried to push itself off the mat—this was wrong, it shouldn't be happening. But he was too tired, felt too weird to actually do anything.

Dimly, he heard a yell from outside the car, but when he twisted around to look back, the seat belt got in the way. He fumbled with the buckle, but his hands were mitten-clumsy, and suddenly the woman had a hard-nailed hand across his chest and was pushing him into his seat.

"Who are you? Where are you taking me?" he tried to ask, but his words were slurred, and he was having a hard time keeping his eyes open.

She looked over at him and smiled once again. Her eyes were small stones in her head, dark and shining very bright. "No questions now. Face front. I have to concentrate on driving if I'm to get us home in one piece. You wouldn't want us to have an accident, would you?"

17

Elliott

"Do you think this is it?"

Elliott glanced down at the patch of asphalt, partially shielded from the parking lot by a dumpster. A hundred cigarette butts, tan and white worms, littered the ground. "Yes."

"I mean, do you think she'll talk to us?"

"She could've said no." Elliott glanced at Amy sidelong. Watched her bite her lip, nudge a flattened soda can with a foot. Put her hands in her pockets, take them out.

He didn't blame her for being nervous. After months of guesswork and planning, she was actually on the ground, about to talk to a person who might, if they were lucky, give her some answers. That kind of discovery brought with it all kinds of emotional turmoil.

The night before, Amy had been almost inconsolable. Tears streaked her face. "I've looked for Lacey for almost a year, Elliott. Ten days isn't going to make a difference."

"Of course it will," he'd said, trying to believe it himself. "We just have to follow through on this information."

She cuffed at her nose. "I want to believe you, but . . ."

"Look, eight years ago, I would've given anything to have ten more days." He squeezed her arm clumsily. "We have to use what we're given. With luck and some hard work, we might just make some headway."

She nodded.

"And don't just think about Lacey," he continued. "This is about getting to the truth, about saving some other parent the same heartache you've been through."

"So what do we do?"

He stood and started pacing, unable to sit any longer. The space was so small he had to turn every four steps. "Someone is out there grabbing kids and, eventually, killing them. We don't know why or for what purpose, but the first psychologically significant thing is, obviously—"

"The birthdays."

"Right. Which could stand for any number of things to this person. Until we know more, we have to go with the basics of what the event means socially for any of us, which is to say they are milestones, transitions, thresholds."

"Departures, too," Amy said, straightening in her seat. "Leaving things behind. Childhood, adolescence, innocence."

"True," Elliott said, impressed. "So, we have to build a psychological model of the person doing this as we move along—what birthdays mean to *him*—so that we figure out which social constructs make the most sense and help us fill in the remaining pieces."

"We have to find the connection, the thing in common," Amy said, then gazed down at her stack of papers. "From the kids who fit the pattern."

"Exactly. And those children had families, families we need to talk to. What did these six kids or families or parents have in common? Did they know each other or share something we can tease out and examine? Talk to enough people, ask enough questions, and we'll be able to build a profile that will get us to the next stage."

"Do we have time for that?"

Elliott spread his hands. "We'll have to make the time."

"That's going to be . . . so hard for them. The parents, I mean."

"Yes. But it's all we have."

Amy shook her head to clear it. After months of struggling in isolation, things were suddenly moving fast. "What will we ask them?"

"Most people want to talk if you give them the chance. And these parents, once they find out we've walked a mile in their shoes, might open up even sooner."

The first name on their list was a girl named Tammy Waters, abducted nearly four years before, her body found the previous December. A Janine Waters was listed in the case file as the mother, but a clumsy black marker smear covered where the woman's address had been—one of the redactions Dave had mentioned. Luckily, Amy had spotted the name of her workplace in the summary, a Tire King on Wheaton Pike.

A direct approach seemed better than a call, so they'd driven straight to the strip mall, where they found the sad little tire shop with its checkered flag motifs stuck between a Chinese takeout on one side and a check-cashing store on the other. From behind the counter, a wary-looking Janine had agreed to talk to them when they mentioned they were with the police, but—with a glance and a shrug at her manager—could only spare them fifteen minutes during her smoke break. The beady eyes of her boss followed them as they left.

They turned as the steel security door opened from the inside with a *ka-chunk*. Janine, wearing a polyester smock with the Tire King logo and her name embroidered in yellow thread, poked her head through, then followed it out when she saw them standing there. She jammed an old plastic cup in the gap to keep the door from closing.

She sized them up, then asked without preamble, "You got a smoke? I'm all out."

Amy shook her head, but Elliott pulled out a battered soft pack of Marlboros, shook one free, and offered it to her. He lit it and Janine took a deep, sucking drag, holding it for a long minute before tilting her head back and blowing the smoke sky-high. Balancing an elbow on her hip, she looked Elliott up and down, taking in the tattered army jacket, ragged shoes, and dirt-encrusted hands.

"Just so we're straight, I don't believe for a second you're with the cops. But if it gets me five more minutes of break time, I'll take it. So, who are you really and what do you want?"

Elliott looked back at her. It had been a long time since he'd talked to someone completely cold. Encounters on the streets—other homeless folks, a cop here and there, maybe a kind stranger—didn't count. The conversations had been perfunctory and uncomplicated. Now that he had something on the line, he was, he found to his surprise, tongue-tied.

Janine was about thirty-six, he guessed. A pack-a-day habit and holding down two or even three jobs kept her trim. And, he knew, whatever those things hadn't done to hollow her out, grief had done the rest. This was a no-bullshit woman who'd already lived a life on the rocks and knew she was barely squeaking through the rest of it. If they wasted her time, she would take the cigarette and leave them with nothing. As if reading his mind, she quirked an eyebrow. The clock was ticking. He turned to Amy, mute.

Amy offered the woman a shaky smile. "Janine, almost a year ago, I was living in a small studio apartment with my little girl, Lacey. Just me and her. She'd just turned ten. We didn't have much, but we had each other and that was almost enough, as corny as that sounds."

Janine took another drag of her cigarette and stared back, her face stony.

"One day, while she was on the way home from a friend's house, someone grabbed her and took her away. I haven't seen her since." Amy paused. "We know something like that happened to your girl Tammy. Someone came and took her away from you."

"Who the hell are you?"

"A mother, Janine. Just a mother. Elliott here is helping me. He's had some experience working on cases like this."

"Cases?" She laughed and waved the cigarette in Elliott's direction. "I told you, honey, I can tell you ain't no cop."

"I'm in deep cover."

Janine looked back at Amy. "Why aren't the police helping you? The *real* police."

"I think you know why," Amy said, holding the other woman's eyes. "They've given up. But a mother can't give up."

Janine shrugged, scuffed at the ground.

"We know that Tammy was kidnapped two years before . . . before she was discovered," Elliott said. "We think there might be a connection between Tammy and other children who were kidnapped over the years. And, maybe, from them to Amy's daughter, Lacey."

Janine paled. "What kind of connection?"

"Tammy had just had a birthday when the police found her, hadn't she?"

"Yeah. Why?"

"Can you tell us about her? How she was kidnapped?"

Janine's lips pulled together, looking like sutures were drawing her mouth shut. "I don't want to do this again."

Amy took a half-step forward. "Janine, I know you don't. I really do. But there are six other kids out there who died a lot like Tammy did. And we're afraid there might be more."

"And the cops don't know any of this?"

"They did as much as they could." Amy gave her a bleak smile. "We're taking it from here."

A shaking hand brought the cigarette up again. She took another drag, exhaled, and shook her head. "I can't. I won't. It's too much." She turned to go.

"Wait." Amy reached out, imploring her. "Please."

"I'm sorry. I—I have to get back to work."

"Janine." Amy scrounged in a pocket. "Look at this before you go."

"What?" Janine turned, but her hand stayed on the door.

Amy held a small photograph in her hand. "Just look at it. Look at her. This is my little girl. Lacey's going to be eleven soon. Her birthday's coming up, and I'm worried about her just like you worried about Tammy."

Janine reached out and took the photo, being careful to hold it by the rippled edge with both hands. She stared at it.

"You took this at White Hills Mall," she said finally, without looking up. "The photo booth by the pretzel shop."

Amy swallowed. "Yes."

"We took the same one." A single tear slid down Janine's face, ran down to her chin. "Just the two of us."

Janine's upper body gave a jerk, like she'd been touched by a hot iron, followed by small tremors that shook her body. Another tear followed the first, and then more. Amy stepped forward and wrapped Janine in her arms, whispering to her. She caught Elliott's eye and he shuffled to the end of the service alley, where he watched the traffic for a long time, naming the makes and models of cars, memorizing license plates, counting the number of stalls in the parking lot—anything to fight the feeling trying to pull him all the way down. The deep-fried stink of the Chinese restaurant set his stomach churning. He stood there for what seemed a long time.

"Elliott?"

He turned. Amy and Janine stood close to each other, no longer embracing, looking wan but composed. Janine stared at the ground. Amy tilted her head.

He cleared his throat. "Janine, what happened the day Tammy went missing?"

She hugged her arms to her body. "I don't really know."

"You don't know?"

"She wasn't with me."

"Okay." He glanced at Amy with a question, but she shrugged. "Can you tell us about that?"

Janine picked a spot three feet up the brick wall, talked to it. "Randy, may he rot in hell, got tired of being a husband and a father, but didn't have the decency—or the guts—to tell me he was through. Didn't like to be pinned down, he told me, was meant to be *free*." She fluttered her hands, and smoke trailed in lines that hung in the air. "I told him he should've thought of that before he knocked me up."

"He left you?" Amy asked.

"Oh no. I couldn't get so lucky." Janine laughed, a harsh sound. She took another drag and glared at Elliott. "The story is boring. It bores me. It has to bore you."

"We'd still like to hear it."

She sighed. "He told me I was a bad wife, that I was lousy in bed, I never showed him enough affection. Once that stopped having an effect, then he told me I was a failure as a mother and Tammy would end up a loser like me, a slut, jumped-up trailer trash." She finished the cigarette and dropped it to join the forest of butts on the ground. "And just when I got over that, I lost my job. He started in on me again, telling me I was too stupid and too ugly to get another. And who did I think was going to hire me at my age."

"He sounds like a real winner," Amy said.

Janine shook her head. "From all of his bitching, you'd think he'd want to get the hell away from me. But no, he said I was his cross to bear."

"Of course," Elliott said. "He needed *you* to leave *him* so he could be the injured party."

Her eyebrows shot to her bangs. "You some kind of shrink?"

He gave her a weak smile. "There was a breaking point, I guess?"

"He slapped me around, but that wasn't it. I can take a punch," she said, running a finger along her nose. "But then he hit Tammy. Just once. I put a screwdriver under his chin and told the son of a bitch I'd kill him if he touched her again. He didn't, but then he *really* started hitting me."

"What happened?"

"Like I said, I can take a punch, but what would he do to Tammy if I was knocked out or couldn't help? So, after the worst fight, I ran to the neighbor, just looking for a little help. She was a nosy old bitch, but I didn't have a choice. Randy had emptied our checking account, and I still had to go to work if I was going to keep the two of us alive. The neighbor let us stay the night and I thought we were safe, so I left Tammy with her the next day."

"She called CPS," Amy said.

"Sure did." She looked around, distracted. Elliott shook out another cigarette from the pack and offered it to her, then lit it. He stuffed his hands in his pockets as she continued talking. "Randy got hauled off for beating on me, but spun some line that I was the one who'd abused Tam. I missed too much time at work going to hearings and lost the job. So, at the final hearing, the judge saw a single mother with no job and a history of a violent household. They put Tammy in foster care and told me I had six months to get my act together."

"And Randy?" Elliott asked.

She waved a hand. "He skipped town after he did his ninety days in lockup. Guess he finally found his reason to leave. Good riddance. Although, if he'd been around so the judge could've seen two parents at home . . ." Her voice trailed off.

"What happened then?"

"The foster parents turned out to be complete space cakes and let her walk to school by herself through a truly shitty neighborhood." Beside him, Amy flinched. "One day, on the way there, someone grabbed her. They didn't report her missing for almost a week. By then, there was nothing to go on. They found her body last year in some gravel lot in DC."

Elliott paused, then asked, "Had she been . . . ?"

"No. Or, at least, not when they found her." Janine seemed unfazed by the question. Her emotions, perhaps, had been blunted by too many nights spent worrying—tears spent, one hand wringing the other—and now her tone was flat and matter-of-fact. "But after two years? Who knows what she went through."

Wet tires on pavement—rolling in, rolling away—was the only sound for a long time.

"All I know," Janine finally said, breaking the silence, "is that I didn't get to see her that last day. I got to visit her in foster care once that week, a ten-minute talk. With a chaperone present, of course, in case I tried to steal her back. My own daughter."

The door popped open suddenly and the manager, a bald, moon-faced man, leaned out. He frowned, gave Janine a pointed look, then retreated inside.

Janine rolled her eyes. "I have to go. Krauthammer gave me my job back but never lets me forget." She dropped the second cigarette, half-gone, to join the other, then glanced at Amy. "I'm sorry. I really am. I hope you find your little girl."

Amy, lips pinched, nodded.

Janine moved to the door, opened it, then stopped and looked back at them. "We didn't have a good life, but we loved each other. She deserved better."

18

Jeremy

He awoke in darkness, which scared him almost more than anything, because he'd fallen asleep with the lamp on, which meant that someone had come in and shut the light off in the middle of the night without him knowing. He fumbled with the lamp and flicked the light on again, then got out of bed and pressed his ear to the door, but heard only distant thumps and whispered voices.

Suddenly, the memories of the night before hit him and he sank to the floor, where he put his head in his hands.

They'd ridden in silence for what seemed like hours.

His head had felt stuffy and he had trouble keeping his balance, even though he knew he was sitting down. Slouched in his seat, he could only see the tops of bright highway lights as they flew by that became intermittent yellow streetlamps that, in turn, became less and less frequent until they stopped altogether.

After a long time, the car had slowed and turned sharply onto a dirt road. The outside was just a smear of darkness interrupted only occasionally when the car's headlights lit up a tree or a shrub. The car first dipped down, then up a steep rise, stopping only when they pulled onto a gravel drive. Jeremy had a momentary impression of a bulky, squat house illuminated by the headlights; then a blindfold came down over his eyes, knotted painfully tight.

A car door slammed, his opened. The woman pulled him out of the car and to his feet, her hand wrapped around his arm above his elbow like a steel band. Wobbly and disoriented, he'd tottered across a gravel drive and up a set of steps, maybe the porch of the house. She'd fumbled with keys as she unlocked a door, then pulled him forward, where he immediately tripped over a threshold and stumbled into a smelly, mildewy room.

The door had shut behind him with a bang, then a series of thick locks clacked into place, setting off a wave of panic inside him. He'd struggled, wanting to run back to the car and find a way home. But the woman had slapped him so hard that he sank to his knees.

"Never disobey me," she hissed, her lips close, touching his ear. "Never again. Do you understand?"

He nodded, not trusting himself to speak.

She'd led him to the second floor, where they'd walked down a hall with wood floors—their footsteps loud in the night—and into the closeness of another room. She sat him on a bed and, without a word, left the room and shut the door. A key turned in a lock, and then he was alone.

He sat for long minutes with the blindfold still in place, terrified that she hadn't actually left. His face where she'd slapped him tingled and began to sting. When he couldn't stand it anymore, he'd reached up and ripped the blindfold off.

Whatever drug she'd given him had begun to wear off, and he was suddenly consumed with rage, rattling the knob and kicking the door, screaming that his mother would sue and the woman would be thrown in jail. There was no answer. He'd stopped when his voice went hoarse and his throat started to burn.

Distraught, he'd explored the room, looking through the few pieces of clothing in the wardrobe and running a finger along the spines of the books on the nightstand: *The Count of Monte Cristo*, *Adventures of Huckleberry Finn*, *Grimm's Fairy Tales*. They were bound in leather and the titles were in gold leaf like the books in his dad's office, but they smelled bad and were spongy to the touch. Drained and terrified, he'd finally climbed onto the bed and cried, until the tears—with no one to answer them, no one to stop them—had dried up.

Covered only by a thin blanket, he'd spent the night shivering and thrashing around on the narrow, musty-smelling bed before eventually falling asleep, comforted only by the weak light of a bedside lamp, a hokey old thing with a cowboy on a bucking bronco as the base. Until he'd woken with the light off and his reality shattered.

A key suddenly rattled in the lock. He scurried back to the bed and sat down, not sure what else to do.

The woman opened the door slowly, peeking her head in before entering and shutting it behind her. He was surprised to see she was dressed like a businesswoman this time—not as sharp as his mom, but less frumpy than what she'd worn last night. She held a large box in both hands.

She nodded and smiled when she saw him sitting on the bed. "Very good." She placed the box at her feet, then took out a stringy pair of jeans and a thin blue T-shirt. "Put these on and give me your clothes."

He was embarrassed to change in front of the woman, but the imprint of her hand still burned on his face. He turned so that she couldn't see him in his underwear, at least not the front. The jeans fit around the waist, but the hem came halfway up his shins. "These are too small."

She pursed her lips. "They'll do. Put the rest on."

He changed quickly and handed his clothes to her, which she dropped by the door. Reaching into the box again, she pulled out a piece of construction paper and a box of colored pencils, then lowered herself to the floor and sat cross-legged. She patted a spot on the floor. "Come. Sit."

He did so gingerly, afraid the jeans would rip. She handed him the paper and colored pencils.

"Take this and write your name at the top. Then draw all the things you remember about your life." The woman's voice was low, gentle, and even. "Your mother, your father. Sisters and brothers. Your dog. Your house. Make sure they're all in the picture."

"Right now?"

She nodded. "Right now."

He shook the pencils out of the box and started to draw, feeling like a kindergartener. Will there be milk and cookies next? He doubted it. Soon, however, the room faded away as he warmed to the task.

His family began as a collection of stick figures, four in all, but he went back and added details to his dad's face and remembered things like Julia's flower dress she'd worn the first time Dad had introduced her. Mom was a black dress with a head on it, and Graham was a scarecrow half again as tall as anyone else on the page. Home was a jumble of different buildings and cars. The house he'd grown up in that had to be sold. So it could be split fairly, they'd said. Apartments and mansions. Big cars and compacts.

"No siblings?"

Jeremy jumped. He'd forgotten the woman was even there. "No."

She raised an eyebrow, then gestured for him to finish, but his concentration had been broken and he wrapped up with a blocky facsimile of school with the flag flying overhead and a yellow school bus in front. It looked like a two-year-old had drawn it, he thought critically, but he'd never been good at art.

He put the colored pencil down and looked up at the woman. She held her hand out and he passed the drawing across to her. She examined it closely, noting each of the figures. She pointed.

"Who is this?"

"My dad."

"And this?"

"Julie. His girlfriend."

"They're not married?"

He shook his head. She pointed again.

"My mom. And her husband Graham."

"Your parents are divorced?"

He nodded.

"Do you love them?"

He nodded again, because this time he didn't trust himself to speak. His throat was tight and his eyes itched. He blinked fast, trying to make it stop—he didn't want to cry in front of her.

"Why do you love them?" The woman's gaze was relentless and hungry. "Why?"

"Because . . ." Jeremy was stuck for an answer. "They're my family."

Relief flooded through him when she nodded slowly. "That's right. You should love your family."

She lowered the paper and smiled at him, although her eyes looked weird. Julie had made him cookies once, with a blue-icing smile and raisins for eyes. The woman's eyes reminded him of those raisins.

"How did your mother and father discipline you?"

"Dad swats me, I guess, when I've done something wrong."

"And your mother?"

"She puts me in time-out. Then I have to"—he stopped, embarrassed—"negotiate my release, she says."

The woman raised an eyebrow. "Which one of them scares you more?"

"I don't like either," he stuttered. "I mean, nobody likes getting spanked, but Dad doesn't do it that hard. And the time-out is just . . . silly."

The woman made a slight humming noise, perhaps to show she understood or agreed, then seemed to change the subject entirely. "Let me tell you about this house. It is quite old. The basement is so dark, so damp, and so quiet you can hear the spiders when they walk. Mold grows on the walls, which are so thick that, if you were to scream at the top of your voice, no one will hear you, even if they stand just outside and listen. I know, because I've done both."

Jeremy was unable to look away from her face.

"Beneath it," she continued, "is an ancient root cellar, where my grandfather and his father before him put their storage for the winter. It is no bigger than that wardrobe over there. It is so cold, so dark, so quiet, it makes the basement look like a carnival." She paused. "Last night, I struck you to get you to comply with my wishes. It stung, didn't it? But the memory of it will fade quicker than the bruise, and soon you'll be asking yourself: 'What can I get away with? What will she do to me if I disobey?'"

He reached for his face instinctively, then dropped his hand.

She watched his reaction with amusement. "What I'm about to say will not fade from your mind. When I say you will be punished, I won't *swat* you. You will not be put in a *time-out*. I will tie you, hand and foot, and take you, not to the basement, but to that old, cold root cellar . . . and I'll throw you in. I'll forget about you. No one will remember you are there. And you will lay there, forgotten, unable to move, screaming a scream that can't be heard."

She paused to see what effect her words had. Then, "Do you understand me?"

"Yes," he whispered.

She picked up his paper again, then took a black marker from her pocket and drew a line through "Jeremy" at the top. "This is no longer your name. You will not speak it again. You will not tell anyone else what it is."

She waited until he nodded, then drew more lines, this time through his mom and dad, Julie and Graham. "You will never mention your father or mother or their girlfriends and husbands or your life from before ever again. If you do, you will be *punished*." She paused, and he nodded to show he understood. "You will meet your new family soon.

You will not tell them about your life from before, and you will not ask them about their lives from before. Is that clear?"

He nodded once more.

"Now, pay attention."

Slowly, ceremoniously, she raised his hand-drawn picture until it hung between them, then tore it in half. She placed the pieces in a folder, put the folder in the box, then turned to him. She was still smiling, he saw, and her eyes had an odd gleam. Bright, as though lit from within.

She placed a hand on her breast as if speaking a foreign language. "My name is Sister. This is your home now. Your only home. Do you understand?"

He swallowed painfully, then nodded one last time. "Yes, Sister."

19

Elliott

"Did you have to give her my cigarettes?" Amy asked, peeved.

Odors of stale coffee filled the car as they made their way down the stoplight-tortured Wheaton Pike. Tire King was behind them, though they'd braved the glare of the manager to grab a free cup of coffee from the lobby before they'd left.

Elliott looked over. "You can't possibly still be smoking. That pack has to be two months old. It looks like it's been through a war."

"I've been trying to quit," Amy said. "But it was my last pack."

"If it was your last, then it doesn't matter, right?"

She shot him a sour look. "Some of us have our dependencies, all right? Don't tell me you never had a crutch or a vice."

He turned to the window. "I've had my share."

"Who hasn't?" Amy asked rhetorically, unaware of Elliott's discomfort. "High school was one big blur, but after I met Darren and started partying like it was a job, the blur got even blurrier."

Elliott looked back at her, curious despite himself. "When was that?"

"Freshman year at UMD. Good ol' CFA, the College of Fine Arts, although most people said it stood for Can't Fucking Add. The majors were music, theater, art, sculpture. The minors were pot, pills, and shrooms."

"Which one were you?"

"Pot, mostly."

He grimaced. "I mean, which major?"

"Oh, art. Mixed media. I'm a decent artist, but I get bored quickly. I started collecting sticks when I'd walk in the woods and crafting these endless spiral arrangements. Real Andy Goldsworthy stuff."

"You stopped?"

"I went from two-dimensional spirals to three-dimensional helixes," she said, making a twirling motion in the air with one finger, "and that got me to thinking about infinity and the power of numbers, which led to . . ."

"Numerology and arithmancy?"

"Exactly," she said, missing or ignoring his sarcasm. "When I saw how profound the Pythagorean ideal was, I kind of lost interest in gluing sticks together, you know?"

"I imagine shrooms helped with the epiphany."

"Not really. Shrooms are too much. They get in the way, like a puppy trying to play with you while you're juggling two plates and a chain saw. I could only do arithmancy when I was straight. Which helped when I switched to math."

Elliott did a double take. "Math?"

"Yep. Double major, math and cognitive science," she said, then glanced over, grinning. "What? Hard to believe?"

"No, I . . . ," Elliott stuttered. "Why aren't you still there? What happened?"

"Lacey happened," she said and the grin faded. A broad silence filled the car.

Elliott took a sip of coffee and looked at his feet. After a moment, he said, "Well, I'm sorry I took your cigarettes, but we needed Janine to open up. Dave told me he learned to keep a pack around to get people talking. Besides, I'm doing you a favor by getting rid of them."

"Yeah, thanks. Anyway, who are we seeing next?"

He looked at the list they'd compiled. "Faith and Gary . . ." He frowned. "Nuxmein?"

"Neumann."

"Your handwriting is terrible."

"Another holdover from art school," she said. "What do we know about them?"

Elliott consulted the list again. "Their son was one of the earliest hits we found, at the edge of the five years of files Dave pulled. He went missing almost six years ago and was found about two years later."

"What was their son's name?"

"Danny."

Amy tugged a long lock of hair out of the headband she wore as she drove, twirling it around one forefinger before dragging it across her upper lip. She did it over and over, unaware of the subconscious tic. "That poor woman has been through a lot."

"Who? Janine? Yeah, she has."

"Did we learn anything?"

"Less than I'd expected, more than I thought."

"What's that mean?"

Elliott put the list down and slouched back into the seat. "I made an assumption. Shame on me."

"Why?"

"I thought the answer would be with the family." He ran a finger along the door frame. "Not that I expected to find a . . . I don't know, a killer birthday party clown in each case, but with Tammy in foster care when she was abducted, a lot of the normal connections I'd planned on following are either gone or much further down on the list."

"You mean like someone they knew? An uncle or a teacher?"

"Yes."

"Where does that leave us?"

"Two connected data points form a line, not a shape. We need more perspectives to build anything resembling a theme, here. You can't make a constellation out of two stars."

"Just like a web isn't made from a single strand of silk."

"Exactly."

Amy paused, then asked, "What's your sign?"

"What?"

"Your sign. When's your birthday?"

He glanced over. "Are you asking me because I said 'constellation'?"

"Just tell me."

"No."

"Why not? You had to be born sometime."

"I was," he said. "I just don't want to tell you."

"I'll tell you mine."

"I don't care."

"January tenth. I'm a Capricorn."

"That's wonderful. Let's concentrate on driving."

She pulled over to a curb, where the Celica bucked before coming to a stop, and turned to him. "Spill it."

"Are you sure you can get this thing started again?"

"If I believe in it enough yes," she said. "But we're not going anywhere until you tell me your birthday."

"It's really that important to you?"

"Yes," she said. "You're helping me find my daughter, and I want to make a connection with you."

"And we're not moving unless I tell you?"

"Yup."

He sighed very lightly. "October."

"October what? The date is important."

He closed his eyes. "The thirty-first. Halloween. A bad omen, right?"

She frowned. "No, why?"

"What do you mean, why? Because it's *Halloween.*"

She waved a hand. "Judeo-Christian crap. There are much deeper mysteries out there."

"Really?" He paused. "So, does it mean anything? Being born on Hallo—on the thirty-first?"

"You're a Scorpio. You're analytical, meditative, resourceful, but ruled by your desires. Fierce and independent."

"Is that all?"

"You're good at hiding your feelings, which can be both good and bad."

"You needed a horoscope to tell you that?" He snorted. "I'll let you guess my weight next time we stop."

Her lips flattened into a line. "It's not nothing, you know. The things I believe in. It's what led us to the birthday clue. Without it, we'd have nothing."

"Maybe. Or maybe we would've arrived at the same place if I'd had two minutes to study the dates more closely."

"The police did that and didn't solve a thing," she said. "Why not?"

"Because they didn't care," he said without thinking. They were quiet for a moment as the truth of it sank in. "I didn't mean it that way—"

"No. You're right. They care, but the way cops care about anything. Enough to keep themselves motivated, enough to take pride in their job. To remind themselves why they do what they do. But maybe not enough."

"They have a lot on their plate," Elliott said cautiously. "You can't fault them for not investing as much as a parent would."

"I'm not," she said. "But maybe it takes a parent to care enough to persevere."

Fifteen minutes later, they arrived in the up-and-coming suburb of Davidson Run, an enclave of closely packed red brick and vinyl-sided homes that promised to have seasonal glimpses of the Potomac River but full-time views of each other's minivans, soccer nets, and landscaping. A white postal truck was just puttering into the neighborhood, completing the picture of suburban bliss.

"What's the address?"

Standing on the sidewalk, Elliott consulted their notes. "5402 Calm Glenn. Probably on the corner up there."

The sun had poked its head out from behind the clouds, sending down a cold, bright light, but there wasn't a single person visible on the trimmed, still-green lawns or precise brick sidewalks. Elliott hesitated, suddenly aware of how much they stood out. The two of them might not be out of place strolling into a tire shop in a shabby roadside strip mall, but an upper-class suburban neighborhood was not their element. A rattling sound distracted him.

"What is that noise?" he asked. "I hear it every time you move."

"Tic Tacs," she said. "Sorry if it annoys you. Want one?"

He shook his head irritably and they walked to the house. A herringbone brick walkway threaded its way from the street to a low, roofed front porch. The lawn hadn't been touched for several weeks, and the tall grass flopped onto the bricks and the slab of the porch. Two wicker chairs, their white paint chipping, were the only ornamentation. Elliott took in the state of the home, then stepped off the porch to glance at the other homes, which were covered with cornstalks and gourds, flint corn bouquets, and silly cardboard turkey cutouts.

Amy tucked the stray lock of hair back under her headband, then opened the screen door and rapped the knocker, a brass fish. It took three tries before a shadow moved behind the front window's gray privacy sheers.

The shadow would peek through the peephole, Elliott knew, assessing and measuring. It wouldn't surprise him if the door stayed shut and the shadow retreated into the depths of the house.

But it opened, revealing a middle-aged man with shaggy white hair. His face was gray and sour, with red-rimmed brown eyes and sagging jowls. A stained, baby-blue polo shirt hung over the waist of baggy jeans. The flesh seemed to hang on his frame, as though a larger person had inhabited his body before leaving for greener pastures, leaving behind something diminished and worn.

"Help you?" The voice was phlegmy and made Elliott want to clear his throat; then the man's breath hit them. His skin prickled as he recognized the look, the smell, the feeling rolling off the man.

Amy asked, "Mr. Neumann?"

"Yes." The man looked from Elliott to Amy with slow, bovine swings of his head.

Amy explained how sorry she was to have bothered him, and did he have a minute, and here's who they were. It was short and to the point, but doubt and impatience crept into the man's face. He began to ease back into the house, a slow-motion withdrawal. "I'm not really interested . . ."

"It's about Danny," Elliott said.

Neumann froze and the eyes, doused before, showed the smallest spark. "What did you say?"

"We want to talk to you about your son," Elliott said, pushing his words into the tiny space he'd made. "Mr. Neumann, we know how hard this is, but we could desperately use your help."

"What do you want?"

"My daughter," Amy began, then stopped, her voice catching. She paused, then continued as if nothing had happened. "My daughter Lacey was kidnapped nearly a year ago. The police have given up looking for her, but I've never stopped. Mr. Nash, here, used to work for the police, and he's helping me try to find Lacey."

"What does this have to do with Danny?"

"We think his disappearance might be related to Lacey's," Elliott said. "But even if it's not, there's still a pattern there that might point to a single person responsible for the kidnapping of several children."

"Kidnapping?" The man looked baffled. "Danny ran away from home."

Nonplussed, Amy glanced at Elliott. "I know it's painful, but can you talk about the circumstances around that?"

"Why do you think there were circumstances?"

"We're just looking for a connection, Mr. Neumann—"

"There's no connection between your . . . your daughter and my son."

"You don't know that, Mr. Neumann," Amy said gently. "And anything you tell us might help."

"How about I tell you that I loved my son?" Neumann said, his eyes filling with tears. "And that it didn't matter a damn."

"I know you loved Danny," Amy said. "But could you tell us what led him to run away?"

"There was no damn reason. He just took off one day, leaving us to our little suburban hell."

"Kids rarely decide to run away on their own," Elliott said. "It's not an idea that occurs to them without reason."

A flush sprung up around his neck, forming a scarlet collar beneath the fleshy chin. "I had nothing to do with it. The kid got it into his head to leave behind a home *I* provided, with money *I* earned, while Faith *sat* here, screaming at me to do something, that it was my fault—"

"Please, Mr. Neumann," Amy interrupted. "We're not accusing you of anything. We're only trying to find my little girl."

Pink blooms sprang up on his cheeks, his forehead, across his chin. His voice was chipped and hoarse. "And who helped me when my little boy left? Who knocked on doors after the first week, the first month, the first *year?* No one. My wife ran from it, my friends ran from it. Only I got to stay and stare at the truth day after day, night after night."

"Mr. Neumann, please—"

But the man swore, took a step back, and slammed the door, rattling the windows. They stood in place for a moment, stunned by the bitterness and violence.

"I don't think he's going to help," Amy said to the brass fish.

"No," Elliott said. The prickling sensation was still writhing under his skin. "Not today, at least."

Defeated, they turned around and headed back down the walkway to the car. As they crossed the lawn, a woman at the next house over—thin, blonde, warm-up pants and a large athletic sweatshirt, a pair of garden clippers in one hand—was busy at her mailbox. Peeking, reaching in, looking into the depths again. Elliott paused, then glanced toward the entrance to the cul-de-sac. The mail truck they'd passed on their way into the community was just now coming down their side of the street, pausing to tuck the day's delivery of junk mail and bills into each house's box.

He leaned close to Amy. "See the lady at the mailbox? Go say hello."

"What? Why?"

"She wants to talk to you." He gave her a gentle push. "Trust me. I'll wait in the car."

Amy gave him a confused look, but headed over to the woman. Elliott walked to the Celica, slid into the passenger's seat, then leaned back. Through closed lids, he watched Amy introduce herself. The woman started, feigning surprise. Free of Elliott's presence, however, her expression opened, showing concern as Amy talked. He was no lip-reader, but a first-year psychology student could've probably scripted the conversation.

Hi, my name is Amy Scowcroft. I'm sorry to bother you, but do you have a second?

For what, exactly?

Do you happen to know anything about Danny Neumann?

Oh. Are you a friend of Faith's?

No, I'm afraid not, though she and I might have something in common . . .

Once the preliminaries were over and social challenges met, he lost the thread; he wasn't psychic. But whatever it was that Gary Neumann hadn't wanted the two of them to know seemed to be the only thing the neighbor wanted to talk about. Arms crossed, nodding at something Amy said, gesturing and nodding again, she was the very picture of interest. She maintained a half turn, however, keeping her back to the Neumann house. The two spoke for a long time and were wrapping up when he caught motion out of the corner of his eye.

Gary Neumann had emerged from his house. Perched on the end of his porch, as though he'd hit an invisible wall, he had to lean to see into his neighbor's yard. He watched the two women for a moment, then yelled something obscene. Even from inside the car, it was easy to see the man's face purpling. Elliott sat up and put his hand on the door handle.

Amy and the neighbor, unaware that Neumann had come out of his house, jumped at the first string of expletives. Without bothering to face him, however, the neighbor turned and walked back to her house, ignoring the shouted insults. When she reached her porch, she paused long enough to wave goodbye to Amy, then went inside.

A little slower on the uptake, Amy was subject to Neumann's abuse as she returned to her car. She'd almost reached it when Neumann started down the brick walk toward her. Elliott yanked the handle down and stepped out of the car, staring at Neumann, who froze in his tracks.

"Why don't we get out of here," he said to Amy quietly as she came near.

"Glad to," Amy said, brushing past him and getting in from the passenger's side.

Elliott stared down Neumann, who veered from insults to threats, assuring them the cops would be pulling them over before they left the neighborhood, though he didn't take another step toward them. Elliott held the man's glare, saying nothing, as he crouched and reclaimed the passenger's seat.

"Let's go," he said.

The Celica caught on the second try. Amy hauled hard on the wheel to make a screeching U-turn in the middle of the lane, then sped off.

20

Charlotte

After the pounding on the door and the yelling came the crying, which lasted much of the night. They all heard it, coming from the last room down the hall. From time to time, Sister cried—long, guttural weeping that came more from the stomach than the throat—but this was higher pitched, the tears of a child. All of them knew better than to leave their beds to investigate.

The sound was frightening and sad, reminding them of their own first nights in the house. None of them were strangers to fear and hard times, but the first night at Sister's was another magnitude entirely, when you realized just how different and isolated your new life was to become. Maggie crawled into bed with Charlotte until they both fell asleep, their arms around one another.

The next morning, Sister went from room to room to tell them to stay in bed and not to move until she called for them. Charlotte and Maggie obeyed, not even daring to whisper, though Charlotte fidgeted the entire time, silently terrified that the pains in her stomach would come back, leaving her with no chance to run to the bathroom. But, to her relief, nothing happened and eventually Sister rang the little brass bell in the hall, summoning them. They slid out of bed, pulled their clothes on, and joined the other two in the hall already there, anxiety plain on all their faces.

"We'd better go," Charlotte whispered, then led the others down the stairs, holding Maggie's and Buddy's hands like Charlie had when they were scared. Treads popped and cracked underfoot no matter how lightly they stepped. They froze when they heard Sister's low murmur come from across the house, then Tina poked Buddy in the back. One by one, they filed down the hall and into the kitchen.

Sister sat at the head of the farmhouse table, hands folded, studying them as they entered. To her right was a boy—gawky, pale, and tall, with a shock of red hair that pointed straight up from his head. There was a livid, kidney-shaped mark on the right side of his face, and the skin around his nostrils and mouth was raw. His eyes, likewise rimmed in scarlet, were locked on the plate in front of him where an open-faced butter sandwich lay untouched.

They filed into the room and took their assigned seats. Charlotte's was next to the new boy, Maggie and Buddy across from them, and Tina at the foot of the table facing Sister. She forced herself to stare at the table and not look to her left. Even so, she could tell the boy's ill-fitting clothes were just like theirs—musty, patched, and fraying—but Charlotte's nose twitched at how . . . *new* he smelled. The heady perfume of shampoo swept down from his hair, intoxicating and fresh. She'd forgotten what real soap smelled like, since Sister made them all share one cheap bar that smelled like cardboard. And when that melted away, they had to make do with nothing but water for weeks until she gave them a new one.

"Good morning, everyone," Sister said as they settled into place. At the look on her face, Charlotte felt her belly turn fluid and loose. She dropped her eyes.

"Good morning, Sister," they said in ragged whispers.

"Now, bow your heads," Sister said in a sweet voice, then led them in a quick prayer. When she'd finished, Buddy reached for the long bag of generic bread in the middle of the table, but a word from Sister stopped him.

"We have introductions to do first." She gestured to her left. "We'll start here."

"Buddy."

"I'm Maggie."

"Tina."

"Charlotte."

Still staring at the table, the boy made no move that he understood. Charlotte's heart started to pound.

Sister leaned toward the new boy. She was smiling, but it was a bare twitch of her lips over her teeth. "And what do we say at breakfast?"

The boy said nothing. Charlotte stole a glance at Buddy, whose face was wrinkled in fear.

The smile dropped from Sister's face. "What do we *say* at *breakfast?*"

The boy whispered something inaudible.

Sister's face twisted. *"What do we say at breakfast?"*

"Good morning." The boy's voice cracked as he spoke.

A flat silence followed. Sister looked from face to face. "Well? Aren't any of you going to greet your brother?"

As one, they intoned, "Good morning, Charlie."

21

Amy

Amy shifted to get comfortable in the cheap plastic seat, feeling like she was sitting on the worst ride at a carnival. Holding the french fry like a specimen, she carefully examined each side before nibbling the crispy sides, then eating the exposed white flesh of the potato. Across from her, Elliott savored the cheeseburger that made up the largest portion of the Happy Meal they'd found the money to split.

"You were right."

Elliott wiped a lick of mustard from the corner of his mouth. "About what?"

"The neighbor, Kathy. She wanted to talk."

"Hmm hmmm."

"She said we could've saved the knock on his door if we hadn't just missed the recycling pickup."

"Empty bottles?"

"A fifth every two days, sometimes every day." She fiddled with the cheap plastic toy that had come with the meal, a purple worm with orange antennae. "How'd you know?"

"I've met a lot of drunks in my life," he said curtly. "Is the wife—Faith—still there?"

"No."

"Was he violent? Abusive?"

"Kathy didn't think so, but said everyone knew the drinking was catching up with him. Drunk by noon, couldn't get into work most days, that kind of thing."

"Did Faith leave him for it?"

"Not at first, but someone reported them as neglectful parents, and I guess the family got hauled into court for a hearing. They elected not to pursue the case."

His face was pinched. "That wasn't enough of a wake-up call?"

"Apparently not."

"Until Danny went missing," Elliott guessed, then held the burger out, offering her half. Amy shook her head.

"The neighborhood turned out to look for him. Held a vigil. The whole nine yards. They thought he'd been kidnapped—which is why you don't see any kids playing on the street, she said—but they had no luck and eventually the search was called off."

"Then the body turned up?"

"About two years later."

"That's right." Elliott said, frowning. "It's not been the case for all the victims, but several have turned up about two years on. Which means they've safely passed at least one birthday. Why?"

Amy chewed on a fingernail. "Kids change a lot in two years. Especially at Danny's age."

"So they reach some kind of threshold?" Elliott said, almost to himself. He shook his head as if to clear it. "What else did Kathy say?"

"The police reopened the investigation, and it came out that Danny had written a note blaming his father and the alcoholism for a lot of things that were going wrong in the family."

"Neumann hid the note?"

"Yes."

"Jesus. He let everyone think his son had been kidnapped?"

Amy nodded. "The neighbors turned against him. Faith left him not long after."

Elliott was quiet for a minute. "Danny wasn't abducted, he was a runaway. Yet he still fits the profile of these other kids who were killed on their birthdays."

"Maybe it's just a terrible coincidence."

"What's bothering you? Besides the obvious."

Amy nudged the worm along the table. The antennae wiggled as it moved. "The obvious. It's not a happy story."

"Wife gone, son dead, no community. Saddled with a lifelong addiction. What's not to love?"

"It's sad."

"Some people would say he got what he deserved."

"No one deserves that." Her voice was husky.

He looked at her for a moment. "No. No they don't."

Amy picked up three fries, dabbed them into a puddle of ketchup, and set to nibbling them, asking between bites, "So, does this help us?"

"It's another data point. But it's still not much to build on. The one connection we have is two broken homes." His voice turned bitter. "Broken, in part, because of two weak-willed and flawed men leading the way."

Amy gave a weak smile. "That can't be our only lead, or we'll be knocking on half the doors in the country."

Elliott bit into the burger, chewing thoughtfully. "Do you have the database with you?"

"Yep." She leaned out of the booth and pulled the thick binder from a plastic grocery bag. She dropped it with a thump onto the little table they were sharing, then looked at him expectantly.

"I know these are summaries, but check the coroner's reports for the kids on our list. Tell me what they say."

"Okay." Amy riffled through the papers. "Tammy Waters died of exposure. Danny Neumann died of an overdose."

"What drug?"

"Fentanyl."

"Signs of sexual assault? Janine said no, but what's the coroner say?"

Amy's lips pressed together, but she ran her finger down the report summaries. "No." When Elliott didn't speak, she said, "That's a good thing."

"Of course."

She looked at him sharply. "But not normal."

He hesitated. "No. Not in cases of juvenile abduction."

"Should we be paying attention to that?"

"Anything unusual is definitely worth remembering." He put the burger down and wiped his hands on a napkin. "Can I see that?"

She slid the binder across the table and watched as he skimmed the six cases in succession. He tilted his head in concentration, then shook it in frustration before pushing it back to her.

"What were you looking for?"

"It's not important."

"Yes, it is."

His face flashed annoyance; then he composed himself. "Sexual predation would be the first thing you'd expect but not the only thing. Certain psychological obsessions manifest in different ways, so I was looking for physical trauma besides the cause of death."

"What kind of trauma?"

"Like if something had been missing."

Amy blanched. "You thought the killer might be . . ."

"Taking trophies," Elliott said. "Yes. But there's nothing listed here. I'm relieved, of course, but all it means is our kidnapper has another form of benchmarking his progress. Our job is to figure out what that yardstick is. Who's next on our list? Maybe that will tell us something."

"Eva Collier. She was—" Amy stopped, then began speaking again. "She was twelve when she went missing, would've turned fifteen just before her body was found."

"Cause of death?"

"She died of . . . hmm." Amy's eyes widened.

"What?"

"She died of an overdose, as well."

"Fentanyl?" When she nodded, Elliott said softly, "That's his second mistake."

"He's drugging them," she said. "Trying to make it look like an overdose."

"Be careful. Two instances isn't a pattern. But . . . yes."

"Why use fentanyl?"

"It's a snap to acquire, whether from prescriptions or on the street. It comes in various delivery forms. Inhalers, patches, pills, lozenges. There's even a lollipop, which would be attractive to kids, of course. It's an opioid, so it's a sedative. No screaming fits. Overdose victims just slip away."

Amy put a hand to her head but said nothing.

"Were the other kids on our list poisoned this way?" Elliott asked.

"What? Oh," she said, then leafed through the database. "One had traces of an unidentified substance. The other three are . . . dang it."

"Redacted?"

She nodded.

"Thanks, Dave." He crumpled the hamburger wrapper in frustration. "You have a Ouija board in that bag? Maybe the spirits have what we need to know."

She closed the binder. "Seriously, what is it with you? Why won't you let go and trust something more than what you can see? Don't you think bigger mysteries exist than what you can put your hands on?"

"Of course. I was—I am a psychologist. The mind is the biggest mystery in the universe."

"But you only trust the mind as far as you can analyze it. Why won't you believe there's something more profound than what you can figure out from a textbook or an interview?"

"I never said there wasn't."

"You don't have to—it's written all over your face."

He sighed. "Look, it's nothing about you or what you believe in."

"What is it, then?"

"I have a professional and personal . . . aversion to hippies. And hippielike things."

"I am not a hippie!"

He gave her a look. "You're a hippie."

"Well . . . what's wrong with that? Where's the distrust coming from?"

"It's inherited."

"Lame," she said, grabbing another fry. "Just because your family hated hippies, you do, too?"

"When I say inherited," Elliott growled, "I don't mean *from* them. I mean *because* of them. *They* were hippies."

"And that's a reason to deny all the varied mysteries of the universe?"

"Yes."

"So narrow-minded, Dr. Nash," she said primly. "I wouldn't have expected that from you."

"Fine." He glanced to the side, weighing something, then looked back at her. "Let me give you an example. Guess what my middle names are."

"Names? Plural? How many do you have?"

"Two." He arched an eyebrow, waiting. "Remember, hippie parents."

She stared back, baffled, until a light came into her eyes, and she put both hands over her mouth to smother a giggle. "You're kidding."

"I kid you not." He sighed. "My full name is Elliott Crosby Stills Nash."

Her crystal peal of laughter seemed to catch him by surprise, and he smiled despite himself. Several tables looked their way when she couldn't stop. "Oh my gosh, that's so funny. At least your last name isn't Young."

He snorted and took a sip of soda. The straw made a squeaking noise as he pushed it in. "Small mercies. They met at some kind of wannabe Woodstock a decade after the real thing, and I was put together in the back of a Chevy Nova. They claimed I was named after a long debate, but I'm guessing it's because CSN was the only eight-track tape in the car."

"This was the late seventies, right? You're lucky. They could've been into disco."

"Grand Funk Railroad Nash?"

"Abba Nash." She had a hard time catching her breath. "Earth Wind and Nash?"

"Yeah, yeah. Anyway, there you have it, the real reason behind my scientific skepticism. Believe me, I earned it pressing tofu and weaving baskets as a kid." He squeaked the straw a little more. "Sorry about the crack about the Ouija board. That was unkind. It might not be how I solve problems, but that doesn't mean you don't find value in it."

Wiping away tears with a paper napkin, Amy said, "What you really mean is, you still think it's a load of bull."

"Of course. But if it makes you feel better, who cares?"

Reaching across the table, she put her hand over his. He flinched. She looked directly into his eyes. "Thank you, Elliott. I haven't laughed like that in almost a year."

He glanced down at her hand, and she wondered how long it had been since someone touched him. "You won't hold my prejudices against me?" he said.

She shook her head. "No. I don't mind if you don't believe what I believe. I know what the truths are."

"I'm glad one of us does."

A young family of four—blond, sunny, smiling—walked past them down their aisle, trays in hand, looking for a table large enough to eat and horse around on. The father's eyes slid over Elliott. He called to his kids and they moved to the other side of the restaurant.

Elliott straightened in his seat; he'd been hunched over his food like a miser. "You ready? We might be able to catch the Colliers before the end of the day."

The two of them stood and headed for the exit. As they pushed their way through the glass door, she saw him glance back at the family where the kids giggled and ducked as they tried to daub ketchup on each other's noses. The father, feeling the stare, raised his head to look at them. She expected Elliott to turn away, unwilling, maybe, to gaze on the scene of family bliss or afraid of ruining it for them. But, this time, he just smiled and followed her outside.

22

Dave

Dave pulled up to the curb and sat in the cruiser for a full minute, staring at the café with the bistro tables, checkered tablecloths, and wicker chairs placed close in pleasant intimacy. Though it was not quite noon, waiters and busboys were already busy in and around the patio's outdoor seating. Most seats were occupied, despite the chill autumnal weather—lunch in DC was serious business.

They weren't comfortable things, these meetings of theirs, Dave thought, full of awkward pauses and unspoken words, but it was something he had to do. When you had so little family—in their case, only each other—you had to hold on to it. Working where he did, he'd seen too many fractured, dysfunctional, abusive families dissolve. Sure, a lot of the time it was because of actions from within, but sometimes it wasn't, and he'd seen the consequences of a family that allowed itself to be torn—or, in many ways, almost sadder—drift apart until there was nothing left.

So, every few months, less often lately, he reached out and arranged a lunch or a coffee. They'd meet at Ted's or Bistrot Lepic or, if he was in a hurry, at one of the chain restaurants. She never made the arrangements, and sometimes he wondered if she'd just as soon stop meeting. He'd suggested it once, but was surprised when she'd vehemently told him no.

He saw her now, walking up the sidewalk, heading for the café, enquiring if her brother was there yet. She was tall and thin, and dressed well, if a little dowdily, making the small gap between their ages seem much wider. In fact, within the last few years, she'd come to resemble their mother. Or maybe that was just his memory playing tricks. It had been thirty years since he'd seen her, after all, and any woman over a certain age began looking, in one way or another, like his mother.

Dave got out and walked over. They exchanged a dry kiss on the cheek, then he allowed the hostess to lead them to an inside table. Political power brokers and lobbyists, forced to sit at the bar and shout their conversations at each other, turned to see who merited a booth in the back. He smothered a grin with his hand. Once in a while, rarely, being a cop had its privileges.

Once they'd been seated, she ordered hot water with lemon and the house salad, her usual, regardless of where they ate. He had a Sam Adams and roast beef sandwich au jus.

The beer went down fast, and he toyed with the glass handle of his mug, tilting it back and forth, as he searched for something to say, settling for, "How have you been?"

Her hands were folded in her lap. She watched his hands as they fidgeted. "Fine, fine. Work is busy, as always. A coworker told me recently that the place would fall apart without me."

"Nice of her to say."

"It was," she said, giving a small smile. "It's rare for anyone in government to get thanked, even by someone else in government."

"Tell me about it," he said with a laugh, surprised and thankful they could find a common thread. His hand slipped, however, and he caught the beer mug at the last second.

"Don't *do* that!" she snapped. Her hand came down over his wrist. "I can't stand when you fidget!"

He looked at her in surprise, the feeling of empathy and connection gone as quickly as it had appeared. She had her foibles, but she hadn't lost her cool in . . . well, he couldn't remember how long. He put both hands up in surrender. "Hey, no problem."

She looked away, her expression peeved. The awkwardness was back, and they let the clatter and buzz of the restaurant swallow them. To his relief, their meals arrived and he dug in. They ate in silence until, picking at her salad, she surprised him by asking, "How is your work? Have you saved any more children?"

He frowned, hearing a whiff of condescension. "You make it sound inconsequential when you say it like that."

"Well, I'm sorry you feel that way. It's just that, from all the cases you've described to me, the children seem worse off than when they started."

"Why? Because they go to foster care?"

She gave an eloquent shrug.

"You might not believe this, but what you and I went through was not nearly as bad as some of the things I've seen on the job. The foster system isn't perfect, but most of the kids in it are infinitely better than where they came from." He wiped his hands on a napkin. "I mean, is your job so very different? We both decided to help children, to make something out of our past instead of . . . I don't know, surrendering to it."

"I suppose. Though, sometimes I wonder just how much good we can do. It seems as though everything is against us," she said, her voice trailing off; then she shook her head as if coming to. "Never mind me. Your work. Tell me more about what you've been doing."

He quirked an eyebrow. She didn't often show this much interest in his job. "There's never any shortage of kids in trouble. Lots of leads, tons of investigations. Oh, there was one we actually saved and not from his own family, for once. An overdose we caught in the nick of time. We almost lost him."

She tsked. "There are so many these days."

"True." He hesitated, wondering if he should mention the peculiar memory that had struck him when he'd seen the boy's clothes, then dismissed it. She wasn't one for whimsy, only concrete facts. "How is the house holding up?"

She sighed. "It's fine."

He lowered the sandwich he'd raised to take a bite. "Something wrong?"

"No. The old pile just needs repairs, as always. I think the roof will need replacing soon."

"Do you need money?" *You know I'll gladly pay to never see that place again.*

"I don't think so, but thank you for offering."

"Sure."

The conversation petered out and, eventually, it was obvious that they'd run out of things to say. Normally, Dave would be the one to try and slip in one or two more topics, just to keep the anemic conversation rolling. Today, however, he looked down at his watch and pushed his mug away.

"Sorry, I have to cut this short. I have to head back to the office and catch up on some work."

She dabbed carefully around her lips with her napkin. "Catch up? Were you playing hooky, Detective *Cargill*?"

She always said it that way, having never quite accepted the fact that he'd taken their foster family's name. He sighed, refusing to rise to the bait. "Not really. I spent time earlier in the week pulling files as a favor for an old friend. All my regular work had to get put on hold, so now I have to pay the piper. And this particular piper is a hard-ass named Lieutenant Green."

"Well, I certainly understand that." She patted her hair. "I should get back, as well."

"Do you want a ride? It's just across town."

"No, thank you. You know I don't like police cars."

They stood, he walked her out, and they exchanged another dry kiss on the cheek. "It's good seeing you."

She looked back at him with the same buttonhole eyes he'd remembered since he was a child. "It's always good seeing you, too, brother."

23

Charlotte

Charlotte dusted the entry table and the lamps, the picture frames filled with their old prints of fox hunting scenes and fishermen, the brass clock-and-barometer set. She slipped the rag in between each banister on the steps and along each patch of oak flooring on the sides of the faded wool carpet runner that smelled like a wet dog.

The others dashed through the work, but she always took her time, moving intentionally from the steps to the living room to the entry hall and into the dining room. There wasn't anything to do afterward, so why rush? Not to mention, Sister punished them if they didn't do the job right, so Charlotte made sure she polished each and every nook.

And today she had another reason.

Lingering by the front door, she ran the rag over the locks and the dead bolt. Two were locked from the inside, two from the outside. The door was ancient and thick, with deeply grooved and beveled panels the size of cookie sheets. Over the years, the panels had warped and developed cracks that were too small to see out of, but big enough to let in a whisper of air.

Charlotte glanced over her shoulder, then ran the dust rag over everything a second, unnecessary time, passing her hand over the knob.

Her mouth went dry as it turned easily.

But of course the locks were the problem. Working quickly, she slipped the key she'd found in Charlie's room out of her pocket, then bent to compare it to the lock. A whisper of a breeze sighed through the cracks in the door, gently pushing at her face and hair.

Her heart sank. The key was ancient, obviously older than the locks, and the shape so different she didn't need to try it—she could tell from looking at it that it didn't fit. She kicked the door in frustration.

"What are you doing?"

Charlotte jerked around, instinctively hiding the key in the dust rag. Tina sat on the steps, elbows on her knees, chin on her fists, watching her.

For how long? Charlotte swallowed. "I was smelling things."

"You do it every time you dust."

"So?"

"Sister wouldn't like it."

"Why not?"

"Because it looks like you want to go outside. To leave."

Charlotte looked at the other girl curiously, her fear temporarily forgotten. "Don't you miss seeing trees? Smelling the grass or the leaves?"

For a brief moment, Charlotte could see Tina struggle with the idea. Then a shadow passed across the girl's face and she shrugged. "It doesn't matter. It's not allowed."

"That doesn't mean you don't want to do it."

"I'm going to tell Sister what you were doing."

An invisible hand clutched at her throat, but she forced herself to stay calm. "Go ahead and tell her."

"You don't care?"

"What more could she do to us? We're already locked up like rats."

"She can do worse," Tina said with a grin. "A lot worse."

"Like what?"

The girl's eyes narrowed. "You've never been in the cellar. She's buried bodies down there. I've seen them."

Charlotte yawned extravagantly. "Nice try."

She shrugged. "Don't believe me. Sister probably wouldn't even be *that* nice. Not after I tell her what you were doing."

"Do it and I'll get the others to give you another whipping."

The girl's grin melted away. A couple of months before, Tina had been on a tear, giving Sister nightly reports and making up things about the other kids when she couldn't find anything wrong. Sister had punished them. Charlotte, sick of it, had gotten the other kids together to exact revenge, with Charlie holding her down while the rest of them beat Tina with rolled-up socks and shirts so that they wouldn't leave a bruise. Tina had stopped tattling for a while afterward, but with Charlie gone, she was obviously bold enough to begin bullying them again.

But the promise of a beating was enough to chase her off today. She said a bad word at Charlotte, then ran up the stairs. Charlotte watched her go, glad to have chased the little snitch away, but her stomach churned at the close call. If the girl had spotted the key in her hand, no amount of threats would've kept her from telling Sister. In which case, Charlotte was dead. But she figured Tina would've found it impossible not to gloat about having something that juicy to tell Sister.

The bigger question was, what did the key fit? Slipping it back into her pocket, she swallowed her disappointment, then bent down again. Tina was right—she did stop at the door every time she dusted, sniffing and thinking of the world outside, and she might as well do the crime if Tina was going to tattle on her anyway.

Scents of decaying wood and grass filtered through, along with a touch of gasoline, still lingering in the air hours after Sister had left the house. Another smell, too, that she couldn't place . . . it reminded her of walking to school in the rain, kicking the carefully raked piles of orange and yellow that had been left in the street and on the sidewalk. That was it, rotting leaves. Which meant it was fall outside. Another season gone.

Charlotte kicked the door again, then reluctantly left the hall and moved to the dining room. Knickknacks and sideboards in the room made dusting a challenge, and doing it properly took an hour. Her routine was to start at the windows and work her way inward. She would tug back the curtains, dust the blinds, and run the rag along the sills, being careful not to get carried away since the paint on the sills was chipping and trying too hard would only make a mess.

When she reached for the curtain at the big window in the corner, however, she paused. What she first mistook for a stain on the fabric disappeared when she passed her hand over it: it wasn't a stain, it was a small patch of light. Pulling the curtain back, she discovered that a marble-size hole had appeared in the plywood covering the window, maybe where a knot in the cheap wood had fallen out.

Glancing over her shoulder to make sure Tina wasn't watching, she leaned over until her chin was almost resting on the windowsill. The hole was small and not entirely round, but if she placed her head just right and squinted, Charlotte could see outside.

She felt as if she could see the entire world through that small circle. At a guess, the window faced toward the back of the property and the view was actually boring—a little bit of overgrown yard and some bare trees leaning in the breeze—but tears filled her eyes. It seemed like forever since she'd seen the outside.

The only man-made object in view was a battered wooden fence that outlined the edge of the yard. In the center of the fence was a gate missing a board in its middle. It didn't lock, and she watched as it banged open and shut in the wind. The disappointment of the key not fitting any of the locks faded, replaced with a tingling sensation that ran from her fingers to her toes and back.

Because where there was a gate, there was a path.

And where there was a path, there was a place to go.

24

Amy

Dusk pushed the day away in pieces, bringing a gloom that swallowed the edges of things until suddenly you had to squint just to make out the letters on a street sign or the numbers on a house. A light rain spattered everything, putting a sheen on the road and the tops of cars.

Cupping her hands around her eyes to shade them from the streetlight glare, Amy peered around the **BANK OWNED—FORECLOSURE** sign into the living room window of the tenement. Dirt and an algaelike buildup had grimed the windows, marring the once-white vinyl edge.

"No one home?" Elliott asked as he rounded the corner of the house.

"I don't think so. Anything in the back?"

"A T-shirt, rotting in the mud. Broken lawn chair. Rusty old grill. They've been gone awhile."

She descended the porch steps, hugging her arms to her body. "If we could get to a library, we might be able to look up the ownership records, see how long it's been since the Colliers moved."

"But not to where."

"No."

"We've got a few more names on the list, right?" Elliott said as they walked back to her car. Neither of them mentioned that time was working against them. "Who's next?"

"The Goldsteins, I think. They live off Florida Avenue, somewhere near Shaw."

"Ten minutes with traffic. Let's go."

With a quarter hour to find parking, it was more like half an hour. Amy looked out at the corner, brick and tar-paper row house from the comfort of the car, her head rocking subconsciously to the rhythm of the windshield wipers.

A simple pipe-and-elbow railing ran from the sidewalk along a cracked concrete walk to the porch. Lights illuminated the bottom two windows of the home like wide-open eyes, while the mouth of the house smirked at them thanks to a set of sagging, sway-backed wooden steps.

They slid out of the car, then walked to the door. Twilight had petered off to dusk. Bright white streetlamps threw their shadow ahead of them as they walked.

Elliott eyed the steps. "How about we go one at a time?"

On the porch, they stood shoulder to shoulder at the door. Amy rang the doorbell, then knocked firmly.

The door was opened by an emaciated man in his thirties, with a sprinkle of gray in an unkempt beard that forked unevenly past his chin. The sharp tips of his shoulders and ridged bumps of his sternum showed clearly through the material of a yellowing undershirt like the bones of a beached fish. Sunken eyes flicked back and forth between the two of them; then he opened the screen door forty-five degrees. The laugh track of a TV show erupted in the room behind him. He stared at them.

Nervous, Amy started her introduction, but he interrupted when she began talking about Lacey, what had happened, and how it might relate to him. "I don't have no kids."

"Sorry?"

"I said I don't have no kids."

"You mean . . . you're not Aaron's father?"

He shook his head melodramatically. "Not me. My cow of a wife had a son after she got knocked up by some guy from work. Never had kids. Just whores and hungry mouths living at my house."

She hesitated. "I don't mean to bother you. Maybe I could talk to your wife?"

"What makes you think I'd keep cows and whores around if I didn't let that kid stay in the house?"

"So, Aaron was here?" Elliott said, leaning forward.

"I didn't say that."

"Sir, this is the last address we have for Aaron. If you could just see your way to helping us a little . . ."

"I don't like whores and I don't like sons of whores and sure as hell don't like people coming around asking about either one of them. A man's got a right to control what goes on in his house, to punish the guilty and throw them out if they don't play by the rules. Anybody who doesn't like that can go screw." The words were quick but stilted, stale with rehearsal.

As if punctuating the statement, the TV gave a hoarse shout from inside the house as a studio audience laughed at something.

"Is that *Who's Got Your Number?*" Amy asked suddenly. "I loved that show."

"What?" Goldstein asked, surprised. He looked behind him as if he'd forgotten it was there. "Yeah. Watch it every night."

"The host was so pretty," Amy continued. She could feel Elliott looking at her, puzzled at the sudden change in direction. *Come on, Elliott, work with me. Weren't you a psychologist once upon a time?* "What was her name?"

"Kathy Higgins," he said automatically. "Finest set of lungs in prime-time television."

"That show must've been on for ten years," Elliott said, catching on. "I don't think anyone's seen every episode."

"Wrong again, bud. With an upper deck like Kathy's, I wouldn't miss a show. Made everyone keep quiet, too, so I could act like I was trying to answer the questions. Though I could've just watched it with the sound off."

"And miss all the canned jokes?" Elliott said. "That is, when you can hear them. Don't you hate it when kids talk during the show?"

"Christ, yes," Goldstein said, then his face turned ugly as he realized what he'd said. He swore. "Why are you wasting my time?"

"There are lives on the line, here. Are you Peter Goldstein or not? It's a simple damn question."

"Elliott, let me—" Amy began, but the man, glaring at Elliott, talked over her.

"Who the hell are you?"

"Elliott Nash. I'm with MPD."

"Who?"

"The police. We're investigating Aaron's disappearance and any connection it has to several other deaths."

"Now why don't I believe that?" He laughed, an ugly sound. "You don't even look as good as the bum I have to chase out of my backyard on trash day."

"Not all of us have badges and work at a desk, Mr. Goldstein," Amy said. "You *are* Peter Goldstein, aren't you?"

"Maybe I am, maybe I'm not," he said with a humorless grin, enjoying himself. "I guess real cops would be able to find out, wouldn't they?"

"Look, we need to know more about Aaron's disappearance and murder. It's important. If you can answer just a couple of questions, we'll be out of your hair in ten minutes."

"You'd be out of it sooner if I shut the door in your face."

"You don't want to do that," Elliott said, his voice tight.

Amy quickly backed away from the door as Goldstein opened the screen and stepped out onto the porch. Her stomach fell and she steeled herself emotionally for more haranguing, for finger pointing and confrontation. She could see it so clearly that it felt as though she'd jumped forward a half minute and watched it develop.

Instead, the film split in an entirely different direction. She squawked as Goldstein's hand shot out, catching her in the shoulder, shoving her backward. She clawed at the rail, but the metal was slick with rain and she tumbled down the steps to land on her back in the mud.

Flat on her back and trying to catch her breath, she watched as Goldstein turned to Elliott just in time to take Elliott's fist driving into his stomach. Spittle flew out of Goldstein's mouth and, thin as he was, he folded in half like a sheet of paper. Elliott grabbed him by the neck and drove his knee upward, missing his nose, but with enough force to snap his head back.

Amy yelled at Elliott to stop, but she could only watch as he grabbed Goldstein by the belt and ran him off the porch. The man landed next to her, belly first, with an explosive grunt. Elliott clattered down the steps, then put a hand on the back of Goldstein's neck and leaned his weight forward, grinding the man's face into the mud.

Amy leaned over, grabbed his arm. "Dammit, Elliott."

He shook her hand away but took his hand off the man's neck. "Roll over."

Goldstein obeyed, looking scared, holding his hands palm up. Elliott knelt on his chest, put one hand on the man's throat, and cocked a fist. "Yes or no. Did Aaron live here?"

"Yes."

"Did he run away?"

Goldstein glanced to the side. His eyes were white in the gloom. "Yeah."

Elliott tightened his grip. The muscles in the man's neck stood out like cables.

"Okay. No. I threw him and his mother out when I found out she was sleeping around."

"Did you smack them? Try to teach them a lesson?"

Goldstein glared at him. "I was angry. What am I supposed to do? I didn't even know if he was my kid." His voice was petulant, demanding. "Some other guy's kid in my house, I'm supposed to keep him around? Feed him, pay for him?"

"You raise this kid for years, *then* you wonder if he's not yours?"

"How do I know how long she cheated on me?"

"Where is she now? Why wasn't Aaron with her?"

He shook his head. "She shacked up with the other guy, but he didn't want him either."

Amy looked down at him. "You just . . . threw him away?"

His face rippled with a half dozen emotions. "Not my goddamned fault. CPS showed up, took him away. Not my kid, not my problem."

Elliott looked down, his expression blank. "What did you say?"

"About what, man?"

"Who came for him?"

"CPS. Why? What's it to you?"

Amy looked at him. "Elliott?"

For a moment, Elliott looked as if he were going to throw a final punch, but then his hand opened and Goldstein sagged. Dazed, he said, "Let's go." He stood and stepped over Goldstein's body, then walked to the car without looking back. Goldstein coughed, then propped himself up on an elbow and called after them. "Hey, man. Hey, man!"

Lost in thought, Elliott waited while Amy crawled into the driver's seat and started the Celica. He slid in after her, then put the seat back so he could lay his arm across his forehead.

Amy glanced over at him as she piloted the car down the street. "Elliott? What happened back there?"

He was quiet for so long, Amy was wondering if he was going to answer. Finally, he said, "I'm putting together some things that piece of garbage said with the few clues we've got."

"Sharing is caring," she quipped, but his silence was heavy and the small smile faded quickly. "Where are we going now?"

Elliott looked out the window, got his bearings. "Keep going on Florida Avenue. I'll tell you when to stop."

They rode in silence. Amy continued to glance over from time to time, but Elliott simply lay reclined in the seat, staring out the window. The lights and life of the city at night passed in a mosaic of color and sound, unseen and unregistered.

Elliott shot out his hand, pointing to a curb. "Here."

Startled, Amy looked at the corner. A throng of people crowded the sidewalk, heads bowed over their phones, nodding to the music coming from a pair of headphones, or talking to one another as they walked. "What?"

"Pull over here."

Amy whipped the Celica over, earning a honk from the car behind her. "I don't think I can park here."

"I don't want you to park," Elliott said, yanking on the handle and popping the door open. He grabbed his knapsack and stepped onto the sidewalk. "I've got some thinking to do."

"You've got . . . hey! What am I supposed—" Amy began, but Elliott closed the door in her face. She threw the car in park and scrambled across the seat to open the door again. "Elliott, wait!"

But by the time she managed to get out to the sidewalk, Elliott was gone, the last view his back slipping into the crowd on the sidewalk, lost in the press.

25

Elliott

Elliott shoved through the crowd on the sidewalk. A few made an effort to step to the side; others, however, he bulled out of his way. The physical contact felt good, but a voice of caution shouted at the back of his head as he saw the alarm growing on the faces in front of him. *Crazy homeless guy . . . angry . . . dangerous.* If he didn't calm down, someone would call the cops and from there, it was a short trip to a night in lockup or a tasing or a bullet. He veered into a thin alley, dim and wet, off the main artery. The sense of relief from the walkers on the sidewalk was palpable.

Thirty feet from the crush of the street, the noise was so muted that he could hear water trickle from a gutter into a drain. Trash lay flattened on the ground, slowly becoming one with the asphalt. Bundled newspapers moldered forgotten in a puddle. A rat scurried ahead of him, pausing to hide in a bunch of trash before bolting again as he followed it down the alley.

Being out of the crowd would give him the chance to slow down, get back to some rational thought, maybe. But it was going to be tough as long as his mind was still in shock from the conclusion he'd made staring down at Peter Goldstein's battered face. What he needed was a chance to reassess what he knew, formulate a theory, then seek confirmation, someone from the outside to say, "Yeah, looks like you're onto something." For that, he needed a place to stop and think.

He found what he was looking for on the corner of Sixth and P. Dirty windows, a neon beer sign hanging next to an ad for the lottery, the reek of bleach thrown into the street gutter. Country music blared through the open door, filling the space around the building and explaining why the place looked so deserted. Through the window, dull, shadowy forms moved inside, obscuring, then revealing, what appeared to be the single light in the place. A chipped sign over the door said Tony's.

A bar? Really? A ripple passed through him. An ancient thirst, one he thought he'd left behind, caught him by the tongue and wrung his mouth dry. *No. We're not here for that.* This had to be about business, about getting to the truth.

The bar looked seedy enough, all right, but he glanced down at himself in the gloom to be sure. As long as it was dark inside and no one got close enough to get a whiff, he should be okay. What he couldn't do was take his knapsack in with him. Drinkers didn't carry baggage—at least, not the physical kind. They walked in with twenty bucks and a mission. He took out the little bit of cash he'd hidden in the seam, then stuffed the sack behind a dumpster in the alley. Walking away from it, he felt nude.

The smells and sounds of the bar hit him as he stepped over the threshold and his mouth instantly felt pasty and dry. Pretending to let his eyes adjust, he paused, then moved toward the bar with as much confidence as he could patch together.

The place was crowded for as early as it was. A few solo practitioners, sitting square to the taps, held the bar down like nails, while small groups gathered in intimate crescents around the tables and in the corners of the main room.

Behind the bar was a big guy in a tight blue shirt, broad as a bed, with long black curly hair and a thick beard—a heavy metal roadie who'd quit the tour. Two bars of white ran through the beard from the corners of the guy's mouth, like the tusks on a walrus. Eyes, small and bright in the big face, looked Elliott over as he approached, then dropped as the guy moved from pulling beers to washing glasses.

Elliott swallowed, but it was like licking sandpaper. *Don't sit in the corner, don't avoid looking at him. No one's ashamed of ordering a beer.* He headed for an opening at the bar left of center and climbed a stool.

The walrus racked the last glass, wiped his hands—front then back, front then back—on a bar towel hanging from his belt, then walked over. He leaned against the bar, hands spread wide, and raised his eyebrows. A blurry tattoo of a whale covered the inside of one arm, and on his shirt was a slap-on HELLO! MY NAME IS tag that read TEDDY in fat block letters.

"Heineken?" Elliott asked, his voice stumbling over the three syllables.

Teddy got a sour look and Elliott thought, *This is it, I'm out,* but he said, "Does this look like a joint that serves Heineken? Bud, Bud Light, PBR, Labatt's."

"I . . . Budweiser."

Teddy nodded and reached for one of the recently washed glasses. Elliott suddenly realized he needed to pay and pivoted away from the bar, hoping to hide the fact that his money was wadded up in a ball. Homeless people didn't carry wallets. But Teddy set the beer down in front of Elliott, then moved off to help someone else without a backward glance.

Out of habit, he cupped his hand around the glass. It was still warm from the wash. Beer had never been his drink of choice—the bourbon, amber and sweet, whispered to him from the rack behind the bar—but he still refused to take a sip. His stomach was clenched like he was expecting a gut punch. It took a conscious effort to release the tension and simply sit there like any other patron.

Teddy, he could see, was keeping an eye on him, or maybe that was his imagination; the bartender seemed to be everywhere at once, scooping tips off the bar, snagging empties, taking orders.

As he cruised by, Elliott leaned forward. "Is there a pay phone around here?"

Teddy quirked an eyebrow. "This being the twenty-first century, no." He looked at Elliott for a beat, considering, then leaned over behind the bar, one hand flat on the top for balance. He came up with an old-fashioned dial phone on a long cord. He banged it down in front of Elliott. The bells inside rang faintly.

"House phone. Local calls only, ten minutes max. It's an antique, so treat her gently. And no sex calls either."

"I wasn't—"

"Relax, man. It was a joke." Teddy moved away as three guys sidled up to the opposite end of the bar, laughing and waving to get his attention.

He stared at the phone, unsure now. But his mind had already analyzed the disparate pieces of information that had been floating through it since Amy had first approached him for help. And it pointed in a direction he didn't like.

Elliott picked up the receiver and brought it to his ear, then dialed the number from memory. It rang on and on. It was late, he realized suddenly and wondered if the whole charade—hiding the sack, buying the beer—had been for nothing when there was a clatter on the other end as the phone was answered.

"Cargill."

"Dave." There was a knot of silence. He hadn't planned well for this call. "We need to talk."

26

Charlotte

Charlotte froze. She hadn't heard the door open, hadn't heard footsteps on the floor. But suddenly she felt a presence next to her bed, so close that she imagined she could feel breath on her face. The form loomed over her, and she shrank back into the pillow.

"Are you awake?" The words were barely above a whisper.

"Tina?"

The girl nudged her. "Move over."

"I don't know if you can fit."

Beside her, Maggie breathed deeply and asked groggily, "Who's that?"

"Shh. It's Tina. Can you make a little room?"

The two of them scooched over and Tina slid into bed beside them. Charlotte, sandwiched in the middle, didn't know what to do.

"What do you want, Tina?" Maggie was apparently not reluctant to ask questions.

"I couldn't sleep," she said, then hissed, "Your bed is cold."

"It's because you're so tall," Charlotte said. "The sheets are cold at the bottom."

"The mattress is lumpy, too."

"If you don't like it, go back to your own room."

They were quiet for a second, none of them sure of what to say. Maggie fidgeted and Charlotte was afraid she was going to tumble over the side, but she wrapped her arms around the little girl until she rested her head on Charlotte's shoulder. Outside, the wind picked up, and leaves swept upward by the breeze rattled against the side of the house like birds' bones.

"Tina?" Maggie's voice was very small.

"Yeah?"

"Do you ever think about home?"

Charlotte gave a small squeak. The word "home," said like Maggie had, glowed and sizzled in their heads. It meant their lives before, and family and friends. It definitely didn't mean Sister's house. As the silence stretched on, Charlotte began to shake, certain that Tina was a second away from jumping out of bed and sprinting to Sister's room with a mouthful of accusations.

But the girl didn't move. Quiet, measured breaths stirred Charlotte's hair. Finally, she broke the silence.

"I don't even know what home is," she said. "I miss my mom, I guess. We did everything together since I didn't have a dad or brothers and sisters. But she was sick or high a lot. Like, all the time. When that happened, it was like she was asleep or dead, and I wished I was on my own. I mean, she'd wake up and everything would be okay for a while, but then it got bad again. So bad, that some government people came and split us up. I thought it was for just a little while, but then I was sent to a new family . . ."

Maggie burrowed into Charlotte's side like a small animal as Tina's voice trailed off. When she started talking again, her voice was distant, as though the story was being told near her, but not from her.

"My new family seemed okay at first, but the other kids, the real ones, were scared of the dad. I didn't understand why. He would drink and smoke and watch TV every night, but that didn't seem so bad. Every night, though, his kids would sit very still, hoping he would just pass out in the chair."

Tina stopped as the wind blew hard against the house and a branch screeched against the side like a banshee.

"One night, after he got really drunk, he picked me up, high in the air, and started swinging me around, faster and faster. He wouldn't stop no matter how much I cried. The more I cried, the more he laughed. Finally, I was so scared and dizzy, I puked. I couldn't help myself. He got angry and I thought he was going to hit me, but he just made me clean it up. Later, the other kids told me that I was really lucky, because when they did something bad, he would burn them with his lighter. The only reason he hadn't done it to me was because the government was going to send someone to check on me. But after that, they said, he'd start burning me, just to teach me a lesson."

Charlotte's heart flopped in her chest like a fish caught in a net. Next to her, Maggie was shivering.

"The night Sister brought me here, I cried. I was scared because it was all new to me and Sister was mean at first. But she's never hurt me, not really, not like *he* would've. And I haven't cried since." There was a long silence, then she grunted and moved in the bed, reaching under her and pulling something out. "What is this?"

Charlotte reached out in the dark. "That's mine."

"It's wet," Tina said, her voice rising with a little laugh. "Charlotte pees in bed!"

"Give me that!" Charlotte felt for Tina's arms as the other girl wriggled around. She caught one wrist and twisted. Tina yelped. Charlotte clapped a hand over her mouth and hissed in her ear, "Shut up and let go or I'll break your arm."

Tina let go of the rag but slid out of the bed and, in a flash, had crossed the room and thrown the light on. She looked back at Charlotte and Maggie in bed, her face triumphant at first. Then the look turned to horror as she saw the bloody cloth Charlotte was holding, then down at the blood on her own hands.

"Oh my god," she whispered, and Charlotte felt a flush of embarrassment at the look on the girl's face.

Charlotte jumped out of bed, grabbing Tina by the ear while simultaneously flicking the light back off. "If you say a word of this to Sister, you'll wish I'd broken your arm. Got it?" When the girl didn't say anything, she shook her head by the ear and Tina gasped. "Do you understand?"

"Yes."

"Good. Now wash up, go back to your room, and go to sleep. Remember what I said."

Without another word, Tina left the room, waiting for another gust of wind to cover the noise of the door opening, then was gone.

Charlotte tucked the rag between her legs, holding it there with pressure, then shuffled back to bed. Maggie snuggled close, but didn't say anything for several long minutes. Charlotte realized she was holding her breath. They were both waiting for the bang of Sister's bedroom door or a sudden shout as she discovered Tina going back to her room. The wind sighed and pushed at the house for a long time.

Finally, Maggie whispered, "Now Tina knows."

"Yes."

"Will you get in trouble if she tells Sister?"

Charlotte swallowed. "I don't know. It's not like I can help it."

"I'm scared."

"Why?"

"I don't know," Maggie said. Her words were muffled, and Charlotte knew she'd put a knuckle in her mouth, a habit she had when she got upset. "Because . . . because . . ."

"Because Sister doesn't like it when things change," Charlotte said, and something about the simple statement was so right and so telling that a shiver went through her. "She hates it."

"Yes." The word was small. Small jerking motions told her that Maggie was starting to cry. "I don't want Sister to hurt you."

"She won't, Maggie." Charlotte put her arm around the little girl, even though she felt like crying herself. "I won't let her."

"How?"

She thought about the key, hidden now under a flap of carpet in the corner of the room, and the lonely path leading into the woods she'd spied through the peephole. Her next sentence amazed even herself. "I'm going to escape."

The jiggling motions stopped. "Escape? Like, to the outside?"

She hadn't actually admitted it, but saying the words out loud made it seem real and possible. "I'm going to try."

"You're going to leave me behind? Like Charlie did?"

Charlotte blinked in the dark. She hadn't thought of it in those terms and she fumbled for an answer. "Only to get help, Mags. If I can get out of here, I might be able to reach my family, and they'll bring the police to get us all out."

Maggie digested that. "I don't like the police. They took me away from my mom."

"They're not all bad. And the good ones will help take us away from Sister."

"Can't you take me with you?"

Charlotte hesitated a hair too long, and Maggie began to cry. To shush her, Charlotte held her tight and whispered urgently in her ear. "I can't take you with me because you've got a really important job."

"What's that?"

"I need you to help take care of Buddy," Charlotte said, making it up on the spot. "You know Tina is always bullying him. She might even hurt him. He needs you. The two of you can stand up to her until I come back with help. Can you do that, Mags?"

The girl was quiet for a moment, then squeaked, "I guess so."

Charlotte hugged her, then talked her into counting sheep until she slowly faded into a deep slumber. Charlotte lay there, listening to the little girl's soft breathing, until the first tiny spoke of light seeped through the cracks in the plywood.

27

Elliott

Modern TV sucked, Elliott thought, looking blearily at the screen in the corner. Every inch of available space was moving or squawking or blinking, all of it BREAKING NEWS whether it was about war ten thousand miles away or a celebrity death or the failure of a stock to perform as expected. Everything was important, which meant that nothing was.

It was early morning, and sunlight filtered reluctantly through the stained windows. Teddy was back behind the bar, lifting and dumping a forty-pound plastic drum of ice into the cooler without apparent effort, hauling racks of steaming glasses from the kitchen in the back, swiping at the counter with a rag. The only sounds were the clatter Teddy made and the excitable drone of the TV newscasters.

After his call the night before, Elliott had sat at the bar, feeling his world being swallowed and spat out. Teddy had left him alone, letting him sit in front of his untouched beer, unmoved by the laughter and shouts swirling around him. Last call had appeared suddenly, with Teddy throwing on the lights and unceremoniously grabbing glasses and dumping them in the sink to get the message across. Elliott had found it impossible to move, glued to the stool, as though years of weariness and disappointment had all come calling at once.

When the bar had emptied, Elliott had raised his head to see Teddy looking at him, arms braced against the bar. Elliott mumbled an apology and reached into his pocket.

"One buck," Teddy said, his expression inscrutable behind the beard.

A bitter taste filled Elliott's mouth. "I don't need a handout. I ordered the beer."

"Did I say it was free?" Elliott stared at him. Teddy shrugged. "We're running a contest. Last man standing pays a buck a beer. Congratulations."

Elliott peeled a dollar out of his ball of cash and slid it across the bar.

"No tip?"

Elliott looked at him.

"You seriously can't take a joke." Teddy swept the bill up and threw it in the cash register, slammed the drawer shut, and began tallying something on a tablet. Without looking up, he asked, "You got a place for the night?"

Elliott stared at the empty glasses across the bar.

"Hard to believe, I know, but I didn't always own a dive bar on a back street named after somebody else." Teddy finished writing whatever it was he was writing. "I've been where you are. Maybe worse."

Elliott continued to stare.

"If you don't have an invitation to stay at the White House, there's a storeroom in the back. I crash there when I can't make it home. It's got a blanket and wooden pallets and everything." Teddy looked at him dead-on. "No joke."

A long minute passed, then Elliott slid off his stool and started putting chairs on tables. Teddy watched him for a moment, then grabbed a mop and a pail from a closet. The two of them worked in silence, cleaning and tidying and putting the bar back into rough shape. By three, they were done. Exhausted, Elliott retrieved his knapsack, then Teddy showed him where he could bunk down.

"Just a couple things about your stay," he'd said. "The main room is going to be locked, so if you feel like starting a fire, keep in mind I've got insurance and you don't have a key. If you need to take a leak, bathroom's at the end of the hall. Steal anything or shoot up or break stuff and I'll kick your head in. I'll be back at ten in the morning. Sleep tight."

After a tortured night, Elliott had been woken by a sharp rap on the door. He'd slumped out of the room to pitch in around the bar, setting up tables and lugging cases of beer from the storeroom until almost noon. Elliott dropped onto a stool, his shoulders rounded with fatigue.

"You know," Teddy said, leaning his elbows on the bar across from him. "That Unabomber look isn't going to cut it with the ladies."

"There's only so much you can do with fingers and a paper towel."

"Today's your lucky day." The bartender rummaged under the bar, then lifted a cardboard box and dropped it onto the counter. He pulled out a pair of scissors and a comb and handed them to Elliott. "Lost and found. It's a mystery what people can manage to lose."

Elliott held them like relics. He couldn't remember the last time he'd groomed himself. "Thanks, Teddy."

"Don't mention it," he said, running a hand over his own beard. "I could use a trim myself."

Elliott went to the bathroom, then washed and trimmed his beard and hair as best he could with the dull scissors. It took a concerted effort to get the comb through his shoulder-length hair and resulted in large tufts having to be pulled out, but thirty minutes later Elliott emerged looking better, if not feeling better.

"That's more like it," Teddy said upon seeing him.

"Do you think I could use your phone again? Last time, I promise."

Without a word, Teddy put the phone on the counter and went to unlock the front door. Elliott sat and stared at the phone, then finally picked up the receiver, made his call, then took his seat by the TV and waited.

Amy showed up thirty minutes later, her hair pulled back in the headband, her face pale. She hugged her arms around her bag of binders, hesitating at the door of the bar. Teddy glanced over, then jerked his head at Elliott sitting in the corner. She approached cautiously, dipping her head down so Elliott could see her before she called his name. He glanced at a stool and she sat.

"You said you listen for the connections in things," Elliott said after a moment. "I do, too. I was trained to look for patterns and repetitions, the structure that holds a person's mind together."

She said nothing.

"When I studied a subject who exhibited violent behavior," he continued, "I didn't take the violence at face value. I asked, why is the person this way? What is the root cause of their behavior? What is it in this person's psyche, stripped of its excuses and defenses, that makes them do what they do? Had I done that with you, instead of believing you, I might've saved both of us a lot of time."

Teddy banged open the front door with a hip, took one step, and heaved a bucket full of bleach water onto the walk outside the bar. It made a fat, splashing sound. On the TV, an enthusiastic white anchor with a crew cut and a block for a head began criticizing a recent decision by the mayor's office.

"Working together, we found that each of the kids on our list had a few things in common." Elliott traced the wood grain of the bar with the tip of a finger. "They were kidnapped, went missing for a year or more, then were discovered dead on or near their birthday. I told you the only way we'd be able to find Lacey was if we took those known facts and built on them, find the patterns and strings that would tie everything together, constructing a blueprint that, if we were lucky, would lead us to your daughter."

Teddy walked to the back, glancing their way as he passed. On the television, the commercial break ended and returned to the local news segment.

"I took for granted that every fact as we knew them—as you knew them—was on the table," he said, his voice reasonable, measured. "To think otherwise made no sense. Why would any mother jeopardize her daughter's life when what we knew and what had been shared was critical to finding her?"

Amy said nothing, but her face tightened.

"But all the cases we looked at, each family we spoke to, each child we investigated, had a second thing in common, didn't they?"

She tugged a lock of hair down and pulled it across her lip. "Elliott, I don't know what you're saying—"

"I'm saying *every* child came from a broken home. *Every* kid was abused or neglected or thrown away." He looked at her. "Including yours."

A tear slid down one cheek.

"I wanted to give you a chance. I thought maybe I'd screwed up. So I called Dave Cargill last night. He told me the rest of the facts about your *case*." His voice turned savage. "Lacey wasn't at a friend's house when she was kidnapped. She was in foster care."

"I was getting her back. I—"

He cut her off. "The cops didn't stop listening to you because of your flaky ideas. They stopped because you're a goddamn addict."

"Was. Was an addict."

"Christ. As if that mattered."

Her face twisted and she pointed a finger at him. "I lost my *daughter*—"

"You were too high to pick her up from school. Neighbors told him you blacked out on the way more than once," he said, his lip curling. "You didn't *lose* anything, Amy. Lacey was taken from you for her own good."

"That doesn't change the fact that she was kidnapped. It has nothing to do with it."

"It has *everything* to do with it," he shouted, turning on his stool to face her. His chest felt like it was cracking in half. "Don't you understand? You're culpable. You're part of it. You made this happen. I helped you because I thought I might have an opportunity to take back a tiny bit of my own history and rewrite it, give someone I thought deserved it a second shot. But you tossed your chance away before I ever came on the scene."

The TV volume suddenly doubled—*"The DMV reports new delays at all statewide offices"*—nearly drowning them out. They glanced over to see Teddy aiming the remote at the TV. He looked at them pointedly. Amy moved closer to Elliott so she could be heard.

"It must be wonderful to be on the righteous side of an argument all the time, to have never done anything wrong," she said, her voice shaking. "To never have a moment's feeling of guilt or doubt about how fit you are to be a mother and a parent."

"Irrelevant."

"So, you've never had to struggle with an addiction? Or failure? Or abuse? Oh, please, Elliott, tell me what it's like to have absolutely no flaws, to be loved unconditionally, to never face a goddamned challenge in your life."

"Never face a challenge?" Elliott gaped at her, outraged. "You have no idea what I've been through. I didn't *deserve* what happened to me—"

"And I did? Who gets to measure that? Who gets to judge whether or not I get my daughter back? Or if she gets to live? Do we just take a kid away from every mom who doesn't quite pass the test?"

"Being a parent is more than biology. You have a responsibility to look after your child, and when you don't, there are consequences."

"So Lacey got what was coming to her?"

"Of course not. Stop being melodramatic."

"But maybe I should suffer, is that it?"

"Why not? I have. I still do."

"And I see you picked a bar to do it in."

"What's that supposed to mean?"

She laughed. It was an ugly sound. "You think a junkie can't spot a drunk? You should've seen your face when Neumann staggered to the door."

Elliott gritted his teeth. "I haven't touched a drink in eight years."

"And I went straight after it mattered, too. But that doesn't keep anyone from passing judgment, does it?" Amy's lip quivered. "My god, you've been wallowing in your own pity for years, totally unwilling to forgive yourself for . . . for whatever it is you did or didn't do, but the real problem is you would never forgive anyone for anything. Isn't it enough—no matter what I've done, no matter what I'm guilty of—that I simply want my daughter back alive?"

Elliott looked at her for a long moment, then lowered his head into his hands. His pulse beat painfully in his neck. Amy sat next to him, crying. Inane noises surrounded him, a soundtrack of meaninglessness—the downshifting of a passing truck outside, music coming from somewhere across the street, the babbling of the TV.

"In local news, a Washington, DC, family is celebrating the return of their son after he went missing four years ago."

Elliott raised his head. A professionally perky woman—young and blonde, with chunky earrings and a bright smile—was delivering the news. After the lead, the screen cut from the anchor to footage of an ambulance pulling around the circular drive of a hospital.

"The Public Affairs office of the Metropolitan Police," the reporter continued, "announced today that Jay Kelly, son of Karl and Patricia Kelly of Washington, DC, has been found alive after being abducted as a young boy. The story made national news after the wealthy husband and wife experienced a messy public divorce followed soon after by the abduction of their son. The couple posted a one-hundred-thousand-dollar reward for any information leading to the discovery of their son, ten at the time he went missing."

Elliott glanced to his right. Amy was watching the screen, entranced.

"No headway was made in the case, and the young man was feared dead until just this past Wednesday, when a construction worker stumbled across a body in a parking lot in the Trinidad neighborhood of northeast DC." The camera switched to a scene of cars and dumpsters. "But the body turned out to be Jay Kelly. Comatose, but alive."

Another cut, this time to a middle-aged woman with graying brown hair and a moon face. Her eyes were red and the skin of her nose blotchy. "We're just so thankful to have Jay back. We never gave up hope, but his birthday was just a few days ago and . . . and . . ." They watched the woman pull herself together. "It seemed a kind of milestone, you know, and the light began to dim. But he's with us now, and that's all that's important."

The reporter wrapped up the story in her singsong voice. "Jay was taken to Mercy General with undisclosed injuries and is listed in serious but stable condition. The police investigation into his abduction has been reopened with these new developments."

The news report moved on to the vagaries of the day, but Elliott was no longer listening. "Your database?" His voice was raw.

"Here." Amy fished it out of her bag and banged it onto the bar. She flipped through the pages, snatching at the next before the first was gone, whispering, "It's here, it's here, it's here."

Elliott stood and moved close, watching over her shoulder, not daring to speak.

"Got it!" Amy said, her finger pinning a slim paragraph to the page. "Jay Lawrence Kelly. Abducted from foster care four years ago." She raised her head to look at Elliott. "His mother said in that report that his birthday was just this past week."

"Found comatose, with undisclosed injuries, in serious condition." His face was grim. "Just the way you'd describe a drug overdose if you didn't want to come out and say it."

Amy grabbed his arm. "Elliott, this boy is supposed to be dead."

"A teenage boy, growing an inch a day. Metabolism of a jackrabbit," Elliott said, thinking out loud. "It would be easy to screw up the dosage if you were trying to make it look like an accident yet didn't want to overdo it."

"We have to talk to him, we have to talk to this Jay Kelly," Amy said, but he was nodding before she said her next words. "He knows whether Lacey's alive or not."

28

Sister

She returned home from work, faintly bothered by her lunchtime meeting with her brother and his talk of saving the young addict. It had stuck with her throughout the rest of the afternoon, a reminder of the important—no, critical—work she was doing to save the children. Certainly more important than her brother's efforts, feeding, as he did, into a system that nearly ruined them both.

The thoughts were still weighing heavily as she came up the drive. She was struck at the sight of her own home, and she let the car roll to a stop as she stared at her house, the house her brother couldn't bear to look at—as if his memories were more painful than hers—the house she'd lived in her whole life. The house she'd chosen as her reminder of, and shelter against, the moment her life had changed.

Angled slabs of light slid through the trees, catching the leaves as they fell, seeming to hold them for a moment before letting them continue their descent. The windows were down, and the same musty smell of rotting earth filtered into the car. A breeze blew through the car, crisp and cool, with the promise of winter riding behind it.

Exactly the same as that day.

It had been her first year of junior high and the everyday choices—coat or sweater? boots or sneakers?—seemed profound, potentially life altering. She'd been so excited to choose for herself, so thrilled for the future. Thanksgiving festivities had wrapped up and a Christmas dance was around the corner, with the holiday break soon after. Mother had been distracted and distant, of no help. All the children had demanded her attention, whining and yelling and crying, none of them seeing something break in their mother's eyes.

Butterflies and stomach cramps had kept her in a state of perpetual nausea throughout the day—she'd been so nervous, had forgotten everything from her locker number to her homeroom assignment—but she'd finished thrilled and exhausted, unable to stop talking to Tom Childress on the way home. On the bus, she'd caught a look in his eye and flushed, feeling confused but excited, filled with the sense that she'd started to cross some kind of threshold.

They'd kept chatting at their bus stop long after the sound of the diesel engine had faded into the distance—she swinging her denim bag back and forth, he with his thumbs hooked in the straps of his backpack like an old man in suspenders—until the realization of just how late she was hit her like a slap on the back of her neck. The Childress boy had gaped as she'd turned without a word and sprinted away, helping confirm a reputation for strangeness she'd gotten through grade school.

She'd begun to tremble as she made the long hike up the drive. Mother didn't abide tardiness and had a number of punishments, large and small, to drive the point home. She was sweating and out of breath when she rounded the bend and came in sight of the house, but relief warred with fear when Mother wasn't waiting for her on the porch as she so often was, arms crossed and one hip thrust forward like an accusation.

The door was open.

Another rule broken, another reason to be anxious. She shut it, then stood in the foyer for a moment, listening.

The house was very still.

The furnace clicked on and warm air shouldered its way through the hall, trailing with it a strange smell.

Three steps in, she stopped, feeling queasy, and pressed a hand into her stomach. Something ugly sat in the air, squat and croaking, calling for her to pay attention.

She opened her mouth to call out, but instinct stopped her and the words died in her throat. Slipping off her shoes, she padded down the hall and peeked into rooms, but there was no one in the parlor or the den or the kitchen or the dining room. She crept up the stairs, pressing herself tight to the wall to keep the steps from squeaking. The pattern of the wallpaper was rough under her hands.

At the top of the stairs, she went down the hall to Charlie's bedroom.

The door was open and the bad smell was strong.

The croaking in her head grew louder.

Hunching her shoulders, she slipped in without touching the door or the frame.

Buddy was on the bed, sleeping. The top sheet, a thin thing with a Western motif, was pulled to just under his chin and had been tucked tight around his body. She whispered his name. When he didn't respond, she put a hand on his chest and felt the complete inertness, the wooden lack of life that was more like a piece of furniture than her brother.

She clapped both hands to her mouth, vomiting into them.

Stumbling out of the room she bumped into the door. It banged against the wall as it swung.

From the bedroom down the hall, Mother called her name. The voice was slurred, drowsy, thick.

Quickly, then, she retraced her steps, the metallic stink of vomit filling her nose, tears welling in her eyes, shaking and flinching as she slipped back down the steps.

Her mother called her name again. Thuds and bumps and footsteps on a tile floor.

She flew down the rest of the steps, grabbed her shoes, and flung open the door . . . then stopped. How far would she get? Her mother was fit enough to run after her or hunt her down in the car.

From the upstairs hall, her mother called for her again, the voice a screech now.

Leaving the door open, she bolted down the hall into the kitchen. Quaking with fear, she went to the oven, opened the door, and crawled inside. Praying that the springs wouldn't squeak, she shut the door quietly, cutting off all light.

Crouching in the dark, she hid in the last place in the world her mother would think to look, shivering and squeezing her eyes shut as the woman stumbled around the empty house, howling her name. She pinched her lips until they were numb as she listened to the screams of her brother and sisters as they came home and were met by their mother and placed in their beds.

The absolute silence that followed was Mother doling out her own final punishment in the upstairs bathtub. Long, long, long after the last sound had died away, Sister lay curled on the floor of the oven, praying her mother was truly dead, that she wouldn't come downstairs and brace herself against the door, then turn the stove on to punish her willful eldest daughter.

The police discovered her the next day, still in the oven. It took two burly officers to pull her out of it. They found Brother three days later, starving, hiding in the bole of a nearby tree, willing to die there rather than come home. After a year of therapy, they learned he had watched Mother kill Buddy before fleeing, running out the door and into the woods an hour before Sister had come home.

In the hospital, the doctor had told them, not realizing the terrible irony his words contained, that they were both lucky to be alive.

29

Elliott

Once upon a time, Elliott thought, Mercy General Hospital in northwest DC had probably been a single, elegant brick building with an elliptical cobblestone drive. Patients would have been delivered to an oak-shaded front door by horse-drawn ambulance, greeted by mustachioed doctors wearing pince-nez and cared for by bonneted nurses. Today, it was a sprawling medical campus with twenty buildings, five entrances, and four multilevel parking garages. It was as busy as an airport—people and cars moved in every direction, passing signs containing a bewildering collection of colors, numbers, and letters.

"Where do we start?" Amy leaned over the steering wheel, squinting at the main building in front of them.

"Pull up to the main lobby and throw your hazards on," Elliott said. "We need some information or we'll just drive around in circles. Literally."

She parked behind a rusty white van and Elliott hopped out, heading for the entrance. Inside, a Christmas tree covered in tinsel and paper cutouts of candy canes took up a corner of the lobby. Next to it sat an information desk where Elliott helped himself to a map of the hospital complex, unfolding it as he returned to the car.

He spread the map on the dashboard and the two of them peered at it, trying to make sense of the blocks and polygons. Amy traced a finger over the paper, tapped it. "Here. We're here."

Elliott studied the legend in the bottom corner. "Most of the buildings don't concern us. They'll be for specialties like oncology or psychiatric care, administration, physical plant, stuff like that."

"He'd be in pediatrics, wouldn't he? Or just general admission? Both are in the main building."

"Unless there's a separate ICU. The news report said he was in serious but stable condition."

Amy closed her eyes. "I had to take Lacey to an emergency room once for a sinus infection. Really bad. They kept her for two nights. I remember the other parents in the waiting room talking about PICU and PIMC."

"PICU." Elliott stared out the window. "Pediatric intensive care unit. The kids on the edge."

"And PIMC is obviously pediatric something-something care." Amy flipped the map over and scanned a more detailed rendering of the core medical facility. "Here. Pediatric intermediate medical care."

"Kids who are out of the red zone, but not out of the woods."

She glanced at him. "Sounds like 'serious but stable condition' to me."

He nodded. "Let's go."

They parked in a garage and walked back to the main campus, hunched over by the cold and watching as headlights and streetlamps flickered to life. It was only late afternoon, but already the sun was low in the late autumn sky and would be setting soon.

Guided by the map, made their way to the PIMC. The halls were colorfully decorated but sterile, smelling of disinfectant and too-brightly lighted by overhead fluorescent bulbs. Nurses and doctors deep in conversation ignored them as they passed, moving with purpose; patients and visitors shuffled along the halls with less drive and focus.

The walls of the PIMC waiting room were a playful purple and blue. A bank of vending machines—snacks, soda, and a combo coffee/tea/soup machine—sat in a small alcove. Comfortable, blocky chairs with rounded arms were placed in discrete clumps of two and three for the adults, while a child-size street sign proclaimed that one side of the room, with its diminutive plastic tables and a basket of toys, was for **KIDS ONLY**. Couples huddled around the room, most with the hollowed-out look of pain and worry held in check.

Elliott threaded the aisles, leading them to a couple of chairs in a far corner. Amy sank into a seat, curling her legs underneath her, while Elliott picked up a magazine and started flipping through the pages.

Amy leaned close. "We're just going to pretend to be parents?"

"Yes," Elliott whispered back. "We need a break, and acting like we belong might get it for us."

"I'll feel like a fraud."

"Act like the night you took Lacey in for a sinus infection. She's not in danger, she's just sick. We're both worried, but you're holding it together for her and I'm holding it together for you."

Stricken, Amy's face fell, and Elliott cursed himself. He put a hand on her arm. "I'm sorry. I didn't mean it literally. Try to remember everyone here is focused on themselves, even the guards and nurses and intake personnel. Look concerned and worried and we'll fit right in. When's the last time anyone asked if you belonged in an emergency room?"

Amy nodded, then glanced at a set of double doors with a lock bar and a phone on the wall. "The patient section is locked down How are we going to get back to see Jay? If he's even here?"

"I'm working on it."

An hour passed before a weary-looking couple on the other side of the waiting room got to their feet. They'd fidgeted for the better part of thirty minutes and engaged in a whispered argument for ten more before coming to some kind of agreement. The woman paused long enough to put on an oversize pink parka, but the man—gaunt and bent at the shoulders—left his denim coat hanging on the chair before heading for the door. A temporary sticker badge had been slapped on the breast of the coat near the collar. The smell of stale cigarette smoke trailed behind as they passed.

Elliott watched them go, then turned to Amy. "Do you have any quarters?"

"A few," she said, automatically reaching for her purse. "Why?"

"I need a cup of coffee. Hurry."

She frowned, but produced a couple of quarters that Elliott snatched from her before hurrying to the vending machines. He bumped his fist on the plastic front impatiently as an indefinable brown liquid poured out of the spout, then grabbed it and tore several handfuls of paper napkins from a dispenser before heading back.

As he passed the seats of the couple who had left for their smoke, he stumbled, spilling coffee on himself, the denim jacket, and the floor. A few people glanced over, then went back to the TV or talking to each other. Cursing, he set the half-empty cup down and made a show of mopping the coffee from the floor, spending extra care on the man's jacket. Once done, he tossed the soaked napkins into the trash, picked up his cup, and came back to Amy.

She looked at him quizzically. "I hope you weren't looking forward to a full cup."

"It runneth over," he said, grabbing her hand and putting something in it. "But I still shall want."

She looked down to see that he'd placed one of the sticker badges in her hand. She looked up, her mouth an "O" of surprise. He motioned for her to stick it on her lapel.

"What about you? Why wouldn't you have one?"

He shrugged impatiently. "I forgot it or didn't get one or whatever. It only matters that one of us has one."

The doors opened with a hiss and the fidgety couple returned. As before, the acrid smell of cigarette smoke pushed through the room with them as they made their way to their seats. As they walked by, the husband continued past them to his chair and grabbed his jacket, but Amy smiled as the wife—plump, with frizzy blonde hair permed to within an inch of its life—glanced at them and returned the smile.

She stopped. "What are you all here for?"

Amy swallowed. "My little girl has a sinus infection. I waited too long and it just got worse and worse."

"Oh no! I had my share of those. What I wouldn't give for one now."

Elliott scooted to the edge of his seat. "Why are you here, ma'am?"

"My little builder," she said with a sigh, "thought he'd put together a skyscraper like the kind his daddy works on. So he made one out of scrap wood and bricks in the lot next door and tried to climb to the top. The whole thing came crashing down with him on top, and he cracked his head open."

"Oh, I'm so sorry." Amy made a sympathetic noise. "Is he going to be all right?"

"If he wakes up," the woman said matter-of-factly, but her eyes were shining. Amy stood and gave the woman a hug. Elliott stood and squeezed the woman's shoulder awkwardly, then offered her one of the paper napkins he'd saved. She took it gratefully and blew her nose.

"We've been back there three times, but he's just the same," the woman said, her voice hoarse. "Doctors say it's just going to take a while."

"What ward is he in?" Elliott asked. Amy shot him a look, but he ignored her.

"Intermediate care."

"Well, that's good then, isn't it? That means the doc thinks he's hanging in there."

"Do you think so?" The woman searched his face, looking for hope.

"I think the ones worst off go there." He lowered his voice and nodded toward the PICU door. "Maybe he's not out of the woods yet, but give it time."

"Oh, thank you for saying that." She sighed and shook her head. "It could be worse, I guess. Like that boy that was missing? The one they found after all those years? He's just down the hall from my Tommy. Can you imagine thinking your baby's gone, only to find out he's been on the streets this whole time?"

Amy made a sound and put a hand to her mouth. Elliott put an arm around her and squeezed. "There's always hope."

"I suppose so."

Her husband approached them, shrugging on his jacket, unaware he'd lost his visitor badge. "Mary, I got to go. I have to clock in at five."

"I know, babe. I'll be here." They kissed, he gave Amy and Elliott a perfunctory nod, and walked out. Mary watched him go, then turned and smiled wanly at them. "He don't mean to be rude. He's worried about Tommy and don't want to show it. At least I can cry about it."

"Well, you cry if you want." Amy stroked her shoulder.

"Would you . . . would you mind going back there with me?" Mary asked, looking at Amy with some embarrassment. "I know nothing's changed, but it would sure help me."

Amy nodded at her in sympathy. "Sure, hon."

30

Elliott

They looked down at the small form. Jay Kelly, slender and inert, was dwarfed by the hospital bed. The light in the room was low, and Amy hesitantly leaned forward to confirm the boy was breathing. The IV tube seemed larger around than most of his veins, blue snakes that stood out under the snow-white skin of his arms and his temples. *I've never seen wrists so thin,* Elliott thought.

He tore his eyes away to take a closer look at a cardiac monitor that stood guard next to the bed, its red and yellow lights blinking garishly in the gloom. Elliott knew enough about medicine that the graph should show an uninterrupted sawtooth edge, but all he saw here was an erratic line of peaks and valleys, no two of them alike. He watched the monitor for a moment, then turned to the IV stand. Two bags of fluid were linked to the same line. Being careful not to touch them, he peered at their labels.

"Saline and naloxone," he said softly.

"Naloxone?"

"An overdose inhibitor for opioids. Cops see so many ODs on the street that they carry inhalers of it now. It might've been what saved

Jay's life. The hospital keeps the dose going and steps it down gradually until the opioid wears off."

"Opioid? Like fentanyl?"

"Yes."

"It fits the profiles of the other children."

Elliott nodded, then his eyes caught something over Amy's shoulder. She turned. Jay, eyes open and cavernous, was looking at them. His mouth opened but no sound emerged.

Amy moved closer to the bed, pulling a stool with her. "Jay? Jay, please don't be afraid. You're safe now."

Jay's eyelids sank to half-mast, then floated up again. He rolled his head around on the pillow to get a wider view of his room, then coughed, a dry, racking sound. Elliott grabbed a large Styrofoam cup from a nearby table and held it for Jay to take a sip. The boy craned his neck to drink, then fell back onto the pillow.

His face a mask of exhaustion, he said, "Where am I?"

"You're in Mercy General, a hospital. Do you know where that is?" Jay nodded.

"You probably want your parents, don't you? They're not here right now, but I'm sure they'll be back later."

Elliott glanced toward the open door of the room and the bright light of the hallway, but there was no one there, only the slight sound of beeping and whirring of medical electronics.

Amy put her hand gently on Jay's arm. "Honey, you don't know me, and I bet it's very hard to trust anyone right now, but I have a really important question. Do you think you're strong enough to talk a little bit?"

He nodded. "I think so."

"The police found you in a bad part of the city just a day or so ago. You've been missing for almost four years. Everyone seems to think you were living on the streets, but my friend Mr. Nash here and I have a different theory. We think you were being held somewhere. Can you tell us . . ." Amy sighed and Elliott heard almost a year of sadness and anxiety in that simple sound. "Can you tell us if we're right?"

Jay's eyes welled up, and a single large tear spilled from each to run down his cheeks. Shoulders jerking up and down, he began to cry silently. Amy stroked his arm, making soothing noises that meant nothing and everything at once. In the middle of his tears, he nodded once, twice, then continued to nod in time to his breaths until they were a spasm.

Amy let him go for a minute until the sobs tapered off. "I'm so sorry to make you remember this, but were there other children with you?"

"Yes."

"Can you tell me their names?"

Jay took a deep, guttural breath, closed his eyes, and threw his head back into the pillow. "Charlotte, Buddy, Tina, and Maggie."

She swallowed. "There wasn't . . . a girl named Lacey?"

"No."

Amy turned to Elliott, panic on her face. "Those weren't their real names, were they, Jay?" he asked. His voice sounded squeezed and unnatural to his own ears.

He shook his head. "No. My name is—" His face twisted. "My name *was* Charlie. We weren't allowed to use our real names or we'd be punished."

"Who would punish you, Jay?"

"Sister."

"Who is Sister?"

"She . . . she's the one who kept us."

Surprised, Amy glanced at Elliott, mouthing the word, *She?* He shrugged, as baffled as she was.

She turned back to Jay. "Who was the oldest?"

"Sister. By a lot."

"I mean, of the children."

Jay gestured weakly toward his chest.

"Then . . . Charlotte, right? How old was she?"

"About ten or eleven?" he said, uncertain.

"What did she look like, Jay?"

"Small. Thin. Blonde like you."

Amy's breath caught. "This next question is very, very important, Jay. Did Charlotte ever tell you her real name?"

Jay turned his head on the pillow and looked at the wall, his lips tight.

"You won't be punished, Jay," Elliott said, gently putting a hand on the thin shoulder. "Sister can't reach you here."

The young teen's voice cracked as he said, "We were best friends. She's the only reason I lasted as long as I . . . as I . . ."

Amy, unable to help herself, grabbed his thin, bony wrist. "Please, honey. What was her name?"

Jay groaned. "She's still back there. I don't . . . don't . . ."

His voice trailed off as his face suddenly clenched like a fist, then his eyelids fluttered crazily as his eyes rolled back in his head. The cardiac monitor's soft beeps changed to a high-pitched squeal as the boy's body was racked with convulsions.

"Oh my god," Amy said, recoiling.

Elliott dashed out into the hall, looking for a nurse, but two were already rounding the counter of the floor station and heading his way. He waved them to go faster as they sprinted down the hall. "Hurry!"

He stepped back as they ran into the room, pushing Amy out of the way as they got to work.

Without looking up from what she was doing, one of the nurses asked, "Are you with the family?"

"Not exactly," Elliott said. "We're out-of-town friends of the Kellys. We heard that Jay had been found and wanted to come see him as soon as we could."

"Wait by the station, please," she said, her mouth a flat line. "All visitors are supposed to be cleared before visiting the boy."

"I'm sorry, we had no idea," Elliott said, backing out and tugging at Amy's arm. "We'll wait for you to come back."

"Did we do that to him?" she asked as he hustled them down the corridor.

"No," Elliott said, his voice angry, uneven. The sounds of the shrieking cardiac monitor chased them down the hall. "This . . . Sister did it. He's in good hands now. But we have to get out of here."

Amy stopped suddenly, grabbing a fistful of his shirt. "Elliott, he *knows*," she whispered fiercely. "Lacey's alive and he knows where she is."

"Yes, she's alive," Elliott said, almost not believing it himself. He turned his head away as they passed the PIMC nurses' station and kept walking, dragging Amy with him. "But we can't go back, if that's what you're thinking. That boy's got no more idea where she is than we do. And it's not going to matter if we don't get out of here."

The bank of elevators was within sight, through a set of open double doors. Next to the elevators was a single door with a stair icon. As he steered Amy toward the elevator, they heard a voice behind them call out, "Sir? One second, please."

Elliott glanced back to see a nurse from the station looking at him. He waved back congenially.

Overhead, the PA system crackled to life. *"Dr. Hahn to PIMC, please. Dr. Hahn to PIMC. Code Red."*

"Stairs," he said tightly to Amy.

"Sir! Stop right there," the nurse called and began jogging down the hall toward them.

Amy banged open the stairwell door with a hip and they sprinted down the three flights in a dizzying circle, their feet making slapping sounds with each step. As they reached the ground floor, Elliott grabbed Amy's arm as she went to bash open the first-floor door.

"Walk," he hissed. "Look normal."

He took her hand, then opened the door calmly. They were in a far corner of the pediatric lobby. Elliott led the way across the lobby to the exit, wincing as the door banged shut behind them. Several people glanced up, then went back to whispering or reading or watching TV. Set on reaching the exit, they skirted the pediatric intake desk and passed through the middle of the rows of chairs.

"Is your little girl all right?" They both jumped, then looked down to see Mary, the mother of little Tommy, looking up at them with a wan smile. They'd walked right past her without realizing it.

"Mary! Yes. She's being discharged tomorrow," Amy said. Behind them, a phone at the intake desk blooped. Elliott watched as the receptionist answered, then stood with a hand cupped over the mouthpiece of the phone as she scanned the room.

Mary frowned. "I thought they were letting her go tonight?"

"Oh, I wish," Amy responded with a weak laugh. "You know doctors, changing their minds."

The receptionist looked their way, nodded, then said something into the phone. Elliott tugged at Amy's hand.

"I'm sorry, Mary," Amy said as they pulled away. "We've got to run. We both have to work tomorrow. We'll be praying for you and Tommy."

"Thank you," the woman said, smiling but confused.

The door clacked open and a burly man—bad comb-over, white shirt and navy-blue pants, hospital security badge—came through, his eyes scanning the lobby.

"Go," Elliott said, shoving Amy in the direction of the doors. Behind them, the guard yelled.

They burst through the doors and ran down the sidewalk toward the parking garage where they'd stashed the Celica. They'd been lucky to find a spot on the first level, but it was deep in the back of the open-air building, and Elliott was winded by the time they reached it.

He cursed as he waited for Amy to get into the passenger side, watching the entrance of the garage with a feeling of dread. There was no sign of the burly security guard. Elliott jumped in as Amy slid into the driver's seat. She slammed the key into the ignition, turned it . . . and nothing happened.

"No, no, no, no, no! Please, oh please. Not now," Amy chanted, turning the key in the ignition again.

Elliott watched out the window for the guard, but saw only the yawning entrance of the garage.

"Maybe they're not coming?" Amy said hopefully.

"Don't count on it."

Amy tried four more times, but each time the ignition simply taunted them with a rapid clicking noise, refusing to start. Elliott frowned, then cracked the door open. The distant sound of sirens cut through the air.

"Elliott . . . ," Amy said, her voice panicky.

"Cops are on their way," he said, opening the door all the way. "Let's go."

"Go where?"

"Anywhere. Nowhere. Wherever we can to help Lacey," he said, grabbing his knapsack and jumping out of the car. Amy crawled out after him, then they vaulted the low pony wall that ran along the garage. They slipped into the darkness as the first of three squad cars came screaming through the main hospital entrance, lights flashing and tires squealing.

31

Charlotte

Charlotte played with the key in her pocket obsessively, running the tips of her finger over the key and back again to feel the dull teeth, the gaps, the skeletal stem. The brass absorbed the heat from her fingers and grew warm, feeling alive in her hand.

It was early afternoon and everyone was napping, leaving the house quiet save for a distant scratching sound coming from above her head. Sister had told them a branch had fallen onto the roof and that it would blow off eventually, but Buddy had whispered to Maggie that it was the body of a dead bird, its dead claws catching on the shingles as the wind toyed with it.

Maggie had gone hysterical and Charlotte had yelled at Buddy for the lie, but now she had trouble getting the image of a big black bird, a wing jutting skyward, being blown back and forth on the roof.

The door to Sister's room, thick-paneled oak reminiscent of the front door, sat in front of her like a wall. The oak's grain was wing shaped, and the image of the bird appeared again. She shivered and pushed the picture out of her mind.

The lock and knob were of chunky brass. Verdigris had gathered in the simple ridges of the escutcheon, but the egg-shaped knob was as polished and bright as a lamp. Charlotte pulled the key out of her pocket and examined it.

Over the course of several days, she'd tried it in nearly every lock she could find on the first floor and in the basement, but either the locks were too new and couldn't fit the fat barrel or, for the few original locks left in the house, the key simply didn't fit. She'd nearly despaired, thinking that Charlie had found a key without a lock and simply hung on to it as a good luck charm.

Lying awake in bed, however, she'd listened as Sister rose early. There were the everyday sounds of her getting dressed and ready for work, then the sound of the door to her room being unlocked, shut, then relocked. The flat, smacking sounds were unlike the sharp clicks of the front door—a thick bolt was being moved, requiring a thick key to move it. Which is when she decided, with a pounding heart, that the key must fit the one place she hadn't dared try.

The idea alone had paralyzed her with fear. Tina might catch her. Or what if Sister had covered the room with traps or telltales? Charlotte had trouble even imagining the punishment. But it was the last place the key could fit.

She slid it into the keyhole and turned.

The bolt slid back with a loud snap that made her gasp.

Charlotte snatched the key out of the hole, ready to run if one of the others had heard the sound and came to investigate. But a minute passed without a sound. She slipped the key back in her pocket, then placed a hand on the door. Her hand shook and her arm twitched involuntarily. In her imagination, the panels were hot and beating like a giant heart under her hand. She closed her eyes briefly, then pushed on the door, and went into the room.

There was someone on the other side, moving in the glum light.

She gave a small cry, thinking somehow, impossibly, that it was Sister. Then she realized the door faced a mirror across the room; she was looking at herself. Moving quickly, she slipped inside, her heart pounding, and closed the door behind her. The room went black and she fumbled for the light switch, then looked around.

Disappointment flooded her. She'd held out hope that this had been Charlie's plan, that maybe Sister's room was different and the windows weren't boarded up, making an escape as simple as jumping or making a rope out of sheets like she'd seen in the movies. And there *were* two windows in the room, but they were boarded like all the others in the house, which explained why it was so dark. She sighed and looked around anyway.

Most of the space was taken up by a queen-size bed with spiraled posts that reached almost to the ceiling. At its foot was a trunk, a block of peeling black leather and brass fittings. Next to the mirror was a simple dresser with flared brass drawer pulls. Sister had her own bathroom, but it was tiny, smaller than the one Charlotte shared with the others, and was filled with a medicinal smell.

She paced the room, eyeing the trunk, but she was drawn to the dresser. Propped on top were a series of old pictures in tripod frames. A department store portrait of a woman with thick glasses and a ruffled blouse. A class picture of a grade-school group.

The largest was of a family, fuzzy and tinted in the too-vivid colors of a bygone process. A woman in a lime-green dress and a bouffant hairdo stood in front of a large farmhouse, holding a baby. A young oak sprouted next to the house. Gray, indistinct woods appeared in the background.

Next to the woman stood a man in a white T-shirt and jeans, with slicked-back hair and an ironic twist to his mouth. One hip was cocked, making his stance casual, sarcastic. His hand was blurry, caught in motion somewhere between his waist and his chin. Charlotte looked closer and thought she made out the glow of a cigarette; he hadn't bothered to stop smoking for the picture.

To the woman's left was a row of children, lined up in descending order like Russian dolls. The first was a young girl, leggy and serious, wearing a spring dress with saddle shoes and short, frilly socks. Her hair was in pigtails and her hands were clasped primly in front of her, but her eyes were so dark they seemed like pinholes in the paper. Next to her was a boy, hair slicked back in imitation of the man's. Then a boy, two more girls, and another boy, their faces indistinct. No one was smiling.

Charlotte stared at the picture for a long time until, shaking her head, she forced herself away from the dresser. She couldn't afford to linger. A quick search showed the bureau was full of underwear, socks, and hose, all neatly folded and arranged. The closet held business clothes. Charlotte recognized all of them as Sister's work outfits.

That left the trunk.

Charlotte padded over to it and gingerly undid the snaps, then lifted the lid. Decorative paper in a cabbage rose pattern covered the inside, peeling from the humpbacked lid like dead skin. The smell of old cardboard and glue wafted upward, making her nose twitch. In the belly of the chest were five large shoe boxes. On the top box was written, in faded pencil, "Charlie" in a swirling script. Charlotte ran a finger under the name, then teased the lid off the box.

Inside was a stack of envelopes. The top was faded and brown along the edges. "Charlie" was written on it again, still in pencil. Underneath the name was written "9/3/87–10/29/90." The envelope crackled like it was made of dead leaves as she opened it.

Inside was a single, fragile sheet of paper, torn in half. She pulled the pieces out with trembling hands and held them together to make a crude drawing. Four stick figures, two large, two small, stood in front of a house. Lines—Sister's signature—had been drawn through them all. The artist had tried to fill in details, but the features were outsize and didn't match each other. The mother's figure had more detail than the father's. A small brown dog with a lolling pink tongue danced on hind legs to one side, part of a rough collage of the boy figure playing with the dog—throwing a ball, feeding it from a trash can–size dog bowl. A black blotch at the top, cross-hatched and scribbled out, was where the name would've been.

A small cry escaped her lips. She'd forgotten about the drawing Sister had forced her to make.

Charlotte slipped the pieces back into the envelope, then placed it on the stack. She rifled through the envelopes in order. Each was marked "Charlie," though as time went on the flowing, serpentine script changed to printed letters and, toward the bottom, block print. Each had a beginning and end date. The dates varied from envelope to envelope, but none overlapped and sometimes were months apart. Peeking inside, she found a torn picture and a crossed-out name in every one, twelve in all.

The last was a crisp white business envelope. On it was written "Charlie" again in blue ink and block letters. Compared to the first few, it had a businesslike, transactional look, like the note she'd brought home from school one time from a disappointed Mrs. Dunlop, her fifth-grade teacher. Underneath the name was written a start date, but no end date. She stared at it. It was the first indication of the passage of time she'd had since being taken by Sister. *Have I really been here that long?* A knot formed in her stomach and she tore her eyes away from the date. Inside the envelope was the single-sheet torn drawing and the name "Jeremy," crossed out like all the others. She lifted the sheet and sniffed; the heady, chemical smell of the marker was still there. It was new.

She put it back and looked at the next-to-last envelope. The beginning date was from four years before. She stared at the end date, penned in recently.

The picture inside was artistic, the best she'd seen so far. A tall high-rise rose in a forest of others. A bird flew around the top floor, and pillowlike clouds bunched above it all. In the foreground was a family of three: mother, father, boy. They stood straight as poles, not touching. Wide gaps marked the space between each. The boy wore a bow tie and a serious expression. Despite the detail, the picture seemed to project emptiness—there was little to look at or feel. She glanced at the top of the page. Written in a kid's blocky script, and crossed out by a single black line, was the name "Jay Kelly."

Charlie. Her Charlie.

Feeling sick, she put everything back in the shoe box, then quickly rifled through the others, finding similar stacks of envelopes for Tina, Buddy, and Maggie.

Last, she pulled out the shoe box marked "Charlotte," written in pencil on top. Inside were the same neatly ordered envelopes. Charlotte . . . Charlotte . . . Charlotte. Fifteen in all, with the dates much closer together than the Charlies, but ranging from yellowed and brittle to a last, pristine white business envelope.

Hers.

She opened it, staring at the picture Sister had made her draw the first horrible night. It was elementary compared to Charlie's. Sister, she remembered—the memory sticking like a thorn—hadn't torn the drawing evenly; she'd carefully ripped it so that she was alone on one of the pieces.

She ran her finger lightly over her clumsy drawing, opening memories up that she'd long since sealed away. Feeling the tears getting ready to spill, she began to put everything back and set it next to the Charlie box when she was struck by a thought.

She picked up her envelope again and turned it over. It sat in her hands like a dead thing. The month, day, and year she'd been kidnapped was written in a clear, steady hand. Next to it was an end date. She knew from the date on Jay Kelly's envelope that it wasn't far in the future.

Her birthday.

32

Elliott

The door clattered open. The driver glanced in the rearview mirror. "Sorry, folks. End of service means this is the end of the line."

Amy nudged Elliott awake, and the two made their way down the aisle, stiff from sleeping on the unforgiving angles of a Washington Metro Area Transit Authority bus seat. Five blocks from Mercy General, Elliott had spotted the bus pulling up to the stop, and for a couple of bucks, they'd hopped on board and had a place to rest and warm themselves for half the night.

The driver stopped Elliott as they shuffled toward the steps off the bus. "Hey, man. There's a shelter on McCandless Street. About two, three miles up Reece. Wish I could take you there, but I gotta get back to the depot before one."

Elliott asked, "Is this Reece?"

"Yeah, man. This is Reece Boulevard." When they didn't say anything right away, the driver looked at them. "You're in Maryland—you know that, right? Up past Olney."

"Sure," Elliott said. "Is there a mall nearby?"

The man's eyes shot to the brim of his hat, but he said, "Washington Center." He pointed out the window. "That's the back of it. Follow the sidewalk until you get to Chambliss, then turn right. But it's closed, man. There's an all-night donut shop next door, but you know . . ."

"I get it," Elliott said. "We'll stay away from the donut shop."

Mumbling their thanks, they dropped off the last step to the curb. The pneumatics hissed to life and the bus shuddered, rising in fits and starts like an old man getting to his feet. Interior lights flickered twice, then went black before the engine roared to life and the bus pulled away, heading down the boulevard and rounding a turn. The engine's noise faded into the night. Elliott turned in place, taking stock.

They were alone at a bus stop, a lonely blister of plastic and steel sitting next to a four-lane boulevard that wanted badly to be a highway. A string of white streetlights ran in regimented order along one side of the road like a diamond necklace. Boxwoods and mulched dwarf pines lined the edges and central median of the throughway in immaculate rows, highlighting a landscaping that was simultaneously pristine and utterly barren.

He grimaced. They were in the suburbs, where life was segregated into discrete, manicured pods—home, school, work, store—but lacked any connective tissue. A city street was gritty, filthy, and usually dangerous, but at least life was *present*, jammed into every available open space, growling and snapping at the edges. Here, you could lie down to die in the three-inch grass, and your body would rot there until the landscaping crew showed up to trim the hedges.

Elliott glanced at Amy. She leaned against the metal post of the shelter, her head hanging down with her chin touching her chest. "You okay?"

She raised her head and nodded.

"We have to find something to eat, find a place to hole up for the night, then put together a plan for the morning."

"What are you talking about?" Amy asked, her voice cracking. "We don't have a car, my phone's dead, and after bus fare I've got all of three dollars in my wallet."

He gave her a brief smile. "I could make three bucks stretch all week. And I've got two, which makes five. Besides, if I know what I'm doing, we won't need to spend any of it."

She put her hands to either side of her head. "What we should be doing is trying to get back to my place."

"The cops have already looked at the CCTV cameras in the garage, which will show us trying to get into your car. They probably ran your plates and traced it back to your address before we'd gone two miles on that bus. I'd be surprised if there isn't a cruiser camped out there right now."

"Did we really do anything illegal?"

Elliott hesitated. "Jay was recovering from what was meant to be a fatal overdose, and opioid ODs are notoriously fickle. If he had some kind of relapse, and it was damaging or worse, we're the ones they'll blame."

"Oh my god. What if we killed him?"

"We don't know that anything we did hurt him," he said, trying to keep her calm. "But even if he recovered completely and is doing fine, the police would detain us and want to know what we were doing there. We don't have that kind of time."

"So we just got the answer we were looking for, and now we can't do anything about it."

He put a hand on her shoulder awkwardly. "One foot in front of the other, okay? We're not out of the game just yet."

Elliott coaxed her into trudging down the sidewalk with him, praying as they went that Reece Boulevard wasn't a regular beat for the local cops—the two of them, walking a lonely road after midnight and looking like they did, would be a sure pickup. But after fifteen minutes only a single car, going fast, passed them. Elliott caught the flash of a young face, tight with apprehension, eyes glued to the road: a teenager trying to make curfew.

Chambliss was another four-lane suburban highway, but where Reece was a connecting artery, this was the showcase, full of the mattress stores, fast-food joints, and other shops that cropped up in the real estate around American malls like mushrooms. The donut shop the bus driver had mentioned was right off the main drag in a strip with a convenience store and a kitchen appliance outlet. Two squad cars sat in the parking lot. Beyond it, bright lights beckoned customers to a grocery store, a bank, and a Japanese restaurant.

Elliott craned his neck back to take in the sign for the mall, a towering beacon that illuminated everything within a hundred feet, then glanced longingly at the tall, cream-colored walls—there'd be warm exhaust grates where the enormous building's heating was expelled, maybe a hidden nook behind a hedge or a low wall to curl up and sleep off the rest of the night. But it wasn't worth it. Circling the mall parking lots somewhere in a little SUV was a bored, underpaid security guard with a flashlight and a phone, just dying to have a reason to call the police.

"What are we looking for?" Amy asked as he steered them away from the mall.

"People tend to throw things away where they buy other things," he said. "Food, clothes, shoes, even electronics. We should be able to find a few things to get us through the night."

They skirted the edge of the mall and headed for the back of the grocery store. Wooden pallets and empty shopping carts shared space with bins and buckets and rattling grocery bags. Behind the Japanese teppanyaki restaurant was a small tub-shaped container with a sign that warned GREASE THEFT IS ILLEGAL.

Using a discarded milk crate as a stool, Elliott peered into one dumpster after another down the line before leading her to the next strip of stores. Amy watched as he pulled out undamaged packages of food, bunches of bananas, bottled water, and a quilted packing blanket covered in coffee grounds. For the next hour, they carefully and quietly sifted through trash cans and dumpsters, filling Elliott's knapsack and several plastic bags, but freezing at each noise, real or perceived.

"How old is your phone?" he called softly to Amy from inside the bin behind the convenience store.

"Old. Really old."

She jumped as he tossed something out of the bin to her, catching it instinctively. It was a phone charger still in its unopened plastic case. "Does that fit yours?"

Tilting the case one way and then the other, she tried to peer through the plastic to check the charger's plug. "Looks like it. Is there a generator in there, too?"

"Probably, but we have to scoot," he said, his head popping over the edge of the bin. "There are cameras on the outside of that bank."

"Oh my gosh." She looked down the alley of delivery bays and dumpsters.

"Take it easy. If they'd seen us, they would've sent one of the cops from the donut shop by now. But there's no reason to take chances."

Elliott crawled out of the bin and led them to the back of another building, a former car rental place by the looks of the peeling logo on the window. Next to a freight door was a raised outlet with weather guards on it. He plugged in the phone and was rewarded with a bloop-ing noise as the screen lit up green and white. He put the phone gently on the ground by the length of the charger cord and got Amy's help to slide several pallets and a barrel in front of the outlet to hide it.

"We'll have to leave it until morning," he said, "but we'll be coming back this way to grab the bus."

Amy slumped against a wall. "What's our plan, Elliott? I'm so tired, I'm going to pass out."

He gestured behind them. "All that junk in those stores has to come from somewhere, and all the customers who want the junk need access."

"So?"

"So, every mall in America is near a highway, every highway has an off-ramp, and every off-ramp needs an underpass."

"I don't like where this is going."

"We don't have much choice. It's two in the morning, we can't go back to your place, and we're miles from the nearest shelter." He spread his hands. "I've done it before, and it'll work for the next six or seven hours."

Amy shuddered, but helped Elliott grab several sheaves of cardboard from a bin, then followed him as he led the way to where Chambliss turned into a sweeping off-ramp of asphalt and concrete. The road was empty in both directions, but Elliott forced them to wait for a moment to be sure, then walked calmly across the intersection, scrambled up the steep bricked slope, and hopped onto the ledge made by the junction of road, slope, and abutment.

Elliott helped Amy clamber over the lip of the ledge. It was only high enough for a half squat. She peered into the darkness uneasily. "Are there rats?"

Elliott pulled out a lighter and held it high, waving it at the back of the shallow, cavelike opening. It was empty save for some gravel, a few pieces of masonry, and a hubcap.

He began laying out the items they'd liberated from the dumpsters. Dinner was two bananas and a peanut butter sandwich, with Graham crackers for dessert, washed down by water and a Gatorade. Elliott had also rescued two pairs of gloves, several winter hats, and three plastic ponchos. Seeing that Amy was shivering, he made her put on the hat and gloves and wrap herself in the freight blanket, then laid down the cardboard as a makeshift barrier against the grit and dirt.

"That's the best I can do," he said, then looked at her. "And, sorry, but the only way we're going to make it through the night is if we share that blanket."

She looked at him. "Are you serious?"

"Would it help if I told you I only want you for your heat?"

She laughed weakly. "I'm so tired, I don't think I'd care either way."

With some convoluted maneuvering, they managed to get into a position where they could simultaneously spoon while making the most out of the blanket. The ground under the cardboard was still cold and hard, but as Elliott wrapped his arms around Amy and put his head down on his knapsack, he felt like it wasn't the worst place he'd spent the night. He said good night to Cee Cee, waited, then sighed and closed his eyes at the silence.

◆ ◆ ◆

This is the way it happened.

They're at the playground. Elliott sits on a bench in the corner, his head in his hands. He agreed to take Cee Cee to the playground, but he's got the mother of all hangovers right now, having spent most of the night in the garage where he keeps his bottles.

"Daddy, look at me!"

He looks up and watches briefly as Cee Cee swings higher than she ever has before. "That's great, baby girl!" he croaks, but moving his head and speaking causes a fissure to split in his skull. His stomach churns, and he wonders if he's going to be sick. Across the mulched play area, a knot of parents huddle, coffees in hand, talking, and he knows he's the topic of conversation this morning. He grimaces and drops his head back into his hands.

"Come push me, Daddy!"

"In a second, honey," he calls. Unable to lift his head, he says it at the ground. The pain that had started in his temples is slipping along the sides of his head and meeting in the back to form a perfect crown of misery. Turning, he reaches into a jacket pocket and pulls out a flask.

He would laugh if it wouldn't hurt so much. A flask at eight in the morning. So trite, Dr. Nash. If he saw it in a movie, he'd walk out of the theater. But it's his life, so he has to stay.

A sip takes off the bleeding edge of the hangover, and five gulps flatten it completely. The last remaining atoms of his self-control keep him from emptying the flask. Cee Cee calls again and he holds up a finger—in a minute—when there's a screech and a wail from the other side of the playground.

He looks up despite the pain. A bundle of kids, trying to go down the sliding board at once, have tipped the entire contraption onto the ground. Children are crying. There are bloody scrapes and bruises. Parents rush over, are hovering, are upset. Elliott staggers to his feet and stumbles across the lot. Uncertain and unable to help, he stands stupidly, swaying in place as noses are wiped and tears blotted. He is mostly ignored, but a few of the parents shoot him looks of disgust—he hasn't been fooling anyone, sitting by himself in the corner.

Drunk and nauseous, he is worse than useless. He turns to go back.

Cee Cee isn't on the bench or on the swings.

She isn't in the playground.

She's gone.

33

Amy

Overhead, a truck rattled across the overpass in the darkness, shaking the struts of the bridge and dropping a cascade of grit and sand that hit her cheek before it skittered down the brick slope. Some instinct told her dawn wasn't far away. Behind her, Elliott's breathing was even and deep, light on her neck.

Amy waited as long as she could, then whispered his name. He stirred, took a sudden breath. "What?"

"Tell me about Cee Cee."

He stiffened. "Why?"

"You must've yelled her name a dozen times last night. You cried."

There was a long pause. His arms, wrapped around her for warmth, were sprung pieces of steel; then the tension in him seemed to melt away. His voice, low and rough, rumbled in her chest. "I told you. Cee Cee was my daughter."

"Tell me more."

"Why?"

"There's something about her you haven't told me. Something I think you want to say."

"Jesus. I don't need any of your New Age bullshit."

"Maybe not, but I need it. Please. I want to know," she said. "I need to know."

He groaned as though pushing a millstone off his chest; then a wash of cold air hit her back as he lifted his arm and peeled away, fumbling for a bottle of water. Amy rolled to face him, waiting. In the gloom, he was an indistinct, rounded shape: a head, shoulders, a torso. He raised a pale hand to his forehead, held it there.

"I don't want to talk about it."

"Please, Elliott," she said. Then again, "Please."

He sat cross-legged, his head cradled in his hand for so long that Amy thought he would simply refuse, that silence was his answer. She thought he might order her to leave, or tell her that he was leaving. Then he began talking.

"I told you about my parents, my childhood. By eighteen, I'd had enough summers of pick-your-own fruit and scoring weed for mom and dad. I wanted the normal life I saw on TV and in the magazines. I went away to school. Made it on scholarships and hard work. Filled a wall with psychology degrees, got a job at a university, found a wife. We had a daughter. We had Cee Cee."

He shifted, and his boot scraped the grit of the concrete floor.

"Life was good, but the job was unfulfilling. It seemed . . . trivial, running trials and writing papers. So, I adjusted course and got the training to go into forensic psych. I worked with police, testified at trials, made a name for myself. Colleagues told me I was doing important work, good work, but most of the time I didn't even know what the verdict was. It started to wear me down, and my big switch from the trivial to the meaningful started to look like a hell of a mistake. I'd started out hoping I was doing something noble, but the futility of it was . . . disheartening."

He picked up a piece of gravel and lobbed it over the ledge.

"Is it trite to say the work drove me to drink? Most alcoholics can give you a reason if you ask. Classic psychological projection. Shifting the blame. *It's not me. It's this shitty job, it's these rotten people, it's this goddamned world.* Everyone in the office, every cop I knew, had a vice, something that got them through. Why couldn't I?

"So, I drank and I worked and I soldiered on, doing the best I could. Or so I thought. I don't think the drinking ever affected my family, but that's a lie that drunks tell themselves. Luckily, work kept me out of the house most of the time. I put in extra hours in the office and on the bottle. My wife got sick of both and gave me a choice: straighten up or she'd leave and take Cee Cee with her."

His voice was bitter, and he ran a hand through his hair.

"I took some time off. I was a good dad, and for a little while, I was even sober. I took Cee Cee to soccer practice and the dentist and to the park. But by the end of the first week, I was taking a nip of booze before we left the house. By the end of the next, I was taking the bottle with me.

"We went to the park a lot. Cee Cee liked the monkey bars. One day, while I was half in the bag, a couple of kids fell off the slide and got banged up. Lots of screaming and crying. The parents jumped up to see what was wrong, giving hugs and wiping noses. When the dust had settled, I turned around and Cee Cee was gone."

Elliott said nothing for long, ponderous minutes. Dull dishwater light slowly filtered into their little nook. Finally, he coughed like an engine coming back to life.

"Dave led the investigation, ran himself into the ground. Weeks passed. But if I'd been drinking before because I was bored with my work, well, now I began drinking in earnest, like *that* was my job. Luckily, Dave and I had grown close, and there was more than one night he poured me into his car and took me home. They never found her body. Just her clothes, her blood, and Kerrigan's threats."

He sighed.

"Those times I was dry enough to focus, I read the case files obsessively, sifting through the letters and weights and numbers and descriptions. Kerrigan's psych profile. Notes and interview transcripts with him, my own and others. All of it, looking for an explanation. Why it happened to us. To Cee Cee. There were no answers. I blamed my wife for not being there. She blamed me for bringing us to Kerrigan's attention. We blamed each other because we had no one else. But I blamed myself most of all, because the *why* isn't really important. Bad things are going to happen. It's *how* you let them happen to you and what you do in response that matters. And what I did was let my little girl get killed because I was a goddamned drunk."

He raised his head to look at her. "What I said to you back at the bar was cruel. Selfish. Hypocritical. It was all aimed at myself. You were right, I don't have the capacity to forgive. Myself or anyone else. But no one deserves what happened to me, what you're going through. What you still might go through."

A horn honked in the distance, followed by the slow buzz of tires on asphalt that grew in volume until a car passed overhead. Silence followed it.

"Thank you," she said finally, or tried to say. "I understand now."

His voice, coming out of the gloom, was grating and thick. "None of my experience will help you. I have no lessons to teach you that you don't already know. We will find Lacey or we won't. The pain you feel now, this poisonous weight in your chest that wakes you up in the middle of the night, will either melt away or it will be dwarfed by what's to come. All I can tell you is I won't quit looking until we find her."

"I know," Amy said, her own voice rusty. She crawled over to Elliott, very close, and folded him in her arms. Hesitantly, he wrapped his arms around her, and they held each other until the light was full and bright.

34

Sister

The news was all over the office.

Did you hear? . . . on every channel . . . the Kelly boy, barely alive . . . behind an abandoned house. . . DC police.

Yes, she'd heard.

Yes, it was wonderful he'd been found alive.

Oh, he'd come through their office? No, she didn't recall the case. You know, so many children . . .

By the third person who'd accosted her, she couldn't take it anymore and sprinted to the bathroom, where she banged open the door to a stall and vomited, standing up, into the toilet. The woman in the next stall pawed at the toilet paper, hurrying to finish her business before heaving noises started again.

When she had the bathroom to herself, she collapsed on the floor, leaning her head against the bowl like a repentant drunk, not caring about the filth from the dozens of people who'd used it since that morning.

Charlie was alive.

The simple statement was the loose thread that signaled the unraveling of her life; she knew it. She'd never failed before, but of course her imagination had envisioned all kinds of outcomes if what she did to the children simply . . . failed.

And now she had her answer.

That child would talk to the police, who were unlikely to be curious about a failed overdose, at least initially. But eventually the truth of where he or she had been for the last four years would burst forth like water from a dam, sweeping away not just her, but all she'd done and all she'd ever do for the children to come.

Talked to the police? She groaned and put a hand to her head, feeling as though it was about to split.

How stupid could she have been? Surely it was Charlie her brother had been talking about over lunch, the boy he'd been so proud to save from the nearly fatal overdose. Of all the people . . . how was it that *he'd* been the one to find one of hers? And what if he was the one who would talk to Charlie, discover the truth about where the young man had been all this time? What if he was on his way to the old house right now? She began to shake at the implications.

Was this how Mother had felt? Abandoned by her husband, saddled with an army of children, her future an endless downward drop? No choices, no hope, nothing. Small wonder she'd snapped, killing everyone around her—had she'd thought of it as an act of mercy, at the end?—and finally, taking her own life. The motivations of a woman she'd spend a lifetime failing to comprehend now seemed clear and lucid.

"Enough." She pushed away from the toilet, getting unsteadily to her feet, then staggered out to a sink, where she splashed water in her face. The door to the bathroom opened and a few sharp footsteps sounded on the porcelain tile, but she didn't bother to look, simply stared at the haggard face looking back, the tight, pinched lines around her lips, mouth, and eyes. Dark brown eyes, her mother's eyes, stared back at her.

Mother probably said the same that day, telling herself to pull it together, didn't she? Just before—

"Stop it! Stop it, stop it, stop it." She slapped herself in time to the words, crying, and the footsteps retreated. Breathing in gasps, she grimaced into the reflection. Spit trailed down from her lips, and the little bit of lipstick she wore was smeared like a clown's.

Closing her eyes, she rested her head against the mirror, the ghost of her mother vibrant and alive in her mind. With a supreme effort, she pushed against the living memory, forcing it into a corner, visualized pushing it into a box that became smaller and smaller as she willed. Her mother shrank from a towering vision to a speck that eventually wailed as it vanished from sight.

Raising her head, she confronted the face in the mirror.

Mother was gone.

It was just her. Only her.

She spat, gargled, and spat again.

Mother had given into her fate, but there was no reason she had to. She would not destroy herself, nor was it certain that anyone else would.

What, after all, could Charlie actually tell her brother or the police? Nothing. The young man knew her face to see her, of course, but what were the chances their paths would cross again? Why would the police—even if they believed the half-crazed story of an apparent teen drug addict—bring him back here, of all places? They'd question the family and friends and the strangers who had visited the wealthy Kelly home. The case would be further complicated by the parents' high-profile, society-page squabbling and acrimonious divorce.

She had to restrain herself, certainly. No more rescues, not for a while. But that was easily done—new Charlie was quite docile, and her other siblings were all nicely behaved. Well, almost all of them. Charlotte, with her sideways looks and the sly rebellion in the eyes, had not been behaving lately. The girl was . . . recalcitrant. Willful.

She pushed on those feelings, examined her own emotions regarding Charlotte . . . and realized she didn't feel the same love for the girl that she once had. She seemed like a stranger, not really like family anymore.

Was it her time, as well? Regardless, could she take the risk and . . . transition the girl, so close to the other? Would the public believe another almost-teenage overdose on the heels of Jay Kelly's?

Of course they would.

The world was full of abusive parents and neglected children and drug-addicted kids who'd been thrown to the street. In fact, there was nothing for the public *to* believe; it happened every day. And while the likes of a Kelly family heir might make the news, another foster child gone wrong would be lucky to make the back page of the newspaper, never mind spark a police investigation.

In fact, she thought as she dabbed at her mouth with a paper towel, wouldn't it be better to do it now, while the region's attention was locked on the Kelly family? She'd never held two birthday parties in a month, never rushed things, but she had felt Charlotte slipping away for some time now, and when she unlocked her own heart and looked inside, deep inside, she saw the well was nearly dry. To her, the girl was less like Charlotte than she was like herself. Really, wasn't that the final, and most important, criteria?

It was worth considering. Once done, she could lay low and dedicate herself to caring for the brothers and sisters she already had. Resist the temptation to save any more, at least not right away. In time, the public would forget, as it always did, about the children who were thrown away or ran away or were scared away.

And when they were, she'd be there to help them, as she always had and always would.

35

Elliott

By seven thirty, they'd made their way, stiff and sore, back to the strip of malls and stores, eating another meal of bananas and peanut butter sandwiches on the way. They picked up Amy's now fully charged phone behind the defunct car rental building and, in exchange for buying a Coke, the kid at the corner gas station let them take turns washing up in the bathroom.

At the bus stop on Reece, Elliott studied the wall-mounted route map and schedule. He poked through their pool of money. "We're going to need some luck and a hell of a lot of walking to get there."

"Get where?"

"Old Town."

"Why there?"

He shrugged. "I know it. I have friends there. Might even get us a place to stay."

"Better than an underpass?"

He smiled. "A little bit."

"Then I'm in." She looked at the money in his hand. "How far can we get on what we have?"

"I promise we can get on the bus," he said. "After that, we'll have to see."

The bus, empty of passengers, pulled up a few minutes before ten. Tickets for the two of them ate up the rest of their cash, but the driver gave them a nod and they tottered to a seat in the back before the bus jerked into motion and headed down the road.

Amy stared at the seat in front of her. "I feel like we know everything and nothing. Lacey is alive, but we don't know where. We know the children are being kidnapped, but we don't know by whom. We know all the kids had a connection, but we don't know what. And we can't go to the police with any of it because either they won't believe us or they'll arrest us on sight."

Elliott was looking out the window, watching the suburban landscape pass by. "When Lacey was . . . taken into foster care, how did it happen?"

Amy, her face stricken, said, "Why would you ask that now?"

He turned to her, contrite. "I'm sorry, Amy. I'm not asking to hurt you. It's a painful subject, I know, but your answers might actually help us."

"Okay," she said doubtfully. "What do you want to know?"

"Tell me the step-by-step process. You can give me just the overview, but don't skip anything."

She swallowed painfully. "Someone must've reported me as an . . . an unfit mother. A CPS worker came out and talked to me, then talked to Lacey. I thought things were okay and I thought I'd dodged a bullet, you know? I promised to get straight; then CPS came out the next morning and took Lacey away."

"Was it the same officer?"

"No."

Elliott frowned. "Hmm. Did you have a hearing?"

"Yes, almost right away. I . . . wasn't in good shape. When they took her, I fell apart and popped a pill to get back on my feet. I didn't realize I'd get a chance to represent myself and I—" She started to shake.

"You were high? At the hearing?"

"Yes," she said, miserable. "And it was obvious. Lacey went into foster care straight from the courtroom."

"Was this downtown? DC Superior?"

"Yes," she said, surprised. "How did you know?"

"I used to testify all the time, remember? Almost never in the juvenile courts, but I walked by them almost every day. And I know foster kids in the District have to go through a review called a CHINS hearing—child in need of services." He thought for a moment. "In fact, if I remember correctly, there's a special stable of judges just for CHINS cases. Do you remember who your judge was?"

"Even high, I'd remember," she said, bitter. "Susan Cranston. Bitch."

The bus made a wide turn, and they swayed in their seat. "Who else was present at the hearing? Literally, in the room?"

Amy made a face. "I barely remember it. There were lawyers and the CPS officer and some clerks, I guess."

"Did you recognize anyone? Had you seen any of them before?"

"The CPS officers who came to the house gave a statement, but everyone else was a complete stranger." She gave him a curious look. "Why all the questions?"

Elliott pressed himself back in the seat. "I have a theory, but I need one more piece of information. Let me see your phone."

◆ ◆ ◆

Dave

Dave was driving home, but he closed his eyes and pinched the bridge of his nose between a forefinger and thumb anyway.

He'd shot the day working just one case. A brother, six, and a sister, eight, children of an abusive father, had been reported missing by a neighbor in northwest DC. By some miracle, Tony had found the brother hiding in a gutter, and it had taken the two of them an hour to talk him out. But there was no sign of the sister, and the son-of-a-bitch father wasn't talking despite their best good-cop, bad-cop, fire-and-brimstone routine. Tony had finally told Dave to go home while he kept on the case, agreeing they could switch in the morning. He'd promised he'd call if he dug something up in the meantime.

So when Dave's phone rang he snatched at it, convinced it was Fracasso with something to tell him. "Cargill."

"Dave." The voice on the other end was scratchy and thick. "It's Elliott."

Horns blared behind him as he nearly drove his car off the road. "Elliott? What are you doing? Where are you? Half of the Metro area is looking for you and Amy Scowcroft."

"Is Jay Kelly . . ." Elliott paused. "How is he?"

"He had a seizure, but they got it under control. The parents are out for blood, naturally, wanting to know how two complete strangers managed to get in to see their kid and attack him."

"Attack him? All we did was talk to him for ten minutes."

"This might come as a surprise to you, but they're a little touchy about their kid right now. What were you thinking, going in there?"

"We were thinking we had to find Lacey Scowcroft. And Jay Kelly had the information we needed."

Baffled, Dave asked, "What could he possibly know about the girl?"

"Amy and I saw the news report about Jay on TV. In it, the reporter hinted that, before Jay disappeared, his parents had a rough divorce. When we looked him up in Amy's notes, we found that Jay had been in foster care, which said to me that things might've gotten so bad that there was a child endangerment hearing."

"You think his *parents* had something to do with his disappearance?"

"No, that's not it. They may be lousy parents, but they didn't put their kid on the street. I want to know what court the Kelly hearing was in."

"The court?" he asked, confused. "Why does that matter?"

"We played a hunch, Dave. And we were right. Amy was right. Jay Kelly wasn't a runaway, and he wasn't living on the streets. He was kidnapped."

"*What?* He told you that?"

"Yes. And he wasn't the only one, there were four other kids being held with him, kidnapped by someone he called 'Sister.'"

"These kids . . . what? Just disappeared?"

"More or less. In each case, the kid ran away, was a throwaway, or simply vanished. Then one or two or three years later, they turn up dead somewhere in the greater Metro or Baltimore area, probably of an overdose of a street drug or exposure."

"Come on, Elliott. A rash of murdered kids? We would've caught some kind of whiff of that."

"How much time do you spend on a runaway or a kid that isn't reported missing for a month? Especially one that's found dead of an overdose? Fifteen minutes? Half an hour?"

Dave was silent.

"Look," Elliott said, "I know this is a lot to swallow, but think about it. Each abduction was separated by months or even years. Same with the murders. There's almost no pattern if you aren't looking for it. But the pattern is there. And before Jay had his seizure, he confirmed it."

"Even if I believe you, how does this get back to the courts?"

"The one connection all of these kids have is that they came from dysfunctional, broken homes—runaways, throwaways, the whole gamut. Almost all of them ended up in foster care. Even when they didn't, I'm guessing every one of them brushed up against CPS at some point, then went missing not long after."

"You think someone in CPS is targeting these kids once they see them?"

"CPS or the court system at large. A social worker, a guard, an admin," Elliott said. "Maybe even one of the ad litem attorneys or a judge who sees the kid at a CHINS hearing. Somewhere in the chain, from the point where the CPS officer visits the house to the final review that sends a kid to foster care, there's someone who sees a vulnerable kid—maybe especially one no one will miss—and takes them."

Dave laughed without humor. "You want me to brace a DC judge on multiple charges of child kidnapping?"

"I was just throwing out possibilities. I don't know if it's a judge. There must be fifty different people who see those kids before they land in foster care. The important thing is to narrow it down, which is why we need you to check those records. If we can find out which court these particular kids had their review in, we might be able to find the kidnapper."

"Because the court records will have a list of all the parties present," Dave said slowly, piecing it together. "The CPS officer who did the investigation, the judge that made the decision, the ad litem attorneys who represented both sides."

"Exactly."

"And you don't have access to the records."

"They don't often grant access to DC court records down at the shelter, no," Elliott said drily. "But a cop who works for Youth and Family Services, on the other hand . . ."

"Jesus, you don't ask for much, do you?"

"Lacey Scowcroft's life is on the line. I'll do whatever I have to get her back."

"You bought in all the way, huh?" Dave asked gently.

"With everything I got," Elliott said. "So, can you help us?"

"That depends. What are you going to do in the meantime?"

"Amy and I are trying to lay low," Elliott said evasively. "We'll hole up until we hear from you."

"Speaking of which," Dave said, "you really *are* on the wire, my man. Assault and battery, endangering a minor, probably ten other things. I'm breaking all kinds of rules just talking to you."

"I know. But we're close. We need to see this through."

Dave sighed, grumbled. "Look, let me pick you up and bring you in. It'll give you a chance to explain everything you've told me. I'll vouch for you, and we can clear this thing up and really get down to finding Lacey."

"I'm sorry, Dave. There's no guarantee they'll see our side of things. Even if they do, you know as well as I do it'll take a week before we're done talking to everyone who wants a piece of us. Lacey's running out of time."

"I sort of hoped you trusted me more."

"It's the system that I don't trust, not you. Please. Can you get us what we need to know or not?"

Dave groaned. "Elliott, getting you some files from the archive is one thing. Scouring court records so you can chase down a CPS officer or a judge and do what? Make a citizen's arrest? I just don't know."

"I know it's a huge ask."

"Huge doesn't begin to cover it."

Elliott took a deep breath. "Dave, I've never really called in a favor like this since Cee Cee's death—"

"God, Elliott—"

"Please, Dave. This is it. This is why I spent eight years on the streets. This is my chance to do some good in the world again, to make just being here worthwhile. But I need your help to do it."

Dave let the line fall silent for a full minute. Finally, "No promises. But I'll look, okay? Keep the phone handy, and don't break into any more hospital rooms."

"I promise. Thanks, Dave."

They hung up and he tossed his phone in the cup holder.

Jay Kelly.

The boy he'd saved in Trinidad. From just another near casualty in the opioid war to the long-lost scion of a wealthy family to maybe the goddamn missing link to finding Lacey Scowcroft.

Jay Kelly.

An image flashed in his mind: the pale, almost greenish face. The strange, poorly fitting clothes. The ridiculous cowboy shirt the boy had been wearing. The robin's egg blue plaid. The white stitching, looping and swirled. Now, in his mind, a picture of it worn not by Jay, not thin and patched and too short by inches, but newly bought, appeared strong and clear in his memory. So strong, in fact, that *I know what that shirt smells like,* he realized in shock. *I know what it feels like.*

Horns blared again. He'd taken his foot off the gas and coasted to under twenty-five on the Beltway, a capital crime to commuters in the District. But this time he didn't care, letting the angry drivers swarm around him, swearing and shouting as they passed. Tears began to stream down his face as a tumult of emotions flooded him.

How? How do I know this?

His sister would know, he thought. She was older than he was, if only by a bit, and had forced herself to remember so many of the things he'd made himself forget. The keeper of the family secrets, he'd called her jokingly one time, but now he'd be grateful if she could put a name to this image in his head.

He picked his phone up from the cup holder and punched in her office number. She was gone for the day, but he could leave a message. Suggest they get together for another lunch.

◆ ◆ ◆

Elliott

"He's going to help us?" Amy asked.

Elliott rolled his head on the seat to look at her. "Yes. Your first intuition about him was right. Dave's a good guy."

"Won't it take time for him to find that information?"

"No doubt."

"Elliott, Lacey's running out of time," Amy said, her voice rising. "We can't just hide until he gets back in touch."

"We're not."

"We're not?" She blinked when he shook his head. "We're not going to Old Town?"

"Oh, we're going to Old Town. We need the break. But then we're heading to DC."

She looked at him, baffled, then said, "Susan Cranston."

He nodded. "We need Dave's info, but there's no reason to sit still while he gets it. Cranston is the one name we have in hand, the judge who presided over your hearing. While Dave digs up those court records, we can start poking around. We might get lucky or we might turn up exactly nothing, but at least we won't be wasting the one thing we don't have. Time."

36

Charlotte

The trips back and forth to the bathroom took forever. Not for herself, but to wash the blood from the rags. There was also a spot on the sheets that she had to clean, which she did by shuttling her single washcloth back and forth from the sink. With five of them vying for the bathroom, it was easiest just to wait until everyone was done and had headed downstairs for breakfast. She was risking Sister's anger, but it was better than the alternative.

The stain on the sheets was incredibly stubborn. She tried to blot it, then scrub it, but nothing had an effect. She pulled the corner of the sheet up and reached her hand under in an attempt to get at it from both sides, rubbing frantically, stymied at how the blood could still be present in a piece of fabric so old and so thin she could see her hand through the other side.

"What are you doing?"

Charlotte whipped around. Sister stood in the doorway, seeming to fill the entire space.

"I was . . . I was just . . ." Charlotte groped for a plausible explanation. "Maggie wet the bed, Sister. I was trying to clean it up before breakfast."

"Oh, really? Let's see," Sister said with a raised eyebrow, coming into the room and revealing Maggie standing behind her, her face tear streaked and red. Charlotte's heart sank.

Charlotte stood in front of the bed. "I'm just finishing—"

"Move."

"It's not her fault, Sister," Charlotte said, her voice breaking, but she gasped as Sister grabbed her by the arm and yanked her away from the bed, sending her crashing into the small dresser she and Maggie shared.

Sister looked down at the sheets and the large blotch of damp fabric, the darker stain in the middle, scarlet when she'd started, now dun colored. Sister stared at the sheets for a long minute.

"How long?" Sister asked without turning around, her voice like a whip.

"I'm sorry, Sister. I should've told you—"

"How *long*?"

Charlotte swallowed. "Two months."

"I see."

Her pulse pounded in her ears. "I was going to tell you, Sister, but I didn't want to alarm you."

The older woman turned and looked at her, but the face was slack and flat, strangely unreadable for a woman who let almost every emotion show. It was an expression of distance and separation, and Charlotte had the distinct feeling she was in a different category of *thing* now. A prickling sensation ran from her scalp to the backs of her legs.

"It doesn't alarm me," Sister said, her voice preternaturally calm. "You're becoming a woman. It's a special occasion. We should celebrate."

Charlotte confused, shook her head. "What?"

"Your birthday is almost here, isn't it?"

"I don't know," she said in a whisper.

"Oh, it is," Sister said, looking at her with her inert face, her vacant eyes. "Which means we should plan on a party, don't you think?"

Without another word, she turned and left the room, her low heels clacking on the hardwood floor. She brushed past Maggie, who looked at Charlotte with dread. She took two short steps into the room.

"Why, Maggie?" she asked, her heart breaking at the betrayal. "Why did you tell her?"

"I'm sorry, Charlotte," the little girl said, her lower lip trembling. "I didn't want you to go. You said you were going to leave us and I thought if Sister . . . if Sister . . . punished you, you'd stay."

The last few words came out as a wail. Maggie turned and ran down the hall to the bathroom, slamming the door behind her.

Charlotte let her go, then sat down at the edge of the bed and put her head in her hands. It didn't matter what Maggie told Sister or the others—that she'd schemed to escape, that she'd hoped to get help for them all, that she knew the ultimate fate of all of the children brought to the house—because none of it mattered. It was only a matter of days or weeks before, like Charlie, she had her party, fell asleep, then was dragged down the steps and into the night.

37

Elliott

Amy and Elliott shuffled down King Street, past hotels and tasting rooms, posh restaurants and boutique stores selling finishing oils and French antiques, looking like old soldiers back from the front.

The trip from Olney to Alexandria, an hour by car, had taken them three days. With almost no money and the constant threat of being picked up by the police hovering over their heads, the journey had been a mishmash of walking, hitchhiking, and hiding. They'd slept under a bridge, in a foreclosed home, and in front of a church. Meals had been dumpster leftovers and whatever they could find along the way.

On the second day, Dave called, repeating his request that they turn themselves in and let him help them. Elliott refused, asking only if he'd managed to figure out which court Jay Kelly had gone through. Dave told them he was working on it.

The waste of time and growing sense of urgency had Amy frantic until a kind tourist couple had given them a pair of Metro passes, useless to someone on their way out of town. Despite the cameras and local police in every station, they decided the risk was worth it and took the last leg of the journey by subway, pulling into Old Town Alexandria on an uncommonly sunny Sunday morning.

Tourists in barn jackets and distressed jeans thronged the sidewalk, taking advantage of the late autumn blush of warm weather. The crowd wanted to be happy, Elliott could see, and a ragamuffin homeless couple weren't making that easy, so the people on the street walked and looked and laughed past the two as if they didn't exist.

It had been a simple fact of his existence for years, but he could see it was a shock to Amy. A week ago she'd walked down this street and been part of the group, accepted and understood. Judged, perhaps, maybe even sneered at, but she'd still been *seen*.

He waited for a lull in foot traffic. "Strange feeling, isn't it?"

"I'm . . . I'm invisible," Amy said. "If they weren't afraid of catching a disease, they'd walk right into me."

Elliott stepped around a family of four cooing at a Labrador puppy being walked by two well-scrubbed thirtysomethings. "It's why some homeless yell or curse people out. They're not crazy; they just want someone to acknowledge they exist."

They continued east down King. Commerce was everywhere, succeeding and failing in waves. A medieval-themed restaurant had a HELP WANTED sign right below CLOSED PERMANENTLY written in white grease pencil. One door down was an empty storefront promising an Italian eatery, coming soon. Next to that was a skinny blue building no wider than a man with outspread arms. Hanging from curlicued ironwork was an ornate shingle for an art gallery, open by appointment only.

Three blocks later, they came within sight of a large colonial-looking building that took up the entire block. An American flag snapped from a narrow cupola atop the building. A large courtyard, a fountain in its center, spread before the building, packed with tents and market stalls. Christmas wreaths festooned with red and gold balls hung from lampposts while evergreen garlands decorated the sides of all the tents. Sweating profusely, a man sold roasted chestnuts in the unseasonably hot weather. Hundreds of people milled about the square, lingering in front of the tents, pushing strollers, and getting in each other's way.

"A Christmas market?" Amy asked doubtfully.

"Just wait."

Trucks and vans—some held together by duct tape and a wish—lined the street around the square. From the corners, street performers blew on trumpets and trombones, strummed guitars, sang opera, all of them trying to be heard over barking dogs that had been leashed to light posts and parking meters. A large woman in pink Reeboks sat on a camp chair on the King Street sidewalk, twenty feet outside the confines of the market itself but close enough to be in the flow of feet heading toward the tents. Next to her was a stack of local newspapers. As pedestrians passed, she would hold up one or two, hawking them for a buck apiece. Elliott headed straight for her.

"Hey, Mama," he said with a tired smile as they walked up.

The woman's pumpkin-round face lit up and a smile split her face. "Elliott!"

He leaned over and gave her a hug. "How's business?"

"Terrible. Everyone gets the news on their little black boxes these days." She squinted over his shoulder. "Who's your friend?"

"This is Amy." Elliott gave a half turn. "Amy, Mama Cass."

Amy shot him an amused look, then surprised the woman by giving her a hug. "How are you, Mama?"

"Better than average," she said, then gave Amy an appraising look. "I seen you before. At Francis House. You weren't there for breakfast."

"That's right," Amy said, surprised. "I can't believe you remember."

"She remembers everything," Elliott said. "I hate to ask, Mama, but we're in a pinch."

"You need a place?"

"Just a night, two at the most."

Her expression turned sour, and she gave him a look that slid off his face to include Amy. "I don't truck with no fooling around, Elliott. You want that, you'll have to go elsewhere."

"We're not . . . together, Mama. Amy's looking for her little girl." He explained their mission in a few sentences. "We're just in a tight spot right now."

Mama searched his face for something. After a moment, she nodded, satisfied. "All right. You can stay. Two nights. You know where the key is."

"I do." He squeezed her arm. "I appreciate it."

"Get going. You're scaring the customers away," Mama said, making a shooing motion with one of the papers. "Don't forget, it's T-shirt day at the Chase Shelter. You could use a sprucing up."

"Thanks, Mama."

"One more thing!" She dug into a fanny pack almost hidden by her belly, then came out with a crumpled fistful of dollars, grimy and looking like the leaves of a dead plant. "Get me something special while you're out, okay?"

Elliott took the money reluctantly. "You're sure, Mama?"

The smile was still in place, but her eyes were shining. "I'm sure, honey. Leave it in the fridge."

Elliott nodded and led them away from the market, gesturing toward a side street. "Let's get off King Street. The cops get a little feisty on market day."

"What was that about a place to stay?"

"Mama looks the part, but she isn't homeless. She's had a house up past the train station for as long as anyone can remember. She inherited it after her husband died years ago."

"A *house*? You're kidding me. Why is she panhandling?"

"She exhibits signs of untreated depression, which has probably kept her from holding down a job for most of her life. With the house falling into her lap, she ended up house rich but cash poor. So, she hangs out at the shelters and sells newspapers on the corner to buy booze and a few other things."

"And she lets you crash at her house?"

"Not just me and not often. She trusts a handful of street people and lets them stay, but never for more than a few nights. She knows people need a hand up once in a while. It'll give us a chance to shower and get a decent night's sleep."

"A night?" Amy's face was stricken. "Elliott, Lacey doesn't have much time. We've wasted days already."

"I know. Believe me, I know. But we look like hell, and if we show up at a courthouse in that condition, we'll get thrown out on our ear. Or worse, they'll hold us and look around for a BOLO that matches our description."

"But, we go to DC tomorrow, right?"

"Yes," he said, smiling grimly. "Tomorrow we go find who kidnapped Lacey."

38

Amy

The shower hadn't been cleaned this millennium—the mud-colored ring around the lip of the porcelain tub said so—while the soap, powdered and in a cardboard box, had the strength and smell of industrial lye. An unidentifiable smell rose from the drain, and the water that came out of the showerhead between a trickle and fire hose strength was hot enough to blister skin when it wasn't ice cold.

And it was pure bliss.

Amy stood under the stream of water for what seemed an eternity, unable to scrub enough, or relax enough. In just a few short days on the street, her hair was tied in knots, while grit and dirt were ground deep into her pores and into the seams of her skin. Sleeping in your clothes under a highway overpass would do that to you. Which meant that Elliott must have felt infinitely worse.

A wave of guilt rolled over her. Elliott was in Mama's living room, waiting patiently for his turn in the shower. She sighed once, then twirled the dial on the shower and watched with regret as the flow slowed to a steady stream of fat drops. She dried off using the threadbare towels, smelling of mothballs and must, she'd found in a linen closet, then slipped on her jeans and sweatshirt. Underwear and bra would have to wait until they had a turn in the sink. She caught a glimpse of herself in the cracked and crazed mirror, a quick flash of sunken eyes and long, wet hair, before she jerked her head away.

Cracking the door open by hooking her finger in the hole where the knob should be, she yelled, "Elliott! Batter up!"

There was no answer. She slipped her shoes on and headed down the hallway. If they'd been any farther south, Mama's house would be called a shotgun shack, a skinny little thing two stories tall but only five big steps wide, with a living room and kitchen on the first floor, two bedrooms and a bath on the second. Big enough for a family of eight around the Industrial Revolution, too small for modern resale, it was just right for a single aging welfare lady and the occasional houseguest.

The house smelled of damp wood and Vicks VapoRub, old frying grease and dirt in the corners. From the kitchen counters to the front porch, there wasn't a level surface in the house, and the walls were so crooked that she had the urge to tilt her head as she walked. She held the banister with both hands as she went down the steps for fear of pitching over the railing.

She followed soft voices to the living room, where Elliott perched on the corner of a sagging velour couch the color of forest moss, while Mama, balancing a wide-mouthed Mason jar on top of her belly with both hands, sat embedded in a blue pin-striped, overstuffed chair. Paperback books held up a corner of the chair where a foot should be.

Elliott raised an eyebrow as she walked in, and Mama beamed to see her. "Feeling better, hon?"

"Incredible, thank you."

"Oh, I'm so happy," she said, wriggling in the chair. "I have trouble with those stairs myself. It's been a while since I've been able to do anything except use the powder room down here. Nothing a little bit of flower water won't cover up, but it's nice to hear someone can make use of this old house."

Amy moved to sit on the couch near Elliott, lighting on the edge of the frame to make sure she didn't sink into the unknown depths of the velour. "I thought you had people over from time to time, Mama."

"I used to, but you and Elliott are the first in quite a while. A few weeks ago, I let Coco and Kirby stay here—you know them, Elliott, they used to hang around the train station on King Street. They helped themselves to my bottle without asking, and I told them to get out if that's how they were going to pay me back. They didn't like that at all."

Elliott frowned. "Were they any trouble?"

"Not really." Mama pushed up a sleeve of her jacket, revealing a yellowing bruise with purple center about the size of a lemon. She looked at it critically, but without rancor. "Coco put this on me when I told him to leave. My circulation isn't what it used to be, so these things take a while to fade."

"Oh my god," Amy said, staring at the bruise. "You're lucky they didn't kill you."

"Luck had nothing to do with it," Mama said. Reaching down into the cushion of the chair, she pulled out a blue-steel revolver in a single, smooth motion. Elliott swore as they sat back instinctively. Mama laughed out loud. "Easy, children. Don't take my juice or talk politics and we'll be fine."

Elliott looked at her uneasily. "Is that thing loaded?"

"Is it loaded?" She laughed. "What good is a gun without bullets? My goodness, Harold would've gone through the roof if he thought I'd held on to his gun but didn't keep it working."

"Harold?" Amy asked.

"My husband, dear. Gone twenty-nine years ago last month." Tears suddenly appeared in her eyes, spilling over and down the cherubic cheeks. Ice clinked as she took a long pull from her glass, draining half of it. When she spoke again, her voice was thick. "We've been apart longer than we were together. Can you imagine?"

She held her glass toward Elliott, who reached down to a paper bag on the floor next to the couch and filled her glass from the bottle inside. Mama took another long pull, then sighed and tilted a look at them. "Speaking of Harold, once you get cleaned up, Elliott, I want you to look through the closet in the back. There are some things of Harold's I can't use—imagine that!—and you could."

"Oh, we couldn't—" Elliott began, but she cut him off.

"I'm not talking about a pair of work pants, sonny." Her voice was tart. "Didn't you just tell me you were going to court or something like it?"

"Yes," he said reluctantly.

"Do you think they're going to let you in wearing a T-shirt? You won't get anywhere if you show up looking like you fell off the back of a caboose. Just take a look in the closet in the back, the tall one near the window." Mama looked at Amy. "Same for you, missy. There are some old things of mine in the other room that I haven't been able to fit into since before Nixon was president."

Elliott smiled. "Thank you, Mama."

"You're so welcome, honey," she said, smiling, but her eyelids dropped to half-mast, then bounced upward only to sink again. She roused enough to take another pull from the glass. Some of the liquor dribbled down her chin to blot on the neck of her fleece. "Haven't been able to help anyone since my little boy left. Miss helping people. Feels good . . ."

Another tear spilled down her cheek as her voice trailed off, her eyes closing completely. Elliott leaned forward in time to catch the glass just as it slipped out of her hands, then placed it on the end table next to the chair. Mama's head fell forward slightly, coming to rest on her many chins. Soft snores rose from her as her hands slid off her belly, stopping perfectly on the arms of her chair.

Amy looked at Elliott, an unspoken question on her lips.

He shrugged. "I don't think Harold or her son had a happy ending. This is how she deals with it."

They watched the old woman sleep peacefully for a moment, before Amy cleared her throat. "Maybe now's a good time for you to take your shower."

He gave her a small smile. "I thought hippies liked earthy smells."

"Earthy, sure. Latrinelike, not so much."

"A rose by any other name."

"Rose is not the word that came to mind."

"Okay, I can take a hint."

"Easier than taking a whiff."

"All right, all right. I'm going," he said, laughing quietly. "Will you watch her? I know this is her routine, but I'd still feel better if someone were here."

"Of course."

Elliott crept away, careful not to wake Mama, but from what Amy could see, it would take a twenty-one gun salute to rouse the woman. Cracks and pops and creaks accompanied Elliott as he climbed the stairs and crossed to the bathroom, followed by the rattle, bang, and dull roar as water rushed through the metal pipes of the decrepit house.

She smothered a groan at the ache in her back. Her short experience with street life had been taxing, and she wondered how Elliott—or any homeless person—managed it, prompting her to promise silently to never complain about her futon again. Even Mama's couch, with the spring prodding her in the butt and the spar of the wooden frame running along her spine, was heaven compared to the benches and sidewalks they'd slept on. She pushed back into the depths of the couch and felt herself relax.

Physically, at least.

Mentally, a clock was running in her head that wouldn't stop, a buzz-saw countdown to Lacey's birthday. Everything they'd done had been necessary, but that didn't make it any easier to watch as the hours slipped by, taking Lacey's chances with them. Anxiety had nearly eaten her up over the last few days . . . at least until exhaustion had made it impossible to care about much except putting one foot in front of the other. She was telling herself to stay focused and calm when she fell asleep.

The sound of someone clearing their throat woke her. She sat up, fuzzy and dumb with sleep, but her eyes popped open as they focused on the man standing in front of her.

Clean-shaven cheeks revealed a narrow, square chin with a dimple in the center. The face was all angles, with sharp trenches running from the prominent cheeks to the bones of his jaw, while the long, aquiline nose only added to his piercing look. Poker-straight hair was combed back in a wave that hung almost to his shoulders, though a lone strand fell into his eyes that he brushed away irritably. He wore a summer-weight charcoal gray suit with a slim black tie and a white shirt. Black wingtips over black socks completed the ensemble.

Elliott tugged at the sleeve at his wrist, an unconsciously sophisti-cated move straight out of a boardroom or a Wall Street office. "What do you think?"

Before she could answer, there was a snort next to her and she glanced over. Mama was awake and looking at Elliott like he'd dropped from the sky. "Oh my word, you look good enough to eat, Elliott."

Amy smothered a smile. With no beard to hide it, Elliott's blush rose from his neck all the way to his hairline.

"We're going to court, not a fashion show," he growled, then turned and headed back upstairs.

Amy caught Mama's eye, and they both gave in to long peals of laughter.

39

Elliott

The Moultrie building was simultaneously nondescript and imposing, a function of both its practical use—taking care of legal matters on a daily basis—and its intent: intimidating people. Solid vertical blocks of gray-white granite and narrow, tinted windows looking like massive arrow slits gave the building the appearance of a tower or castle. The angular construction seemed part of the message: the justice dispensed inside would be straightforward, unbending, severe.

Elliott looked at the building from the curb on Indiana Avenue, unable to move. Since hitting the streets all those years ago, he'd scrupulously avoided this place, knowing that just seeing it again had the power to unhinge him. And he wasn't wrong.

From the moment they'd came up the Metro escalator at Judiciary Square, raw, unexamined memories had swept right through the shell he'd painstakingly created around himself, battering him like an artillery barrage. Each step from there to here—the walk past the bronze lions of the stirring but melancholy National Law Enforcement Officers Memorial, through the manicured lawns of the DC court system, alongside the Metropolitan Police Department headquarters—triggered memories of a previous life.

Not all were bad. Most of his professional triumphs had occurred within a block of where he stood, many of them in the building across the street. But that same edifice was where he'd sat in the gallery, watching as John Jeffery Kerrigan was tried and sentenced for the abduction and murder of his daughter.

Although he told himself the two things had nothing to do with each other, his mind strove to force a connection, attempting to link the aggregate of who he had been as a person with the single most important, and tragic, event of his life. But if they were supposed to add up to something, he couldn't see it. He was blind to whatever the universe was trying to tell him, a sad, broken man tapping a stick in the dark, trying to find the edges of things.

"Elliott?" Amy was looking at him, concern etched on her face.

"I'm fine. Just fighting memories."

She smiled hesitantly. "Should we go in?"

He stared at the courthouse a moment longer, then nodded, a short, sharp jerk of his head. "Let's go."

He plucked at his cuffs and fiddled with his tie as they crossed the street. He had a hard time believing they would blend in: he for the years spent on the streets, but Amy for what she was wearing. Unlike Harold's somber and subdued collection of suits, Mama's wardrobe had been a time warp back to the craziest part of the seventies, ranging from a matching red, white, and blue plaid blazer and pants combo to a purple one-piece jumpsuit. Most of it was too outlandish to wear and would attract too much attention, so Amy had settled on a plaid jacket over a silk gold blouse and black bell-bottoms.

"You look like Farrah Fawcett in *Charlie's Angels*," he'd said when she'd first tried on the combination.

"Thanks, I think, but I could do without wearing something from the sexual revolution," she'd replied, trying to pinch together the blouse. The topmost button, by design, stopped between her breasts. "Do you think we could find a safety pin somewhere?"

A line of people were queued up outside the courthouse, awaiting their turn to go through a quick bag search and a trip through the metal detector. Once through, they joined the swirl of people crowding the main lobby. Some moved with a purpose, others aimlessly. Lawyers wearing Ferragamos and thousand-dollar suits mingled with gangbangers in torn flip-flops and sweatshirts. The escalators that normally moved people from the large lobby to the courts were closed, so Elliott led them to a bank of elevators, only to find that the line was ten deep.

"Family court is on the second floor, if they haven't moved it since I was here," Elliott said, impatient. "Let's take the stairs."

The stairwell was wide and industrial-looking, with shallow steps and a no-nonsense steel handrail, the whole thing big enough to accommodate all of the traffic they'd seen in the lobby. As they started up, their footsteps echoed loudly on the concrete steps. An answering clip-clop was descending and, precisely at the halfway point, they rounded the first curl of the stairwell to face a woman in her late forties or early fifties. She was dressed in a leaf-green wool business suit that was as vintage as Amy's outfit.

Elliott nodded as they passed, but kept his eyes on the stairs in front of him. The woman smiled at them, and as they continued up the steps, her hard-heeled footsteps proceeded down. Keeping her smile frozen, Amy forced herself to climb at a steady pace, resisting the urge to break into a run.

The second floor of the Moultrie building was labyrinthine, but Elliott moved confidently through the crowd, heading for the family court in the east wing. Large monitors displayed the docket agenda, the courtroom name and number, and the presiding judge.

Elliott grunted. "It used to be printed on paper."

"There," Amy said, pointing. "Judge Susan Cranston."

"JD court," Elliott said. "We're in luck."

"What do you mean?"

"Child endangerment hearings are usually closed, but judges in the domestic relations courts, like Cranston, also do delinquency hearings which are open to the public about half the time. If she was doing custody or endangerment cases today, we wouldn't get in the courtroom."

They followed a shuffling mass of people through the great oak doors. The room beyond was long, with a low coffered ceiling and wooden benches in two rows on either side of a center aisle. A low-napped carpet with an inoffensive but distracting pattern covered the floor, a mess of colored vertical lines that led the eyes directly to a raised dais. Two TV monitors, one to a side, hung from the ceiling. Each had a split screen, with one camera's focus on the judge's seat and the other the docket list. They stood, hesitating, in the aisle.

Elliott looked over at Amy. "Bride or groom?"

"I don't know," she said. She seemed shrunken, pulled in on herself, her mouth drawn in a straight line.

"I guess we're with whichever side gives us a good look at the judge."

Amy picked the end of a bench on the left, with a clear view down the aisle of both the judge's seat and the witness stand. They sat in silence, watching the others in the courtroom file in. Each small cluster of people picked seats close to the aisle or, as those seats were taken, equidistant from the next group of people, until there were no more empty spaces. A low, nervous murmur filled the room, swelling as minutes passed, then checked sharply as the bailiff called the court to order, followed by a quick recitation of the do's and don'ts. Without ceremony, the judge walked in through a side door and took her seat on the dais.

Susan Cranston was of early middle age, her blonde hair cut in a fashionable, low-maintenance bob. She wore a neutral, passive expression, but her eyes were her most arresting feature: brown pits in a thin face, unnerving whether on-screen or from forty feet away.

Elliott felt an odd movement to his left and looked over. Next to him, Amy was trembling. Her hands were clasped so tightly that the tendons on the back of the fingers were bright white lines along her knuckles. Her eyes, however, were locked on the screen, drilling into the picture. He reached over and put a hand over hers. His hand shook with the force of the tremors in hers.

"She took her," Amy whispered. "She took my little girl."

"Amy." Elliott squeezed her hands until she tore her eyes away from the screen and looked at him. "We don't know that. Not yet."

"I don't care if she isn't the one who has her *now*," she said. "She took her first."

Elliott had nothing to say. He kept his hand on hers, tight, while they watched the court go about its business. The bread-and-butter cases were over in minutes, resembling nothing like popular TV legal dramas. The few cases that didn't come to a decision were often postponed until a critical piece of information could be provided; then they were shoved out of the way for the next case in a never-ending procession of legal matters.

Elliott ignored the cases, concentrating instead on those people who were fixtures in the court: the bailiff, the attorneys, the judge. As he did so, he felt the first stirrings of doubt. He was sure of his theory that *someone* in the court system was responsible for the kidnapping, but half of the people here were women, which made them all potential suspects, but more importantly they represented the tip of the iceberg. While they sat, listening to the testimonies of everyday heartbreak, all around them were courtrooms with their own bailiffs, attorneys, and judges. Their lead was Cranston, but any number of staff could be the woman they were looking for.

Half an hour passed, then an hour. Finally, he nudged Amy and jerked his head toward the door. He led the way down the aisle and out of the room. No one watched them go.

"What are we doing?" Amy asked, searching his face as the doors closed on the drone of justice behind them.

"We're not getting anywhere. Cranston might be a crazy kidnapper by night, but she's in her judge's persona right now. We won't learn any more here than we already know."

Amy clutched a fistful of his suit coat. "We can't leave now. Elliott, please—"

He gently disengaged her hand. "I didn't say we were leaving. Cranston is just one part of the puzzle, but that doesn't mean we have to confront her directly."

"What are you thinking?"

He turned and started walking down the hall, motioning her to follow him. "Every judge has an administrative clerk and a law clerk. Maybe they can tell us something."

After a half dozen lefts and rights, they found Cranston's chambers tucked away in a corner of the building, seemingly a mile away from the courtrooms. Elliott led the way into the small reception area. Behind a waist-high counter, a young man in a tie and button-down dress shirt, looking barely out of high school, worked at a computer at a standing desk. He glanced their way, clicked something with his mouse, then stood and walked over to the counter. "Help you?"

He gave the young man a confident smile and held out his hand. "Elliott Nash."

Despite the awkward height of the counter, the young man reached across and shook. "Noah Green."

"Let me guess, interning for Judge Cranston?"

"Yeah."

"It's an honor, but you've never worked this hard in your life?"

"Something like that," Noah said with a hesitant smile. "How can I help you, Mr. Nash?"

"I'm a forensic psychologist working on a consultancy with my associate, here"—he inclined his head toward Amy—"and Detective

Dave Cargill of the MPD's Youth and Family Services on a series of cases involving foster children who have been abused after placement. We're doing some preliminary background work to follow the chain of custody, so to speak, of those kids."

"Okay."

"We've already interviewed the staff at the Child and Family Services Agency. We're now at the point where the kids go through the hearings, trying to—no offense—find out if it falls apart earlier in the process."

"I can't give you access to custody or foster information," Noah said doubtfully.

"Oh, we already have the case records from CFSA," Amy cut in breezily. Elliott turned to her, quirking an eyebrow. "We're moving on to the litigation side now and just wanted to confirm which judge presided over which case. Afterward, we'll schedule follow-up interviews with each judge—at their convenience, of course—and start tracing how the children progress through the system."

"Okay," Noah said, chewing it over, then shrugged. "How can I help?"

"We thought we'd start with Judge Cranston and see which hearings she presided over," Amy said, smiling. "Would that be possible? I have the names of the kids in question."

"Let me log on first." Noah went back to the computer in the corner and began typing. "Okay, what were those names?"

"I've got six cases to start with. Can you look those up, see where we're at, then we can move on from there?"

"Sure."

Amy gestured at Elliott, who held up a paper like he was reading the names, but actually recited them from memory. "Tammy Waters, Lacey Scowcroft, Daniel Neumann, Eva Collier, Aaron Goldstein, and Jay Kelly."

"All righty." Noah stared at the screen, eyes flicking up and down. "The Honorable Susan Cranston presiding."

Elliott's stomach roiled like a snake was wriggling in his belly.

"Okay, here we go," Noah said. "Waters, Scowcroft, and Neumann, yes. Collier, yes. Goldstein, yes. And Kelly . . ."

Elliott held his breath. Beside him, he could hear Amy do the same.

"Nope," Noah said, looking up. "Not one of Cranston's. Pardon me, *Judge* Cranston's."

"What?"

"Not one of hers, Mr. Nash. Sorry." He clicked around a few more times. "Kelly comma Jay, right? That was Judge Edelman's."

Elliott blinked. "Edelman?"

"That's what it says."

"But how does that fit?" he asked rhetorically, then realized Noah was looking at him expectantly. "Would you be able to check on that case, as well?"

"Sorry, no. I only have access to Judge Cranston's cases." He snapped his fingers. "But you know what? Kim could tell you."

"Who?"

"Kim Reston. The administrative clerk. Judges share clerks a lot to keep costs down. She's the clerk for three of the judges here: Cranston, Edelman, and Curry." Noah's eyes darted past them. "In fact, here she is now."

Elliott and Amy turned to see the woman they'd encountered earlier on the steps. Her dark brown eyes—stones in the wells of their sockets—widened in surprise, then flicked to Noah and back again. "Can I help you?"

Elliott introduced himself. "We're working with the MPD, Ms. Reston, investigating the cases of several children who've gone through this court."

"Is there some particular reason you're doing that?"

"Some of the children appear to have been the subjects of abuse once they reached the foster system," Elliott said. "We're creating timelines and following the cases through the system, trying to find where it breaks down. Obviously, CFSA and the mayor's office would like to cut down on that number."

"Naturally," she said, then tilted her head. "Do you work here at the courts, Mr. Nash? I feel like I know you from somewhere."

Elliott smiled back at her. "Years ago, I served as a consultant to the police department and used to come to the Moultrie building quite a bit."

"But not anymore?"

"I do fieldwork now," he said. "Mostly on the streets."

"I see." Reston turned her head and stared at Amy for nearly a full ten seconds. "And have *we* met? You look quite familiar, as well."

Amy smiled. "Only in the stairwell this morning. We passed each other on the steps."

Reston nodded slowly. "That must be it."

"Regarding those cases, Ms. Reston," Elliott said, clearing his throat.

"Yes?"

"Noah, here, was kind enough to confirm that most of the cases we're looking into were reviewed by Judge Cranston. But the outlier is Jay Kelly, the young man who was just discovered in Trinidad. We believe his case was seen by Judge Edelman. And since Noah told us you are the administrative clerk for both judges, we were hoping you could confirm if that's correct."

"What were the names of the children?"

Elliott rattled off the names of the other kids. She seemed to think about something, then nodded once. "Let me check the records."

Noah cleared his throat as she headed for the office door. "Sorry, Kim?"

She turned, her smile pressed tightly on her face. "Yes, Noah?"

He held out a slip of paper. "Your brother called and said he won't be able to meet you for lunch today."

"Thank you, Noah," she said, grabbing the note. She jammed it in a pocket without looking at it, turned as if to head back out of the office, seemed to think better of it, then lifted the hinged section of the counter and passed through a door.

40

Sister

It was her. It really was her.

She passed through the judge's chambers in a dream state, unable to believe that just beyond the door, in the room she'd just left, was the mother of the little girl she'd saved nearly a year ago.

Her lip curled. She'd barely glanced at the woman at the hearing more than a year ago, but she'd read the file obsessively. It had told her all she needed to know. Amy Scowcroft: an addict, hooked on painkillers, blacking out on a routine basis. She'd been high at her own daughter's hearing, for goodness' sake. As soon as the girl went to foster care, she'd made sure that Amy Scowcroft would never be able to torment her daughter again.

But now, all her charitable acts were about to come crashing down around her. Seeing Amy Scowcroft and this man Nash asking questions, rattling off the names of her last six brothers and sisters, one after the other . . . it had completely unnerved her.

How had they known all the names? Where had they gotten the information to get this far? How had they known to come to *her*? Surely, the two of them were lying about this so-called investigation they were on. Nash looked vaguely familiar, the memory of him tantalizingly out of reach, but the idea that Amy Scowcroft was on the MPD payroll, helping with an investigation, was laughable. The two of them had made it all up. But good guesses hadn't pointed them to Cranston's office. They would've needed some source of information to piece it all together.

She gasped as the answer came to her.

Brother.

He had every piece of information they needed to find her. But, she thought in confusion, why wasn't he here, then? If he knew, actually *knew*, she was behind the disappearances of all those children, he would've shown up himself. She harbored no delusions: her brother had dedicated his life to the police force and would've sadly, reluctantly—but certainly—put the handcuffs on her, no matter how hard she might try to explain herself.

Unless he was already on his way.

What if he'd cancelled their lunch, then sent Nash and Scowcroft to "investigate" as some kind of delaying tactic, to throw her off balance, while he collected the warrants and papers for her arrest?

Or—and she gasped in pain at the thought—they were getting a task force to raid the house while she was being distracted. She could see it now: the police and a cadre of social workers, kicking down the door, "freeing" the children only to send them back to their biological or, worse, their foster families, thinking they were perpetrating justice when in reality they were committing the poor things to lives of misery.

She couldn't let that happen.

Sister twisted her hands together as she walked through the back office. Despite all her worrying, her second-guessing, it seemed impossible that her life—and her life's work—was about to disappear. But better for her to end it, on her terms, than let her charges be sent back to their hellish existence by some blundering government system. It was up to her to save them one last time.

Tears coursed down her cheeks, but she didn't feel them. She was untethered from herself, hovering outside her own body, watching dispassionately as she walked through the judge's portal and into the courtroom. Accustomed to the occasional comings and goings of clerks, the bailiff and the judge didn't even spare her a glance. Until, that is, she passed in front of the bench, across the intervening space, and toward the bar. The shrew began shouting at her, then, but the words made no sense; they were just sounds that held no meaning for her.

Eventually the yelling stopped, though she was aware that the entire courtroom—from the attorneys at their tables, to the defendants in their seats, to the crowd in the gallery—watched in stunned silence as she floated past. With only a little bit of effort, she pushed through one of the double doors to the hallway beyond.

And with that, the spell was broken. The import of what she'd done and was about to do fell on her like the sky had collapsed. Wailing softly to herself, she fled the courthouse, running to save what was left of her family.

41

Elliott

After a few awkward moments passed, Elliott said, "You looked like you wanted to say something a second ago."

"Oh," Noah said, smiling wanly. "It's nothing. It's just that Kim's office is there." He gestured to a small door to one side of the office. He hiked his thumb toward the more ornate door Reston had gone through. "That goes to the judge's chambers. There's a computer back there, too, of course, but I would've thought she'd just use her own."

"Ms. Reston seemed . . . distracted."

Noah looked over his shoulder. "She gets like that."

"Like what?" Elliott asked.

"Oh, you know. A little trippy, a little out there. Like she's taking a call from outer space," he said, then hastened to add, "I mean, she's a great worker. I've learned a lot just being here. This office is a finely oiled machine thanks to her."

"But she's got . . . issues?"

"Well, I know she's scared to death of the elevator, which is probably why you saw her using the stairs."

"Claustrophobic?"

"I guess. I heard she went through some kind of freaky trauma as a kid, a murder or something. I don't know the details. All I know is she survived, but still lives in the same house." Noah shuddered. "She claims she can't afford anything better, but I'd rather live under a bridge."

"You'd be surprised," Elliott murmured, then frowned, thinking. "Noah, you said you don't have access to the case information for the other judges, right?"

"I can see judgments, if that's what you mean."

"Right."

"What about access to the personal information of the defendants and plaintiffs? Names, phone numbers, addresses, that kind of thing."

"Not if it wasn't one of Judge Cranston's cases."

"Who does?"

"Have access? Well, the judge, of course. And the law clerk for that judge."

"And the law clerks only work for particular judges? They're not shared like the admin clerks?"

"Right."

"But the administrative clerks *do* have access to all that information?" Next to him, Amy gasped. "For all the judges they work for, right?"

Noah smiled uncertainly, confused by the intensity of Elliott's questions. "Oh, sure. They have to type and file all the records pertaining to the cases, so they see all that information for all the judges they're assigned to."

Elliott turned to Amy, but just as she opened her mouth to say something, there was a bang as the ornate door behind Noah flew open. Judge Cranston stood in the doorway with a look of fury on her face and her robes billowing behind her like wings.

"Noah! What the hell is going on?"

The young clerk straightened like a marionette yanked by its strings. "Your Honor?"

"Kim just marched through my well like she owned the goddamned place, ignored my warning, then walked straight down the damn aisle like a goddamned bride at a wedding. Is she on drugs?"

Elliott grabbed Amy's arm. "Thanks for your help, Noah."

As they left, they heard Judge Cranston bark before the door swung shut, "And who was *that*? What in the world is happening?"

"It's her, isn't it?" Amy said as they hustled down the hall, her voice tight. "That woman was Sister."

"I think so," Elliott said. "Can you call Dave? We don't have a clue where she lives or where she's going."

Amy pulled out her phone and speed-dialed the detective's number as they walked. "No answer."

"Shit," Elliott said, frustrated. "All right. Let's get out of the building, at least. If Judge Cranston is on the warpath, we're going to get swept up by security."

"But then what?"

"I don't know. We can find her address somewhere. Tax records, maybe, or some kind of internet search. Maybe phone the utilities and try to con them," Elliott said, but his voice faltered with doubt even as he said it.

They hurried down the stairs, through the lobby, and burst out of the glass doors, earning a glance from the security guards.

"If we can get a taxi, we'll just talk him into driving us and worry about paying him later," Elliott said as he scanned the street. He swore. There wasn't a cab in sight.

But as they stood there helplessly, a nondescript blue Crown Victoria pulled to the curb. The passenger's side window came down, revealing Dave Cargill's bald head and accusing stare.

42

Charlotte

Holding her breath, Charlotte opened Charlie's wardrobe with trembling hands.

It had taken forever for the others to move around the house until she could be alone long enough to get into Charlie's room. No matter how many times Charlotte forgave her, Maggie wouldn't leave her side, weepy and apologizing for betraying her secret to Sister. New Charlie was morose, moving quietly around the house with his head down like a haunted spirit. Buddy was manic and sprinted up and down the steps shouting until she thought she was going to kill him. Tina stalked the floors, tracking the others with watchful eyes.

Finally, hours and hours after Sister had left for the day, the others had settled into their routines—New Charlie in the living room, Maggie asleep on their bed, Buddy in the kitchen banging on the table, Tina probably in the cellar planning her traps. Occupied long enough for her to slip into Charlie's room unseen.

She didn't know why today was particularly dreadful, but from the moment the front door had slammed, she'd felt a knot forming in her belly. Maybe it was a stray look from Sister over breakfast or the accumulation of the too-deliberate kindnesses the woman had been showing her lately. A month ago, Charlotte would've been bewildered at the treatment.

Now, she was just scared. Knowing what she knew about Old Charlie, about the trunk in Sister's room, about Sister's plan for a birthday party for her soon . . . circumstances felt like the arms of a giant clock—second, minute, and hour—coming together at midnight, a fairy tale written just for her. Except in this story, she knew, there were no pumpkins or princes; at the stroke of twelve, Sister would kill her.

So, she'd made up her mind to do whatever it took today, *now*, to try and escape. With any luck, she reasoned, the little knot of wood that had fallen out meant that the plywood covering the dining room window was old and rotting. If she kicked and pushed and pounded on it for the rest of the day, she might just be able to punch a hole large enough to squeeze through.

It was hardly a plan at all, but she was running out of options and time. The only other thing she needed was Charlie's little bundle, his escape stash.

Stretching, she ran her fingers along the inner frame of the wardrobe, frowning when she couldn't find it. In a panic, she climbed halfway into the wardrobe, pawing at the far corners until she hissed as she caught a splinter in her thumb.

"Looking for this?"

Charlotte whipped around. Tina stood in the doorway, smirking, holding the bundle looped over one finger.

"Give me that," Charlotte said, trying to make her voice sound commanding, but it came out with a quaver.

"Why? It's not yours," Tina said. "It's Charlie's, if it's anyone's."

"I found it first. And I need it now."

"Why?"

Charlotte stared at the girl, wondering if a lie would mean anything at this point. She was minutes away from kicking her way out of the house, for crying out loud; there was no hiding what she was planning now. "I'm leaving, Tina. I'm getting out of here, and I'm going to get help."

"You're not leaving," Tina said with a little laugh. "No one leaves here."

"I am. And I need that bundle to do it."

"A couple of quarters? A tiny knife? That's going to get you out of here?"

"It can't hurt," Charlotte said. "I'll use whatever I can to escape."

"Why?"

"Why what?"

"Why do you want to leave? Why can't you just do what she wants?" Tina's voice cracked. "Why can't you just be part of the family, like the rest of us?"

"Because you're *not* my family," Charlotte yelled, suddenly furious. She'd wanted to scream the words since the moment she'd come here. "She's not my sister."

"She could be." Tears filled the girl's eyes. "She's better than what we came from. What you'll go back to."

"No, she's not," Charlotte said.

"You wouldn't know, because you've never tried," Tina accused.

"Tina, this is not our home. She is not our sister," Charlotte said, struggling to find the words. "She collects us, then kills us. She killed Charlie."

The other girl froze, her face stuck in an expression of disbelief. "Charlie left."

"Left where, Tina? Where do you think Charlie went? If you know, tell me."

Tina's mouth opened and closed silently. "He's just . . . gone. We have a new Charlie, now."

"She killed him, Tina. I watched her drag his body down the steps," Charlotte said, then paused dramatically. "And, you know what? You're next."

"No."

"We're all next, Tina," Charlotte said, holding the girl's eyes with her own. "She. Kills. All of us."

"You're just saying that because you're . . . you're bleeding."

"That's part of it," Charlotte said, nodding, her voice low and reasonable. She started walking across the floor toward Tina. "Sister doesn't like change. She doesn't like me. But soon it'll be your turn. She'll throw a party for you."

Tina's face screwed up. "Shut up."

"There'll be big glasses of milk . . ."

"Shut up."

". . . and cake . . ."

"Shut up!"

". . . and candles. You'll fall asleep and, in the middle of the night, Sister will wrap you in a blanket and drag your body down the steps."

"Charlotte, shut up!"

"My name's not Charlotte. And yours isn't Tina."

"My name is Tina!" the girl screamed. "It's Tina, it's Tina, it's Tina!"

Suddenly they both froze. Even through the walls, they could hear a rushing sound emanating from outside, growing in intensity. The sound of tires on gravel. The sound of Sister coming home.

Tina's face, twisted and distraught a moment before, lit up triumphantly. With a whoop, she spun on a toe and ran for the stairs.

Behind her, Charlotte sank to the floor, knowing she was about to die.

43

Sister

Never in her life had she felt like this, almost drunk with confusion, her head ten times its normal size and filled with helium, ready to float away. The paper flower that was her heart was being crushed in a fist. The feeling was so strong she groaned and rubbed her chest.

And, on top of it all, the horrible, pressing sense that time was finally running out, a sense of urgency so strong that she could taste it on her tongue like a squeeze of lemon. Chased by it, she flew through the intersections and down streets, onto ramps and along the highway faster than she'd ever dared before. Some kind of strange luck was with her—traffic melted away, and the police were absent. There were no sirens, no flashing lights, no cars chasing her down.

Her car fishtailed as she spun onto the long dirt road to the house. Gripping the wheel as though it was a life ring, she flew up the final hill, her tires spitting rocks and debris as she went. She came to a rocking stop in front of the door, then dashed out of the car and onto the porch. Cursing and crying, she unlocked the door with shaking hands, finally throwing it open with a bang. Momentum shut it with a soft click.

In the hallway near the steps, eyes wide as saucers, cowered one of the girls. *Which one was it? So many children . . .*

"Tina," she said, then sprang forward and pulled the girl into a hug. "Where are the others?"

"They're . . . they're around," the girl said. "Charlie and Buddy are upstairs and Maggie's in the living room. But, Sister, Charlotte is—"

Without letting go of the girl, Sister staggered over to the foot of the stairs and called, "Charlie! Buddy! Maggie! Come down here, now! This instant! Where is Charlotte?"

Feet hit the floor nearby and a moment later the two boys peeked down the hall, Buddy from the kitchen, Charlie from the living room. "Yes, Sister?" Buddy asked.

"Come here. Quickly! Grab the others. *Do it!*"

"Yes, Sister."

In a moment, the children had gathered in the hall, looking at her warily. She forced herself to slow down, if only for a moment, looking at them one at a time. Tina, loyal sweet Tina, looked ready to cry, as if she sensed what was coming. Buddy was as blank as ever, while Charlie—the new boy—still had the look of a whipped dog. Charlotte was surly, rebellious, and Sister felt her eyes narrow as she looked at the girl. She regretted having not removed her earlier, but there wasn't any help for it now.

She gestured impatiently for them to come close, close enough to touch. Reluctantly, they shuffled around her, but now that the time had come, she felt herself choke up. She swallowed the pain and the grief, trying to smile.

"I know this is very strange, my coming home like this. I have what may sound like an odd request, but you must not question me. Is that clear? Good. We're all going to take a little afternoon nap right here in the kitchen. I want you to go grab all the pillows and blankets from the living room." When she saw that only confused them, she groped for some incentive that would make them stop thinking. "Afterward, I'll go out and bring home pizza for all of us. How does that sound?"

Their little eyes lit up so brightly she almost burst into tears. As they left to grab pillows, she turned and went into the kitchen. It took all of her strength to shove the farmhouse table against the far wall away from the center. She then took the threadbare tea towels and aprons from the drawer and shoved them into the gaps in the plywood covering the windows. Once she was done sealing the room, she walked up to the stove and spun the dial on the oven. The sharp stink of natural gas was immediate.

She turned when she heard the children come back, trailing the square cushions and pillows and blankets cannibalized from the couch and chairs. They stood in the doorway uncertainly.

"Come, come," she said, gesturing. She pointed at the floor in front of the stove. "Over here, lay the pillows here. Get close, now. Yes, lay down, Buddy."

"Sister?"

She raised her head. Charlotte was looking at her with wide eyes. "Yes? What is it?"

"There aren't enough pillows for everyone," she said, gesturing. "Should I grab some more from upstairs?"

She glanced at the floor. The girl was right. Even with every pillow from the couch, there were only enough for a few of the children and none for herself. For a moment, she considered simply lying down—*did it really matter?*—but the thought of her last moments on that cold linoleum floor repulsed her.

"You're right, Charlotte. You and Tina grab what you need from the bedrooms, please, and come right back." She called after the two as they turned to go. "And some pillows for me, as well."

Tina had an odd expression on her face, reluctant and questioning, then turned and followed Charlotte out of the kitchen. Seeing that look, she started to call her back, but Maggie chose that moment to tug on her sleeve. She looked down at the little girl.

"Sister, you look scared. Should I be scared?"

She got down on her knees to be on the same level. "No, honey. There's no reason to be scared at all. No one's going to hurt you like they did before. I'd never let that happen. Do you believe me?"

Maggie smiled, her cherub's cheeks round. "I believe you."

The look on the girl's face broke her heart and this time, she did start to cry. She pulled Maggie close in a hug, aware that the others looked at her in alarm, but there wasn't anything she could do about it. Waves of fear and loneliness and hurt built up over decades came plowing through her relentlessly, and she could only sob and squeeze the tiny doll in front of her.

44

Elliott

Elliott looked at Dave, shaking his head. "How in the . . . ?"

Dave looked over and grimaced. "You might have a bunch of psychology degrees, Elliott, but I've got twenty years on the street."

"You knew we'd head for the court."

"Of course," Dave said. "Once you'd sunk your teeth into that lead about Cranston, I knew you'd head for the court. I've been hanging around Moultrie waiting for you for so long the guards started to get nervous."

"Thank god you were there."

"I guess so," Dave said. "But where are we going?"

Briefly, Elliott told him about their encounter in Cranston's office with Noah and Kim Reston and filled in all the parts they'd surmised.

He stopped abruptly. His friend's face had drained of color, leaving it the same shade as his stained white collar. "Jesus, Dave. What's wrong? Are you all right?"

"I'm fine," Dave rasped. "I . . . just can't believe this has been going on right under my nose this whole time."

"Years, maybe," Amy said.

"So you think she's the 'Sister' Jay Kelly mentioned?" Dave asked, wiping a hand across his face. "You're absolutely positive?"

"As sure as I can be of anything right now," Elliott said. "The intern said that Reston had a traumatic childhood, possibly even a murder in the family. And the woman is obviously on the run. When we started naming the children, she must've panicked."

"Speaking of which," Amy said from the back seat, her voice tight, "can we please talk about it on the way?"

"Can you look up the address by name?" Elliott asked Dave, gesturing at the police laptop mounted from the dash. His friend turned the laptop on its pivot so that it faced him and tapped the keys.

Ten seconds later, he grunted and turned the laptop off. "Split Ridge Road, past Rockville. Almost to Poolesville."

"That was fast," Elliott said, looking at Dave.

"Modern technology and big data," the cop said. "Hold on." They pulled away from the curb fast, cutting off another car. Dave hit his police squawker and punched the gas. Elliott frowned, looking at the sweat that had popped out on Dave's forehead, and opened his mouth to say—

Amy tapped him on the shoulder. "Elliott?"

"Yes?" he said turning, his question forgotten.

"Why is she doing this? It's what I don't get about the whole thing. What is her motive?"

"I've been asking myself the same thing," Elliott said. "We're missing the why."

"Maybe there is no reason," Dave said gruffly. "Some people just snap."

"There's always a reason," Elliott admonished, then thought of something. "Your phone has internet, right?"

"Of course."

"May I see it? We already know a couple key things about Reston. Maybe we can dig up some more."

"You sure you know how to use that thing?" Dave said.

"No, but Amy probably does."

Reluctantly, Dave fished his phone out of his pocket and handed it over his shoulder to Amy. Elliott turned in his seat to face her.

"Noah said he thought there might've been a murder within the family and that she still lived in the house where it happened."

"So search for Reston, Split Ridge Road, murder, I guess?" Amy said, tapping her way through the search terms.

"She looked to me like she was in her midforties, so whatever trauma she experienced 'as a kid,' as Noah put it, would've been thirty to forty years ago. Look for a scan of an archived article."

Bent over the phone, Amy picked her way through websites and search screens for several minutes. "Found it. 'For five generations, the Reston family lived in relative isolation in the last house on Split Ridge Road . . . until the tragic events on Friday night.'"

"Can I see that?"

Amy handed Elliott the phone and he skimmed the contents, grunting once or twice as he read the article. When he'd finished he put his head back, thinking.

"Find anything?" Dave asked, his voice tight.

Elliott sighed. "The mother apparently had a psychotic episode after the father abandoned her for another woman. There were seven children, and she killed them one by one as they came home from school. Only Kim Reston and a brother survived."

"How did they do it?" Amy said in a hushed voice.

"Reston hid in the oven until the police found her. The brother they found in the woods."

"That's terrible."

"But do you see what she's doing? Psychologically speaking?"

She thought about it. "She's trying to put her family back together."

"Yes. But just the brothers and sisters. She must hate her mother. That's probably why there's no sexual or physical trauma component with the kids we're talking about—that wasn't a trait she inherited, so to speak. The mother, before she snapped completely, never abused the children."

"Not physically, anyway," Dave said, his tone grim. "But why, for god's sake? Why is Sister killing them? Why would she commit the same crime as her mother?"

"Oh my god," Amy said suddenly. "They grow up."

Elliott nodded. "They age past the point of the sibling they're supposed to have replaced. One day, Reston looks at a young man instead of a boy or a young woman instead of the little girl she thought was her sister . . . and doesn't recognize them anymore. The fantasy breaks."

"That's why she kills them on their birthday," Amy said. "She anticipates them being too old."

"Exactly."

"How has she held it together for this long?"

"She tells herself she's helping these kids," Dave said, his voice harsh, "saving them from broken homes where they would've been abused or assaulted or worse."

Elliott looked over, curious. "I think you're right, Dave. All those years working in the dependency courts? She must've seen hundreds of cases, a lot of them worse than what she went through. I doubt it was much of a stretch for her to believe she was doing them a favor. She probably rationalizes even their murders this way. She helps herself while she helps them."

Amy asked, "If she thinks this is all coming to an end, what is she doing right now?"

"She won't see any way out. Her rational side knows the law. Multiple accounts of murder and kidnapping—and who knows how many more than what we've uncovered—is going to lead to a dozen life sentences."

"That's her rational side. What about her deranged side?"

"She would never let her brothers and sisters go back into a system that would return them to a broken home," Dave said, staring straight ahead at the road. His voice was flat, emotionless. "She'll kill them rather than give them back."

45

Charlotte

The choice was obvious, which is why Charlotte didn't take it.

She'd been at the top of the stairs when Sister had made her explosive entrance and had seen immediately that the woman had forgotten to lock the door in her haste to get all of them into the kitchen. It was a shame Tina had been sent with her, but it was easy enough to take a fake step into her room and back out. With Tina busy in her room gathering blankets, she'd flown down the steps with her heart hammering in her chest and right out the door.

As she had snuck down the porch steps, each board squeaking like a mouse, with the sun sinking over the woods, she glanced past the aging Cadillac at the driveway beyond. She knew that, almost certainly, it led to a road, and that road led to a street or a boulevard or another road, and eventually to people and homes and safety.

But what if it didn't? She thought back to the conversation she'd had with Charlie and how they'd never heard a car pass by or a knock on the door. What if the driveway was a mile long, with nowhere to hide? What if the road it led to was deserted or went on forever? Any minute now Sister would discover Charlotte was missing. She would dash out of the house with her keys in hand, jump in her car, and catch up to her in no time.

When she'd seen the door cracked open, she knew she had to go now or, instinct told her, she'd never get another chance. With her arms wrapped around the blanket and a pillow she'd pretended to get for Sister, she'd gone right out the door—no plan, no thought except *freedom.*

If she could hide in the woods for a day or two, three at the most, Sister would have her hands full with work or taking care of the others—there'd be no time to worry about Charlotte, by which time she'd have a chance to look for a way to escape for good.

Her stomach turned over on itself at the thought that she was abandoning the others. But maybe, if the track in the woods led somewhere where she could get help, she might still be able to help them. If not . . .

The dark thought disappeared as soon as her feet hit the ground. A shaft of light hit her full in the face, and a piercing, deep cold breath plumbed the bottom of her lungs—she was *outside*, she wasn't a prisoner anymore. A giggle started deep in her belly that raced through her chest and up through her head. Clapping a hand over her mouth, she ran to the back of the house, across the yard, and through the gate she'd spied so many times through the knot in the plywood, not noticing the pillow as it dropped to the ground.

◆ ◆ ◆

Tina

With her arms full, Tina could barely see over the mound of linens and nearly tripped down the steps. Her heart was hammering in her chest. The look on Sister's face had been a terrifying blend of panic and peace, certainty and hopelessness—more frightening by far than the fury that twisted her features during her temper tantrums. Something terrible was happening, something final.

When she got to the bottom of the steps and caught the piercing smell of gas, she knew what it was.

A memory from her early childhood hit her, a vision of sleeping on the couch in their tiny apartment after school. Mom, having given up on dinner, was passed out at the kitchen table. Canned soup, bubbling gently. The stink of natural gas filling the apartment. A neighbor, pounding on the door until he finally gave up and kicked it in, then dragged them both outside, slapping the two of them awake. Tearful thank-yous and promises to never do it again, because the phrase *you could've died* was repeated so many times it began to sound like the lines from a song. Her mother, true to her word, had made sure it never happened again. She didn't always keep things together, herself most of all, but she'd never put them in danger that way again.

But now, the smell, the request for blankets and pillows, the look on Sister's face—it all made sense.

Charlotte had been right. She was going to kill all of them.

Even as the thought coalesced in her brain, she suffered another shock as a cool whisper of air brushed her face, pushing the stink of gas away. She turned, and froze. The foyer, normally cavelike and dim, was lit by the thinnest crack of sunlight coming through the front door.

Tina dropped everything in her arms and walked forward, step by step, as though she had a fever. With a trembling hand, she put her hand on the knob and pulled on it. The door swung open and she stepped cautiously onto the porch, eyes watering as fresh, chill air washed over her. She blinked away the tears and gazed at the scene in front of her.

The front yard was a collection of crab grass and dirt, with a gravel drive disappearing down a hill to her left. A car, an old clunker, sat just feet from the front porch. She turned and scanned the side yard where she gasped softly as she caught sight of a pillow on the ground. From around the side of the house came a squeal followed by a wooden clack. A gate or a door, swinging in the breeze.

Charlotte. She'd actually done it, she'd run.

She ran her hands up and down her arms, fidgeting and staring into the forest beyond the gate. There wasn't much time before Sister came looking for them. If only Charlotte hadn't talked back so often, hadn't forced Sister's hand, none of this would've happened.

Then again, she'd thought sometimes that her mother's drug use was *her* fault for being bad, but no matter how good she tried to be, her mother still used them. It had been her mother's choice to keep doing the wrong thing. Like maybe Sister was unable to do the right thing.

Tina chewed her lip. No matter how bad she was, though, her mother never blamed her the way Sister blamed the children. For the briefest moment, she imagined herself running after Charlotte, joining her in escape, seeing her mom again, being part of the world again. Maybe she missed her mom more than she'd been willing to admit. Did her mom miss her? Was she looking for her right now? Or had she given up and moved on with her life?

She glanced back into the house, at its comforting closeness, the walls and floors and ceilings that had become so familiar to her. The house that, no matter what Sister had in store for them all, was now her home.

Why was she even asking herself these questions? It didn't matter. There was no escape for her, no real escape for any of them. She could hope and dream all she wanted; she would never see her mom again. But maybe . . . maybe if she caught up with Charlotte, dragged her back, redeemed them all, there would be a chance to put Sister's mind to rest, maybe reverse the terrible decision she'd been forced to make, and they could go back to how things were before.

Tina ran down the steps, around the house, and into the woods.

Sister

Minutes passed and eventually the wrenching feeling eased inside her. She released Maggie and led her to a blanket on the floor. "Lay here, Maggie."

Wiping her eyes, she looked around. Charlie and Buddy were lying down, ramrod straight, pretending to be asleep. What was taking the two girls so long? Weary and drained, Sister pushed herself to her feet. Although the smell of gas had dissipated, she knew that carbon monoxide was slowly filling the room. It wouldn't be long now, but they had to be together or it would all be for naught. A surge of fury rolled through her. *Why, of all the times, do I have to follow up on them now?* "Close your eyes, everyone, and try to sleep. I'll be right back."

Stepping daintily over the children, she flew out of the kitchen, ready to rip strips off the girls, when she froze.

Late-afternoon light spilled into the house through a wide-open front door.

Shock ran through her like she'd been dropped into an icy sea. *Betrayed.* Not just by Charlotte—that was almost to be expected—but by Tina. Tina, her favorite. One of the few sisters she'd ever wondered if she could save, not for a few years, but forever. And, now, both were gone. They must've plotted their escape together, kept it secret from her and the others for *months*, even faked a rivalry with each other, just waiting for the right moment to flee.

With a scream, Sister bounded out of the house and tripped down the steps, her heart in her throat and a pounding in her neck like there was something in her veins trying to get out. Pulling out her keys, she raced to the car and jumped into the driver's seat. In her mind's eye, she saw Charlotte and Tina trotting down the drive, their eyes full of hope, completely unaware of just how far freedom was. She grimaced with some slight pleasure as she imagined plowing into the girls, driving them under the grill of the car, smearing them into the road.

She hauled on the wheel to make the U-turn down the driveway, then froze.

Something in the yard, a lump or a bump on the ground, caught her eye. She slowly got out of the car, her long shadow falling across the yard, and walked to the object.

It was a pillow. She turned it over and over in her hands, a vision of her mother plumping it before placing it back on the couch, seeing the children who had slept on it, seeing her own face pressed against it to blot the tears. Seeing it falling out of the hands of one of those little bitches as they ran away.

All the fear and pain and hatred swelled up from her chest, through her throat, bubbling out of her mouth. "You won't make it," she screamed into the woods. "You will never break up our family! I won't let you."

A breeze rattling the dead brown leaves on the beech trees was the only answer. Poor man's wind chime, her mother used to call it. The pillow fell from her hands onto the ground. In a daze, she walked to the gate, then broke into a run as she entered the woods.

46

Elliott

Amy pointed from the back seat at a green and white road sign leaning at a thirty-degree angle and nearly hidden by a low-hanging oak branch. "There, that's it."

Split Ridge Road was a loosely packed dirt lane. Dave took the turn fast, and the car spat gravel before he got it under control and followed the road cut through the hillside. Rusted barbed wire and the husks of fence posts lined the embankment to either side. An occasional break in the berm marked where drives and trails may have once been, but all were overgrown and weedy. Shafts of late-afternoon sunlight filtered through the sweetgums and tulip poplars, the leafless trees throwing long, thin shadows across the road and highlighting motes of dust hanging in the air like sprites.

"She just passed through," Elliott said, pointing to the dust. "How far are we?"

The detective kept his eyes on the road. "A quarter mile."

"Should you call for backup?" Amy asked from the back seat.

Dave looked in the mirror. "You're still fugitives, remember? This one's on us."

The road dipped into a cracked concrete swale with an inch of water in it, the washout for a tiny creek, then climbed a hill for a long minute.

Dave slowed as they crested the top of a ridge and the forest opened into a clearing, revealing a ramshackle four-square farmhouse. Pallet-size chunks of shingles had blown free of the roof and were scattered around the modest yard. A rotting wooden fence ran along the perimeter, doing little to hold back an overgrown copse of brambles, snags, and leaning trees. Inside the fence, weeds and thistle swayed knee-high.

Uneven wooden steps led up to a decrepit porch. A broken porch swing dangled from a single intact chain. Plywood panels had been nailed to the outside of every window. Dave swore.

Sitting at an angle at the foot of the steps, as though ready to drive up onto the porch, was a dusty brown Cadillac from a different era. Its driver's side door hung open and the headlights were on, pointing to the back of the yard. Dave stopped short of the Cadillac and threw the cruiser in park, but left the engine running.

"Oh god," Amy groaned. "Lacey's here, I can feel it."

"Stay put," Dave said, his voice strained as he got out of the car and ran to the house.

Amy popped open her door. "There's no way I'm going to sit in this car."

"Amy!" Elliott called, then cursed and jumped out after her.

Moving gingerly, Dave mounted the steps along their outer edge, then approached the door from an angle. Keeping the thick brick wall between him and anyone inside, he reached out with his off hand and banged on the door, shouting something at the same time. The door, apparently unlatched and unlocked, swung open.

His face turned stormy as he noticed Amy coming up the steps with Elliott trailing. "Get back in the car!" he said.

"I can't," Amy said. "Lacey's here, I know it."

"Do you smell that?" Elliott said, interrupting whatever Dave was about to say. The other two started as the smell reached them: the sharp tang of natural gas.

Dave swore and pushed into the house, reared back as the fumes hit him head-on. "Cover your mouth with your shirt."

Elliott shoved his nose and mouth into the crook of his elbow and pushed in after Dave, getting a quick impression of hundred-year-old furnishings and musty wall hangings barely lit in the gloom of the boarded-up home as he ran after the detective.

Dave charged down the length of the hall without pausing, then turned right. Elliott followed him into an old-style farmhouse kitchen, complete with soapstone sink and a rough-cut plank table shoved up against the wall. In the far corner was an ancient white porcelain stove. The door to the oven was open; a hissing noise emanated from it. Lying on an impromptu bed of couch cushions and throw pillows were three small bodies, seemingly asleep.

Elliott pushed past Dave, who had frozen at the sight of the children, then vaulted over the bodies to kick the oven door shut. He frantically spun the fat dial to its OFF position.

"Amy," he barked. "Get them out of here!"

As Amy bent to scoop up a tiny girl no more than five or six years old, Dave turned to an interior door and opened it, revealing a set of rickety steps leading down into darkness.

"Dave, what the hell are you doing?" Elliott called as he watched the detective flick the light on and start to descend the steps.

"You two get the kids out of here," he called back. "We haven't cleared the house. That lunatic could be loading a shotgun right now."

Elliott reached for the nearest child, a pale redheaded boy with arms like sticks, and heaved him over a shoulder. He loped out of the kitchen and down the hall, trailing Amy, who had her hands full with the other two.

Dave

Dave moved around the cellar carefully but confidently. The single bare bulb did little to illuminate the place—it was really just to keep you from breaking your neck coming down the stairs—but he pulled out a flashlight and scanned the gloomy, dirt-floored level. It was just like he remembered it. A washing machine and dryer in one corner with a soapstone wash sink nearby, the accumulated debris of five generations stacked neatly in another.

Some of the junk had obviously been piled and propped up to form little traps, the kind he used to make when he played fort with his brothers, but more dangerous. Near the steps, the broken shaft of a yard rake had been threaded through the springs of a child's hobbyhorse—it had been Maggie's, he remembered—like a lance, its vicious point aimed precariously upward. A few feet farther on, a jump rope had been stretched across the narrow gap of junk at ankle height, obviously meant to trip unwary explorers. Beyond that, an evil conglomeration of spikes, baling wire, and corroded utensils were balled together in a box carefully set for the tripped person to fall into.

Above him, he could hear the quick, erratic steps of Elliott and Amy as they moved the kids out of the house. He didn't have much time. With something like a sigh, he lowered his hand and rested it on the butt of his gun. "Kim? You there?"

No answer. He moved to the back of the basement until he stood in front of the primitive wooden door to the root cellar. The must and damp tickled his nose. Memories—of hiding, of crying, of whispering—pressed down on him. He yanked the door open.

Cobwebs, silence, and darkness.

He sighed and closed the door, then made a quick circuit of the cellar, listening and moving, his eyes flicking into each corner, until it was obvious he was alone in the space under the house. But that still left the top floor.

◆ ◆ ◆

Elliott

"Get them out on the grass," Elliott shouted.

"Is that Lacey?" Amy asked, even as she lowered the children to the ground. "Is it her?"

"I don't know."

Amy's eyes flicked over the little cadre, devastation in her voice. "She's not here."

"Dave will find her if she's here. But you and I have to get these kids breathing."

The next few minutes were a blur as Elliott moved back and forth from one child to the next, performing CPR, feeling for a pulse, chafing and slapping and breathing for them. Sweat poured off him, rolling down his back and pooling at the base of his spine. His hands were shaking from the effort, but he kept at it until the little girl gave an enormous gasp, turned on her side, and vomited, then took huge, heaving breaths of air. A little boy was next.

"Come on, come on," he growled, pushing on the thin, washboard chest until he saw a flicker of eyelids and another gasp of air. Footsteps clattered on the porch, and he glanced up to see Amy running up the steps and back into the house. Too tired to yell, Elliott went from child to child, making sure each was breathing on his or her own.

Dave

Dave stared at the door. The others had been open to some degree or another, but this one, the last, was shut and clearly locked. The look of it had stopped him cold. Footsteps pounded up the hollow wooden steps behind him.

"Is she here? Is Lacey here?" It was Amy, desperate, her voice breaking. "Did you check?"

"She's not in the other rooms," he said dully, then shook himself like a wet dog. "Watch out."

He backed up two steps, then lunged forward and planted his foot next to the lock. Or tried to. Just before he made contact with the door, his foot twisted slightly and hit the knob. With a flat crack, the wood around the lock splintered and the door sagged open, but he gasped as a sharp pain lanced up his ankle. Amy brushed passed him and scanned the room, looked under the bed, then raced back out of the room.

"Amy! Wait!" Dave made a grab for her arm, but she was already out the door and tumbling down the steps, leaving him to hobble after.

Elliott

Amy rushed out of the house, her face a twisted wreck. "She's not there, Elliott. Dave checked every room and the basement."

"No sign of the woman either?" he asked, looking up from the older boy.

"None."

Elliott wiped his forehead where the sweat was already cooling in the chill air. "The front door was unlocked when we got here . . ."

They turned to look at the backyard, where the once-white gate of the picket fence yawned open, revealing a thin, meandering path that led into the woods.

"That's got to be it. Lacey made a break for it and that . . . woman followed her." Amy made a beeline for the path.

"Amy, wait!" Elliott jumped up and glanced toward the house. "Dave?"

No answer. He looked down at the kids, made sure they were all breathing on their own. He cursed, torn, then made his decision and sprinted after Amy as she headed down the path, joining her in time to plunge through the gate and into the trees beyond.

◆ ◆ ◆

Dave

Using both hands on the banister, Dave limped down the steps. He'd heard the quick conversation, then Elliott's garbled shout, but by the time he made it onto the sagging porch, they were gone.

He spared a quick look in the direction of the row of small bodies. All were breathing on their own; two or three moaned softly as they came to.

"Jesus, Kim," he said, feeling sick. "What were you doing?"

More importantly, he thought, what am *I* doing? He pulled out his phone, began to dial a number, then stopped. He glanced at the woods, back to the house, then the woods again. Memories and half-recalled conversations played through his head like an old film, poorly spliced and put back together. A shudder shook him. He punched the final number on the keypad, spoke briefly, then put the phone back in his pocket before clenching his teeth and limping painfully through the gate and down the darkened path.

47

Elliott

"Is there a flashlight on that phone?"

Amy shook her head. "Too old."

He bit back a curse and kept walking, trying simultaneously to scan the ground, glance at the path ahead of them, and keep an ear cocked for a sound, any sound. The sun was, at this point, over the horizon, its afterglow barely touching the bottoms of the long, wispy clouds, turning them into blushing streaks in the sky. The reflection was enough to light their way, but he knew the effect was temporary—already the trees were silhouettes in his vision, painted black for all the difference the light made. Darkness was almost upon them, and with it would go any chance of staying on the unfamiliar path, not to mention catching up with Sister or Lacey. The thought made him clench his jaw to the point where his teeth made cracking sounds.

Dead branches and forest debris crackled under their feet as they hurried along the narrow track of dirt and gray-green moss. More than once they had to catch each other as they stumbled over tree roots and half-buried river stones.

The wind sighed through the trees, rustling the leaves in small bunches. A solitary mockingbird chirruped a handful of times, then fell silent. Elliott heard Amy's breath catch at a crashing noise that sounded just like a person stumbling through the woods . . . only to find out it was a squirrel dashing along the ground. The damp smell of rot and thick, fecund dirt was overwhelming and sat heavy in the air, catching in the throat and nose.

"Wait," Amy hissed, holding up a hand.

Elliott stopped obediently and listened until he was nearly deaf from his own pulse pounding in his ears. Canting his head, he willed his hearing to be sharper, clearer.

Nothing.

He waited longer, trying to pick out anything from the long, low sigh of wind, waiting so long that the silence itself took on a sound. Still nothing. He opened his mouth to tell Amy they should keep moving when, somewhere ahead of them, someone screamed a string of words, incoherent but full of rage and pain and hate. Amy clutched his arm.

Paralyzed, they waited as the sound faded away, swallowed by the woods. When it was clear there wouldn't be another like it, they threw caution away and sprinted down the path.

◆　◆　◆

Charlotte

Charlotte cried out as she tripped on a root and went sprawling, momentarily dropping the blanket, but she was up and moving almost before she was aware she'd fallen. She'd heard Sister's shouted threats from the yard, but told herself it was just the typical bluster from the woman. Anyway, it didn't mean Sister hadn't taken the bait and headed down the driveway to the road.

But then she'd heard a scream from the woods behind her, an animal howl that began guttural and nearly subsonic, ending on a high, birdlike screech before it was followed by a horrifying tumble of words and noises, rising and falling in pitch and timbre. The sound wasn't normal, barely human, and scared Charlotte more than anything she'd ever heard.

Sister hadn't been duped by her little trick to escape to the woods and not the road. She was following her, and wasn't far away.

It was cold. The tip of her runny nose and her chin were tingling—she wrapped the blanket around her shoulders as she ran, but only managed to get it around her neck as a kind of shawl. The clutter of leaves and downed trees made the path hard to follow—it was easier to look where the path *wasn't* and hope that she'd chosen correctly.

Her breathing was ragged and her chest ached. Trapped in the house for so long, with no chance to run or play, her muscles felt shrunken and unused; moving faster than a walk on legs that hadn't stretched much in what seemed like an eternity was difficult. The cold air cut through to her lungs and made her dizzy. But then she imagined hearing Sister's footsteps through the dry leaves, felt the long, bony hand reaching out for her shoulder, and she suddenly found the energy to push herself forward.

She was moving fast enough, in fact, that she nearly ran headlong into the bole of a large, gnarled oak that split the path. Without giving it a thought, she went with her instinct, stumbling deeper into the darkened wood.

◆ ◆ ◆

Tina

Tina flinched at the yelp, then gasped at the rage-filled screams that rang through the forest. Already terrified from being in the woods, having difficulty even getting accustomed to a world larger than the four walls of Sister's house, she sobbed and broke into a run. Plans to catch up with Charlotte were gone—the only thing left was flight. She crashed through the underbrush, narrowly missing a large tree, and swerved down an overgrown path.

Behind her, so close she imagined she could feel the ground shake, came the heavy footsteps of an adult in pursuit.

Sister

Sister paused as she came up to the ancient oak that split the path in two, unable to help herself. She hadn't seen the tree since she'd been a little girl, and a flood of memories washed over her as her eyes traced the twisted, almost grotesque branches that radiated outward from the massive trunk. She slowed as a memory, tucked away and forgotten until now, thrust itself to the forefront of her mind, digging its claws in deep.

She'd played at the base of this tree with her brother, daring each other to climb higher, neither of them having the courage to go more than fifteen or twenty feet off the ground, the distance they felt they could fall and survive.

One day, he'd displeased Mother and run into the woods rather than face her discipline. He'd climbed nearly to the top of this oak, refusing to come down even after Mother followed him into the woods and threatened him with all manner of punishments, each of them more horrific than the last. Finally, with the sun setting just like it was now, Mother had ordered Sister to gather kindling. Then, pulling out the box of matches she always carried with her to light the stove, she set fire to the small nest of twigs and leaves, letting him smell the smoke and promising to burn him up if he didn't come down.

Terrified for him, Sister had cried and begged Brother to come down, even if it meant facing a whole new frontier of punishment and pain. Eventually, he'd slid down the trunk in a hail of bark and branches, then stood silent as Mother—furious—had ordered him to take off his shoes and walk back to the house barefoot. Sister had brought up the rear of the silent trio, watching as the footprints—clear and clean to start—became bloodier with each passing step.

She slapped herself, hard. Memory was an unforgivable luxury right now.

She bit her lip, considering. Charlotte and Tina had already proven themselves cunning, and Sister was sure, given the choice, they would continue to pick the clever choice. Most people, being right-handed, would choose the right, no doubt. A clever person would reverse that. An older, more conniving person would know *that* and return the choice to the right. But were two little girls conniving or clever enough?

Sister paused, uncertain, until the clear sound of movement came to her through the brush. With a hiss of triumph, she took off after it.

◆ ◆ ◆

Elliott

Amy stared at the tree, then at the path. "What now?"

"We've got to split up," Elliott said, squinting down the right-hand track snaking away into the gloom.

"What if it forks again?"

He shook his head. "Make a choice and go with it. What we can't do is stand still."

She turned to the left, but before she could move, he grabbed her and pulled her into his arms.

"We're going to save her," he whispered into her hair. "I know we are."

She squeezed him, hard, but didn't answer. They hugged each other for a quick moment longer, then separated. He held her at arm's length.

"First one to find her yells out and keeps yelling."

"What if . . . what do we do about Sister?"

"Do whatever you have to," he said, and his voice sounded strange to his own ears.

He shoved her gently toward the path on the left, then turned and hurried around the thick trunk to the right, trying to maintain a shred of optimism, but his mind, analytical and relentlessly logical, refused to stop calculating their chances of success. Every answer seemed to result in failure.

A million variables could keep them from Lacey at this point, from Kim Reston's malevolence to the simple, natural fact that the day was ending. Lacey might die of exposure while they stumbled around the forest, calling her name, or Reston might have found her already and taken her back to finish what she'd started in the kitchen. There'd be no way to know until it was too late to do anything about any of it.

Profound helplessness welled inside him, drawing him back irresistibly to his past. The bitter taste of those long, barren days of asking and waiting and looking for his little girl filled his mouth as though he'd drunk from that cup yesterday, not almost a decade ago. He remembered with near-perfect recall the moment when he'd realized that not every question had an answer and that some situations simply were.

He'd been standing on his porch at midnight, looking out onto the street, waiting for something—anything—to happen, for anyone to appear. Marilyn had tried to coax him inside, but he'd ignored her. Cars had passed occasionally, but none had stopped, and they soon became as much a part of the tapestry of the night as the yellow-orange streetlights and distant barks of dogs and smell of newly cut grass. He'd stood there so long his knees had locked and his hands had gone numb from squeezing them together.

A cancerous black hole had opened in his heart, and a part of him decided that it wasn't his heart that was real—it was the hole. Everything was nothing, and the sooner he came to grips with that fact, the sooner he'd be able to move on. *Let go,* a voice inside his head said. *Just let go.*

He'd wanted to. Dear god, how he'd wanted to. When it was obvious Cee Cee would never come home, that this was a wound outside of time's ability to heal, that there would be no recovering from it, ever.

But he'd never quite done it. The hole was still there, but so was what was left of his heart. He'd never stopped caring, never stopped hoping. It was what kept him going and what kept him from giving in.

He touched his face. He was crying again, the tears stiff and not quite frozen on his cheeks. He cuffed them away and pushed ahead.

"I'm coming, Cee Cee," he choked out loud, pushing his pace to a jog, then a run. "I'm coming."

◆ ◆ ◆

Tina

Tina's tears had stopped, nearly frozen to her face, replaced by the growing belief that she was going to die, lost and alone in the woods, but a deep, instinctive fear kept her from calling for help. Despite her wish to atone for whatever Charlotte had done, she simply couldn't find the courage to turn herself over to Sister—the woman's anger had no end, and she was terrified at the thought of what she was capable of.

Hiding seemed the only option. Hide and try to find her way out of the maze of trees in the morning. Stepping gingerly from the path, she was just about to lift a wide evergreen branch when a hand came down on the back of her neck.

"I'm so disappointed in you, Tina," Sister said in her ear. The words began in a voice that was terrifyingly calm, only to rise insanely fast on an upward scale. "So very disappointed."

Amy

Out of habit, Amy wrapped her arms around her chest, but realized she'd pitch directly onto her face if she snagged a foot on a tree root or slipped on one of the millions of round river stones in her way if she didn't have a way to catch herself. *And,* a voice whispered in her head, *if you come across the woman who took your little girl, you'll want to have a hand free.*

The path, flat to this point, began to climb, and Amy's thighs were soon burning as she pushed herself to keep up a fast pace. The air, crystalline with cold, burned her lungs, and she cupped her hands across her mouth to warm the air as she breathed in.

Overhead, the clouds were ridged lumps, their edges fading as the light slipped away. The path suffered the same, disappearing just thirty feet ahead. In the dim light, she found she needed saplings and the trunks of trees as a guide, moving forward by moving from one to the other. The gloom seemed to engulf everything around her and, as she looked around, the impossibility of what she was doing caught up with her.

What if Lacey had chosen the other path? Or a third branch she and Elliott had missed? What if Sister knew a thousand different shortcuts to get through the woods? At this very moment, the woman might be behind them and heading back to the house with Lacey trussed up and thrown over a shoulder like a trophy. Amy leaned against a tree and let the feelings wash over her.

"Lacey!" she cried, then cupped her hands to her mouth. "Lacey, honey! If you're out there, I'm coming!"

You can't give up. You've come too far. She pushed herself away from the tree and staggered down the path.

From somewhere just in front of her came a muted shout, a high-pitched voice suddenly smothered, followed by whispers—strained, intense, and unintelligible. It was too dim to see and, struck by a thought, she fished out her lighter and flicked it on and held it high.

Standing at the edge of the path was the gaunt, tall figure of Kim Reston, struggling with a smaller figure. Even as she grappled with the child, Reston's dark eyes snapped upward to lock with Amy's.

"Lacey?" Amy screamed, trying to see through the shadows. "Is that you, honey?"

Reston's breath was thick and hoarse, rags of sound that cut through the quiet night. She made a keening noise in between breaths, a sound on the edge of human hearing, something between a moan and wail that sent a shiver down Amy's spine. Snake quick, she spun the girl around and wrapped a long, bony arm around the child's neck.

48

Charlotte

Charlotte stopped to listen, wiped her nose. She thought she'd heard something behind her, something new, not the same scream she'd heard before.

Why are you stopping? she asked herself. *No sound is good.* But she knew the answer. She had stopped because she was tired, because she was scared, because she didn't know where she was going. It was one thing to decide to run away, it was another to set out with no idea where a path led or what was on the other side of the woods. *If there is another side,* she almost said out loud, then clamped down on the thought and kicked it out.

Her heart jumped in her throat as she heard a distinct thrashing behind her. Not squirrels or the wind, a steady crashing of feet through the dead leaves. Terror washed through her and she took off running, barely able to make out the path in the twilight, but willing to take the chance she'd trip and fall rather than get run to ground by Sister.

The path sloped ever higher and, as it crested a ridge, the undergrowth began to thin out until only the massive trunks of evergreens and beech trees remained. Everything became a path and she sprang forward, taking advantage of the clear sailing to break into a real run, stretching her stride out as far as she could, flying over the roots and half-buried boulders. Ahead, open sky appeared through the trunks and branches of the trees, signaling the edge of the forest.

But suddenly she gasped as a feeling like a rubber band snapping hit her in the back of her leg. Atrophied from underuse, a muscle spasmed and tore, sending a shiver of pain from the back of her knee to her butt. She cried out and tumbled to the ground, rolling on a soft layer of pine needles that carpeted the floor of the forest.

Behind her, she heard an answering cry, a note of triumph in the voice. Dropping the blanket, she clawed desperately at the roots and the dirt, scrambling to her feet. From the woods, Sister yelled again, calling a name—*her name?*—but it was garbled and indistinct, a low and guttural sound somehow worse than anything she'd heard to that point, and it spurred her to ignore the pain in her leg and sprint for the edge of the forest.

Stealing a glance behind, she made out a figure shambling from the undergrowth at the base of the slope. The sight gave her the extra surge she needed, and she flew past the last tree . . . barely catching herself at the last possible second from dropping into the swift, but silent, waters of the river forty feet below.

◆ ◆ ◆

Elliott

Elliott caught the hint of movement at the top of the ridge, just one more vertical outline in a forest full of them. He charged up the hill, calling Cee Cee's name as he went. His head swam with the visions of his past. A trip to the library. Holding hands as he walked her to her first day of school. The look of surprise when he opened a can of soda with its loud pop.

A smile broke across his face as he saw her, then, silhouetted against the sky, her slim little form weaving and teetering on the edge of the world.

"Hold on, honey," he called, or thought he did. He reached out a hand. "I'm coming."

Then his world slowed, pivoted, and crumbled inward as the girl glanced back, then—with a look of both terror and triumph on her face—jumped.

Elliott screamed and raced to the top of the ridge, holding on to a sapling as he stared down into the swirling waters of the Potomac. What little light was left glinted off the lapping edges of the river. The base of the bluff was crowded with snags and branches, mud and leaves. White water frothed, stirred by underwater boulders and the roots of stubborn, sodden trees that hung out over the river. His eyes panned the surface, but saw nothing except the wide, wide river.

Like a fire reaching a flashpoint, the hole in his heart bloomed wide, consuming the tiny bit of life left along the edges. It was, strangely, almost a relief. For eight years, he'd danced without comprehension or understanding on the edge of that hole, fighting the irresistible force pulling him inward. Now, despite the struggle, he felt himself pitching forward, falling into the center of that abyss, and it felt . . . good.

The surface of the water was a concrete slab, but it was the nearly freezing temperature that shocked his system, clearing his head instantly and blowing away the cobwebs of memory. The plunge had sent him deep beneath the water, where his feet sank into the muddy bottom, threatening to trap him there. He kicked desperately to free himself, then fought his way to the surface.

He sucked in a lungful of air as he broke through, bobbing like a cork. Warmth spilled from his body. Elliott flailed in place, trying to get his bearings while the current tugged him downriver and away from the shore. A clot of branches and snags had caught in the eddies and he splashed toward it when he saw, floating twenty feet away, a small brown lump with a profile different than anything else on the water.

"Lacey!" The girl's name came out as a croak.

He kicked and floundered. Aided by the current, he began to close the gap, but at an achingly slow pace. He called the girl's name again, and her head moved sluggishly. She moved weakly, trying to paddle away from him.

He kicked harder, drawing from the strength of so many failures, and so much pain. With his heart slamming in his chest, unable to feel his feet or hands, he drew even with the log and put his arm around the little girl. She was so tiny he felt as though his arm would go around her twice.

She cried out and pushed against him.

"It's okay, honey," he choked as he held on. "It's okay. Your mom sent me. Your mom loves you. You're going to be okay."

"Who are you?" The voice was weak.

"I'm here to get you back to your mom, honey."

He didn't have the strength to say any more. It was all he could do to hold her tightly and kick toward shore with every ounce of his remaining strength. The current fought him like a living thing, and it became clear they weren't going to make it. Floundering, he snagged the branch of a downed willow tree as they floated past, a desperate gamble to keep from being swept away altogether.

But his feet were numb, and it felt like claws were being plunged into his arms and shoulders. The shore, tantalizingly close, seemed an impossible target. His mouth filled with river water as he called for help, a desperate, last-ditch effort that his brain, coldly analytical, told him was ridiculously unlikely. Only if Amy or Dave had been following directly behind him would there be a ghost of a chance. His hand slipped on the branch.

Daddy, the voice whispered in his head. *Try anyway.*

"Cee Cee?"

Try.

With legs like lead and his heart near bursting, he let go of the willow branch and plunged toward the shore. The Potomac's bitter water splashed over them both, and he sloshed his way forward in a clumsy paddle.

"Kick, Lacey! Kick!" he choked. The current—constant, inexorable—swept them perilously far off their line of approach. In only a minute, they were yards downstream from the rocks Elliott had aimed for.

"Harder!" he yelled, and they splashed together for the shore. A swift running channel was coming up, he could see, a bottleneck where branches and leaves were being swept away by the frothing torrent. They were going to lose to the endless swell of water.

This is the way it happened.

Elliott Nash, a drunk and a failure, having already ruined his own life, tried helping a mother and redeeming himself in the process. Struggling to overcome his own judgmental and unforgiving nature, he managed to come within an arm's length of succeeding, only to fall short of the courage to make it a reality, drowning not only himself but a young girl in the process—

"No!"

Elliott pushed himself, reduced to only two functions: keeping his head above water and pumping his legs. Burning needles were piercing his thighs and shoulders, and he'd long since lost feeling in his hands. Only when he slammed his feet into the muddy ground of the shore did he realize they'd made it. With their arms around each other, they stumbled over the slimy river stone and sandy beach until they finally collapsed to the ground in a shivering heap.

"Hang in there, Lacey," Elliott tried to say through chattering teeth. "Your mom's not far behind."

The little girl raised her head. "Sir?"

"Call me Elliott, honey," he said automatically. "What is it?"

"My name isn't Lacey."

Amy

"Mom?" the girl cried, the terror in her voice heartbreaking. "Mom?"

"Lacey! I'm here, honey," Amy shouted.

"Mom, help me—" Reston tightened her grip on Lacey's throat, choking off the rest of the words.

Amy stopped short, holding her hands out in supplication. "Oh my god! Don't! Please, don't!"

"Why not?" Reston asked. "Why shouldn't I? So she can join you, instead? So your family can be reunited and you can go back to ruining her life? So she can grow up and someday destroy her own daughter?"

"Hurting her won't help."

"I've never *hurt* any of them," Reston said, looking down at the top of Lacey's head. "I've only ever wanted to free them of the burdens of their parents. Of parents like you."

"Please," Amy said, searching for something to say, something to form a connection with this woman. "I know your childhood was terrible, that you went through the kind of trauma that no one should. And I know you think you're helping these children. But can't you see I've come this far because I love my daughter? I didn't abandon her. I'm here for her."

"You expect to be rewarded for doing what any mother should?" Reston asked, her voice almost curious. "Where was your sense of duty before?"

"I don't want a reward. Just a chance," Amy said. "I've made terrible choices, I know that. But that doesn't mean I can't carve out a new path for both of us. I can make amends. But only if you let her go."

For a thin moment, it seemed as though Reston's grip loosened on Lacey's neck. Then her face hardened. "You already had your opportunity as a mother. And you wasted it."

"Kim." A bright white light suddenly lit Reston's face from over Amy's shoulder. "Let her go."

Reston blinked at the harsh glare, then laughed. "Late again, David? Sure you don't want to hide in the tree and leave me to clean up the mess again?"

"I had to save myself that day," Dave said. "I'm sorry I couldn't save you, too, Kim. Or save the others. And I'm so sorry for what happened to you."

"Happened to me?" she screeched. "What happened to me, David? What exactly do you think *happened* while I listened to our mother murder our brothers and sisters?"

"Something no child should go through," he said, his voice gruff. "Which is why you need to stop. Right here, right now. Let Lacey go. Let the others go. It's time to give these kids back their lives."

"Give them back to their sick, abusive, ignorant families? Return them to their alcoholic and drug-addicted parents?" Reston spat. "No, Brother. I'm not going to do that. I'm not giving them back to people like her."

"You stole her," Amy shouted. A primal, instinctive anger surged through her. "You took my *child*."

"Of course I did. I saved her from you and the rest of the terrible parents out there. I gave her a life. I gave her a family worthy of the name. What did you ever do for her?"

"I'm her *mother*."

"You gave birth to her, but 'mother'? No. The word is nothing but a label. You don't deserve her."

"No, I don't. And neither do you."

"Are you sure? Should we ask her?" Reston asked, loosening her grip on Lacey. "If I let you go, would you really rather be with your drug-addict mother? Or me? Who hurt you more, Tina? Who loves you more?"

Lacey struggled, crying. "You're not my mother. You're not my sister!"

"But who is this woman to you, Tina?" Reston said, giving her a shake. "This *addict* who left you a dozen times to fend for yourself? Who sent you away to that terrible foster family?"

"I don't care what she did before," Lacey said, sobbing. "It doesn't matter. She's my mom. I love her."

Reston's face suddenly twisted, full of hate. She yanked back on Lacey's neck so hard her eyes bulged from their sockets. Amy screamed and ran toward them.

A shot rang out—flat, muted by the surrounding trees, but unmistakable. Reston stumbled back with a shriek and crumpled to the ground. Amy raced forward and swept Lacey into her arms, trying hard not to crush the thin body, the little bag of bones, in her embrace.

Dave ran to his sister's side, his gun raised; then he holstered it and knelt beside her. She moaned, a wail that rose and fell, like her chest, in time to her erratic breathing. Her arm traced manic half circles in the air, and her heels beat a tattoo of pain on the ground. Dave fumbled for her hand, trying to calm her, speaking to her quietly until the motions slowed.

She raised her head weakly. "Tina?"

Lacey pulled away from her mother's grasp. "No, honey," Amy whispered, "don't. You don't owe her anything."

"Mom," Lacey said, looking up at her. "I have to."

Reluctantly, Amy let her go, and the girl walked over and knelt by the woman. "Yes, Sister?"

The dark eyes, gleaming dully, locked with hers. "Why?"

"She's my mom," Lacey said, her voice small. "She deserves another chance."

"She'll . . . damage you, Tina. Like my mother did to me."

"No, she won't. She didn't come all this way just to do it all over again." Lacey glanced back at her mother. "I know we're both afraid of pain, Sister. But no one's going to hurt us now. Either of us."

The woman scrabbled for Lacey's hand. "I did this for you, Tina. For all of you."

Lacey swallowed. "I know, Sister."

Reston let go of the girl's hand, and her head sank to the ground. Her breathing grew ragged and fluttering. "I . . . should've . . . helped them."

Dave bowed his head. Behind him, Amy drew Lacey away and they held each other as the distant sound of sirens wove in and out of the night air.

49

Elliott

"I better get going. The a.m. shift is still going to be there in the morning." Dave Cargill stood and stretched, the vertebrae in his back popping audibly.

Elliott pushed himself to his feet. "I'll walk you out."

Two days had passed since the ordeal at the house. Amy and Lacey were on the futon, sitting close but not touching. Scattered on the coffee table were soy packets, chopsticks, and the devastated remains of a Chinese takeout meal, a makeshift dinner that had started awkwardly, then warmed up as suppressed appetites had kicked in. They'd stuck to safe, mundane subjects and made small talk on a topic that all of them but Dave had previously given up on—the future.

"Dave," Amy called, and he turned from the door. She surprised them both by vaulting the table and giving him a hug. "Thank you for everything. And I'm so sorry."

He smiled sadly. "You're welcome, Amy. Thanks. I'll be in touch."

"Please." She gave him an impish smile. "I think we all have a connection now."

"If you say so," he said with a laugh. He looked over her shoulder toward the futon. "Good night, Lacey. I'm glad you're home."

The girl looked back at him, her face wavering between different emotions. Her eyes were glistening. "Thank you, Mr. Dave. I'm sorry you had to . . . had to . . ."

"That's okay, honey," Dave said quietly. "I'm just glad you and your mom are together now."

Amy returned to the couch and knelt by Lacey, taking both her hands in one of hers and speaking to her in low tones. The two men stepped outside, their breath steaming in the air.

"They're going to need a lot of time," Dave said after a moment.

"Time and love. I think they have plenty of both." Elliott put his hands in his pockets and hunched his shoulders against the cold. "How is the girl?"

"She's still in the hospital for observation and treatment for hypothermia, but one of the detectives told me she'll probably be released soon. Remarkable kid."

"She is. Do we know anything about her?"

"Her real name is Alex Martinez. Her parents abandoned her as a toddler, and she was raised by foster parents for about as long as she can remember. Kim—" Dave coughed, went quiet, then started again. "The theory is that Kim simply took a liking to her one day after looking through old records and decided she needed to be 'rescued,' even through by all accounts she's a foster system success story. Her foster parents have been in the hospital with her twenty-four seven since we brought her back."

"What about the other kids?"

"They'll be reunited with their foster or biological parents as circumstances dictate, I guess. No one knows what the hell to do. Who's ever seen something like this before?"

They stood and watched the cars roll by, the red lights winking as they passed to the end of the block before fading away.

"You're on suspended duty?" Elliott asked finally.

"Any event involving the discharge of a weapon," Dave said, shrugging. "They'll judge it justified, have me watch video for a few weeks. At least it's full pay."

"Followed by psych profiles and surveys."

"Naturally." The words dropped between them, and they let the silence rest for a moment. He coughed. "There's just no way to make sense of it, is there?"

"No," Elliott said. "Your sister was . . . broken, Dave. We'll never know exactly how she processed the horror she witnessed the day your mother snapped, but I think I can say that what she went through would've damaged any of us."

"I think about that," Dave said softly. "What if I hadn't run into the woods that day? What if I'd hidden behind a door or down in the cellar instead of in the woods? Or even just run down the road and stopped Kim before she saw . . . what she saw?"

Elliott reached out, squeezed the other man's arm. "Don't ponder the what-ifs. Deal in the moment."

"The inside of my head is no playground," Dave said, his voice husky, "but how did I turn out the way I did? Why couldn't Kim get past what our mother did and I could?"

"There's no way to know. How do you measure intent against action? Kim did all the wrong things for what she thought were the right reasons. If we could talk to her now, I think she'd still say everything she did was for the children."

"My god. Mother used to say that."

"I'm rusty, but I have some time slots open if you need help working through that. People tell me I used to be a pretty good psychologist, once."

Dave gave him a look, then they both laughed ruefully.

Dave buttoned his peacoat to the neck. "Can I . . . drop you off somewhere?"

Elliott shook his head. "I'm good."

"Good. 'Night, Elliott."

"Good night, Dave. Thank you."

Dave threw him a wave as he trotted down the steps to his car. Elliott watched him leave, then went back inside and lowered himself onto a milk crate across from Lacey and Amy.

"I'm so embarrassed," Amy said, looking at him balancing precariously on the plastic bin. "I can't believe I made you sit on that thing."

"I can handle it. Dave, on the other hand, must've gained forty pounds since I worked with him. He's as big as a beach ball."

Lacey laughed, surprising them, then covered her mouth to smother the sound. Gently, Amy reached out and peeled the little hand away. "You don't have to do that anymore, baby. You make as much noise as you want."

"I will." Lacey turned her face toward Elliott. "Did I hear you say Jay was doing better?"

Elliott smiled at her. "He is. Detective Cargill and I were talking about maybe getting you up there for a visit if it's okay with your mom. And Jay's parents, of course. We might even be able to get some of the others there, so you can see you're all safe now."

The girl's face, a younger version of Amy's, screwed up with uncertainty. "I don't know if I can. I wasn't very . . . nice to any of them." Her eyes filled with tears. "I—I wanted to make Sister happy, to please her, and didn't know any other way to . . . to . . ."

Amy reached over and pulled Lacey close, and this time her daughter collapsed in on her mother and they held each other tight. Elliott made a motion to get up again, but Amy stopped him with a wave. He sat in silence until Lacey's sobs slowed to a sniffle. She had a lot of trauma to get past—they both did—but, looking at the two of them, Elliott knew that if any mother could save her child twice, it was the one he was looking at now.

Amy cleared her throat, then asked Lacey, now that they'd had Chinese, what would she rather have for her first real night out, her birthday night: tacos or pizza? The question sparked a long debate on the merits of both and whether there was a third kind of food that should be included. Elliott tossed in a comment from time to time but let the other two do most of the talking, content to observe a normal conversation, the kind that could be held in any living room anywhere.

The final decision was that pizza was easier to eat than tacos, which broke apart and got all over your hand, so overall pizza was the superior food and would be *the* choice on their big night out.

Lacey turned to Elliott. "You'll come with us, won't you, Mr. Elliott?"

He traded glances with Amy, who smiled and raised an eyebrow. "I wouldn't miss it. Just let me know when we're going."

The two talked about all the things they were going to do together to make up for the lost time. A strange falling feeling blossomed in his chest as he listened to himself being included in their plans. Amy shot him a look as he stood and headed for the door again. "I'll be back. Just need a minute."

He stepped outside onto the tiny concrete porch and leaned against the railing. It sagged against his weight, but held. The sky was a cloudless, blue-black winter arc. Stars like pinpricks in a black curtain sparkled and the night was still. Someone had warned them of an impending snowstorm, but he couldn't see it yet.

Elliott dropped his eyes to the street and watched a light breeze lift the leaves in a patch of cyclone-fenced yard, then pass, letting them drop back to the ground. A shiver ran through him and he shook his head. If he thought this was cold, he'd never make it on the streets this January. If that's where he was going to be.

Earlier in the night, Amy had told him he had a place with them, if he wanted it. *I don't know what that means,* he said. *It's whatever you need it to mean,* she'd told him. He had no answer for her, but they'd embraced. Feeling clumsy and self-conscious, he'd tried to pull away after a quick hug, but Amy had held him tightly and refused to let go until he'd said he'd think about it.

Even when they'd separated, she'd held on to him and looked into his eyes. "You know, what we did . . . we saved those kids' lives. Theirs and more to come. It means something, Elliott."

"It better," he'd quipped. "I almost drowned."

"You know what I'm saying." She'd grabbed him by the arms and squeezed, hard. "I got my do-over, and I'm not going to blow it this time. You could turn this into your own second chance."

He paused. "I know."

"Will you?"

"I don't know," Elliott said, looking away. "All I know is that I was supposed to help you find Lacey. We did it. But what does it mean? Nothing will change what happened to me or my little girl. What's done is done."

Amy had placed a cool hand on his face. "It's not about the past, Elliott. It never was."

And, now, he stared into the sky, watching the unmoving stars wink back at him. Another errant breeze, stronger than the first, blew through, pushing sticks and leaves down the street. It passed, and he was left gazing overhead, looking for answers. *They're not up there,* he thought. *All our answers are inside.*

He rubbed his eyes with a quiet groan. He'd been holding on for so long, he'd almost forgotten how to let go. Maybe all there was left was . . . to do it. He looked up at the sky one last time.

"Good night, Cee Cee," he whispered. "I love you, honey. I always will."

Head tilted, he waited. Minutes passed; his fingers and toes went numb and the breeze slid an icy hand down the back of his neck. A shudder rippled through his body. But, at last, the answer came. He let out the breath he'd held in a long, slow sigh, smiled, then turned and went inside, ready to try again.

ACKNOWLEDGMENTS

I'd like to thank the following people for making *Birthday Girl* possible.

My wife, Rene, provided the support that—amazingly—seems to come with the territory, but also spent *countless* hours kicking around various permutations of the book with me during walks around the neighborhood. Thank you, honey.

My extended family at Thomas & Mercer not only brought this particular book into being; they made this phase of my career possible. Endless thanks to Jessica Tribble, Sarah Shaw, Tara de Nicolas-Duckworth, and the entire team at T&M, as well as Amazon Publishing at large.

I owe my developmental editor Caitlin Alexander a byline. Without her help on and belief in the project, *Birthday Girl* would've been just another wreck on the Boulevard of Broken Books. Jon Ford, my copyeditor, saved me from making some colossal mistakes and added immeasurably to the whole. Thank you, Caitlin and Jon, for all your help.

Jacque Ben-Zekry was the first person to see the idea that lurked behind the book and offered me wise counsel on where and how far to push the story, not to mention the key insight that got Sister her job in the court system. Thank you, Jacque, for your help and friendship.

Fellow mystery author, forensic psychologist, and professor Rick Helms was kind enough to give me the benefit of his technical expertise on the psychological results of Sister's trauma and provided great overall advice besides. You should read his award-winning books (www.richardhelms.net) and buy him a drink if you see him at a conference. Thank you, Rick.

Jil Simon and Chris Day offered their friendship and several needed conversational distractions from writing, but, most importantly, they dispensed advice on the legal front that proved critical to the book.

Dekey Y. Tenpa and Mike Graham didn't hesitate to share their experiences in nursing and medicine, which gave me the insight I needed for several key moments in the book. Dave Green of the Arlington PD did likewise on the law enforcement front, as he has for damn near a decade on the weird and wide variety of subjects that only a crime writer can ask.

Dave Jacobstein and Joe Hart read early drafts that helped shape the final outcome and have provided immense help in other ways, as well. Pete Talbot, Amy Talbot, Frank Gallian, and Carie Rothenbacher provided constant friendship and were sounding boards for whole swaths of the book, as they've done for years, now. Thank you, dear friends.

I used several sources to research Elliott's life as a homeless person, but Mike Yankoski's *Under the Overpass: A Journey of Faith on the Streets of America* was exceedingly helpful.

For musical inspiration, I can't recommend the moody and evocative works of Roque Baños and Gustavo Santaolalla enough.

I've never thanked the mystery writer community at large before, but this past year has pulled me into the orbit of many writers and fans who are also just wonderful people. Make the time to attend a local or national mystery fiction conference and find out for yourself how open and welcoming this group of people can be.

Lastly, thank you to the readers who've made this career possible. Your support means the world to me.

AUTHOR'S NOTE

Readers who know the area around Washington, DC, may recognize that several landmarks may seem familiar—St. Andrews' School, Mercy General Hospital, Washington Center Mall, for instance—but they aren't actually where they're supposed to be or are slightly off in description or name. This was done intentionally to allow myself some poetic license in where and how I got to represent them in the novel. Please don't tie yourself in knots trying to place these locales on a map or in your memory; they either don't exist or not in the way they are in real life.

ABOUT THE AUTHOR

Photo © 2014 by Sally Iden

Matthew Iden is the author of the suspense novel *The Winter Over*, a half dozen books in the Marty Singer detective series, and several acclaimed stand-alone novels. He has visited seven continents, and written on several of them, but lives in Alexandria, Virginia.

Visit him at www.matthew-iden.com, on Facebook at facebook.com/matthew.iden, or on Twitter @CrimeRighter.